"Did you see that? Ellie smiled," Kate said.

Conner chuckled. "I told you, she likes you."

"We're going to do this." Kate looked deep into Conner's eyes. "We are going to save this baby, so help me, God." She meant it as a prayer and a vow, and when Conner nodded, she felt as if they had joined hands in mutual agreement.

There welled up within her a sense of something sweet and powerful. She tried to tell herself it was the same sensation she got whenever she helped her father, saw a baby or a child or an adult improving and knowing she had a hand in it. Only the feeling was unlike any she'd ever before experienced, and she could not dismiss it so easily nor fit it into a tidy slot in her brain.

When she was satisfied the baby had taken all the milk she would, she hurried to the kitchen…in need of an escape from the intensity prevailing in her thoughts while sitting so close to Conner, hearing his deep voice murmur to the baby. And knowing all the while that baby Ellie's mother belonged where Kate now sat.

Linda Ford lives on a ranch in Alberta, Canada, near enough to the Rocky Mountains that she can enjoy them on a daily basis. She and her husband raised fourteen children—four homemade, ten adopted. She currently shares her home and life with her husband, a grown son, a live-in paraplegic client and a continual (and welcome) stream of kids, kids-in-law, grandkids and assorted friends and relatives.

Books by Linda Ford

Love Inspired Historical

Big Sky Country

Montana Cowboy Daddy
Montana Cowboy Family
Montana Cowboy's Baby

Montana Cowboys

The Cowboy's Ready-Made Family
The Cowboy's Baby Bond
The Cowboy's City Girl

Christmas in Eden Valley

A Daddy for Christmas
A Baby for Christmas
A Home for Christmas

Lone Star Cowboy League: Multiple Blessings

The Rancher's Surprise Triplets

Journey West

Wagon Train Reunion

Visit the Author Profile page at Harlequin.com for more titles.

LINDA FORD

Montana Cowboy's Baby

HARLEQUIN® LOVE INSPIRED® HISTORICAL

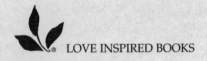

Recycling programs
for this product may
not exist in your area.

LOVE INSPIRED BOOKS

ISBN-13: 978-0-373-42530-3

Montana Cowboy's Baby

www.Harlequin.com

Printed in U.S.A.

God is our refuge and strength,
an ever-present help in trouble.
—*Psalms* 46:1

To my editor, Tina, who guided me through the tangled threads of this story. Thank you.

Chapter One

Bella Creek, Montana, summer 1890

Twenty-two-year-old Kate Baker walked out of the big house on the Marshall Five Ranch. She'd completed her errand and was intent on returning to her home, four miles away, in Bella Creek. She'd taken two steps toward her buggy when a wagon rolled up to the house.

A stranger got down, retrieved a basket like the one Kate used for laundry and handed it to her.

"For Conner Marshall."

Before she could think to ask who he was or what he'd delivered, he jumped back to the seat, flicked the reins and drove away.

She turned to look in the basket and met the dull brown eyes of an infant. Not a single rational thought came to her mind. What was she to do with this baby?

Think, she ordered herself. Who would bring a baby to Conner? He wasn't even married.

Grandfather Marshall was inside—she had delivered some new liniment for him from her father, the local doctor—but he was in no shape to take care of a baby.

Grandfather, as everyone called him, had said everyone else was away. Wait, hadn't he said Conner had stayed on the ranch to keep an eye on things...meaning the older man?

She glanced around. Did she detect movement in the corrals by the barn? It could be one of the hired hands or Conner.

"Conner," she yelled. "Conner Marshall."

The movement turned into a body that vaulted the fence and raced toward her.

She watched Conner approach. The middle Marshall son was twenty-four years old. He was a big man. Blond as all the Marshalls were with piercing blue eyes. His dusty cowboy hat tipped back from his pace, allowing her a view of his strong, angular face.

He reached her side. "Is something wrong? Is it Grandfather?" He clattered across the wooden veranda toward the door.

"Not Grandfather." Her words stopped him and he slowly turned. She pointed toward the basket that she had lowered to the ground. "Someone brought this for you."

"Me? What is it?"

"You best look and see."

He did so. "A baby? Why would anyone send me a baby?"

Exactly her question. They stared at the solemn infant.

"Look, there's a note." She pointed to the piece of paper tucked by the bedding.

He seemed incapable of moving, so she picked it up. "It has your name on it."

He plucked it from her fingers, unfolded it and read

it aloud. "'Conner, this is Elspeth. She's yours. Take care of her. Thelma.'"

Kate lowered her gaze, unable to look at the man. He had a baby? And obviously no wife, unless she had left him. "You're married?" She kept her voice low, revealing nothing of the shock this news provided.

"No, of course I'm not."

He'd fathered a baby out of wedlock? She'd known him since she and her father had moved to Bella Creek in the spring and would never have considered him the sort to act this way. It left her stunned to the point she couldn't think how to respond.

Drawn by the sound of their voices, Grandfather came to the doorway.

"You should be resting," Kate said in her kindest voice, knowing how much his legs must hurt. He'd been injured a couple of years ago and his legs had never healed properly.

"Can't rest with all this commotion. What's going on?"

"A baby." Conner sounded as shocked as he looked. He handed the note to his grandfather, who read it and grunted.

Grandfather hobbled over to peer into the basket. "So you've fathered a baby?" The disapproval in the older man's voice hung heavy in the air. "She's awfully still." He pulled the blanket covering the baby lower. "And thin as a stick." He waved Kate forward. "I've seen how competent you are at helping your father. You'll know what to do with this baby. Have a look at her, would you?"

Kate's father was the local doctor. Her mother had been his assistant before her passing, and since then,

Kate had assisted him. This was what Kate knew. She stared into the eyes of the little girl. Her heart stalled. Something about the look in those eyes begged for Kate's help.

She drew in a deep breath. She touched the baby's cheek, found it dry. Kate slipped off the tiny bonnet and ran her hand over Elspeth's head. She guessed the baby to be about five or six months old. Conner would have a better idea of the age of his daughter.

"She's badly dehydrated." She refrained from giving her assessment that this child was also undernourished. Her throat constricted at the idea that the baby had been neglected. It was all she could do not to scoop the little one from the basket and promise to protect and care for her. Instead, she waited for Conner to take responsibility for his child. "She needs to be fed," she added for good measure. Still no response. What must she do to get the man moving?

"You need to feed her," she continued. A nursing bottle with a skin of sour milk lay beside the baby. She picked it up and held it toward him.

He lifted his gaze from studying the baby to stare at the bottle.

"Come, I'll help you." She made her way to the door. Grandfather hobbled after her, but Conner didn't move.

She sighed. "Bring the baby."

He jolted into action, gingerly lifting the basket and carrying it after her as she crossed through the large entryway into the big, homey kitchen. She cleaned the bottle and got cooled milk from the pantry. As she waited for the milk to warm, she watched Conner.

He scooped the baby from the basket, and although

he appeared to be a little uncertain how to hold Elspeth, he smiled gently as he studied the little girl.

A warm feeling filled Kate's heart at the tenderness in his eyes. She handed him the bottle and prepared to leave. Father would be expecting her home.

She didn't like to leave him too long. He'd had a buggy accident a year ago and afterward he'd been unconscious for three days. It had taken a long time for him to be able to think clearly. He seemed to be well now. Still, she was reluctant to leave him, knowing fatigue and hunger brought on mental confusion.

She took a couple of steps toward the door but stopped. It was a scene she hated to leave…an opportunity to see the strong, noble Marshall men cope with a tiny baby. Her gaze returned to the baby sheltered in Conner's arms. Her eyes stung.

She must make sure this little one was doing well before she left. It was her only reason for turning back to the room.

Conner held the baby in the palms of his hands. Should he lay her on his lap or in the crook of his arm? He settled for holding her against his chest. A protective feeling—so powerful and unfamiliar that his lungs forgot to work—filled his heart.

He stared into the eyes of the baby. Solemn, maybe even guarded, as if wondering whether or not she would be welcomed. Why would Thelma say the baby was his? He knew without a doubt it wasn't because, despite Thelma's teasing, they had never gone that far.

He hadn't seen Thelma for over a year and a half… since she'd left town to join the traveling show. He'd met her a year prior to that when she moved to town to help her ailing aunt. He'd been moved by her dedication to helping the older woman. It hadn't taken him long to fall in love with her. She said she felt the same overwhelming love for him.

When she'd announced her intention to leave town, he had reluctantly agreed to go with her and suggested they marry before doing so. But then she left, leaving him a note saying she could do better on her own. It had hurt to know she found him a hindrance. He'd been devastated and humiliated to have his sorrow witnessed publicly. He'd found solace in the bosom of his family and vowed to always put them first after that. He considered it his service to the Lord and prayed he would not be diverted by his emotions.

He didn't plan to ever trust another woman with his heart. What did love mean if it was so easy to walk away from it?

The baby gave a thin cry.

"She needs to eat," Kate repeated in a patient tone.

"Of course." He could do this. He poked the rubber nipple between the little lips. The milk ran out the corners of the baby's mouth and dribbled into the creases of her neck.

Grandfather made an explosive sound. "Conner, you don't know the first thing about babies."

"I've nursed an orphan calf. It can't be all that different."

With a muffled groan, Grandfather leaned back in his chair.

Conner looked at the infant in his arms. Her mother was missing. How long had she been alone? Somebody ought to care about her. He would. "Come on, baby, swallow your milk." He again jiggled the bottle in her mouth.

The baby blinked and swallowed once, then turned her eyes away from him and stared. He followed the direction of her gaze and saw nothing.

Milk ran out her mouth.

He tried as hard as he could, but the baby wouldn't swallow again.

He gave Kate a pleading look. "She won't eat for me."

Her eyes gentle, she took the baby from his arms and the bottle he handed to her. It was good to have her here…someone with medical know-how.

Kate smiled. "I'll show you what to do and then you'll be able to do it." She eased the nipple into the tiny mouth. "Come on, little Ellie."

Ellie. He liked that far better than Elspeth.

"You need to eat. That's it, sweet girl." Kate's voice drew the baby's eyes and she swallowed. Once. Twice and again. And then she stopped.

Kate crooned to her. "You can do this."

The baby drank another swallow and then her eyes drifted closed.

"She's done for now. She'll be okay if she's fed every hour or more often until she is taking a full feed. It's going to be a time-consuming job for a few days."

She handed the baby back to Conner. Her eyes were steady, her gaze intent. "She's a Marshall. Your daughter." Kate spoke calmly, encouragingly. "It's up to you to give her what she needs, and at the moment that's lots of love, frequent feedings, and it wouldn't hurt to use gentle, kind words around her." She gave a few instructions about feeding the baby and keeping her warm and comfortable. "Now I must return home in case my father needs me."

Although the baby wasn't actually a Marshall, there had to be a reason Thelma said she was. Perhaps the baby was in danger from some of the people in the traveling show. Or maybe Thelma had married and her husband was cruel. Until Conner knew the facts, he would give Ellie the protection of the Marshall name. That meant keeping the truth hidden. He pulled the baby tighter to his chest.

He watched Kate put on her bonnet and reach for the black bag she had brought in and panic clawed up his throat. "Wait. You can't leave. There's no one here but me and Grandfather. We need help." He knew he sounded needy and it wasn't like him, but being in charge of a weak little baby frightened him more than anything he could remember.

He glanced desperately at the door. Where was his family when he needed them? Everyone had gone about their business, that's where. Pa and Conner's two brothers were checking on the cattle and might be gone several days. His sister, Annie, went to visit her friend for a few days and didn't say when she'd be back. Even his recently acquired sisters-in-law had disappeared to their own pursuits.

His gaze shifted to the window and the corrals visible beyond where the horses he had been breaking and training milled about. That was the kind of work he understood.

He brought his attention back to Kate. "You're a nurse."

"Doctor's assistant," she corrected in a distracted way.

"This is the kind of thing you understand. I don't."

"I'll show you how to prepare her bottle. You know how to feed her now."

"Okay." He put the baby in her basket and listened to Kate's instructions. It hardly seemed enough knowledge to care for a weak baby. "I can do this." He would care for this child as if she was his. But he had to grit his teeth to keep from calling Kate back as she left the room. A few minutes later, a buggy rattled from the yard. It scared him to death to be responsible for such a tiny baby, but he'd never let anyone guess.

Grandfather studied him with steely eyes. "Did you know you had a baby?"

"She's not mine! I can't believe you think she is."

"You're sure?" Grandfather's voice was full of doubt.

"As sure as I am that the sun will set tonight and rise again tomorrow." He gazed at the baby, expecting her to be asleep, but she stared up at him. He touched her cheek and played with her hand, curling and uncurling her fingers. "I can't believe Thelma called the little thing Elspeth." Except it didn't surprise him. Thelma had admired a singer of that name.

"Why would she say she's yours? Why would she send her here?"

Indeed. He met Grandfather's piercing gaze with his own steady one. "I can't answer for her choices. But perhaps the baby is in danger." He let that sit for a moment.

"What kind of danger?"

"Some of the people in her traveling troupe were a little…" He held up a hand to indicate uncertainty.

"What are you going to do with her?" Grandfather asked, his voice not unkind.

"Seems to me this little one needs a family to care for her and protect her. I'm willing to do that."

Grandfather cleared his throat. "Every child deserves to be surrounded by love and care. I guess Thelma knew what she was doing when she sent her to you."

"Except she likely didn't think it would be just you and me caring for her."

"Don't worry, son. We'll figure it out as we go. 'Sides, doesn't it say in the Bible that God cares about even the little sparrows? She is of far more value than a hundred sparrows. We'll trust God to help us."

Conner nodded. "I think we'll be keeping God busy for a few days." But hadn't he learned how sufficient God was in the painful days after Thelma had left? His family had gathered round him and helped him as much as they could and for that he owed them his faithfulness. They'd help him with the care of this little scrap of humanity as well. Just as soon as they got back. In the meantime, he and Grandfather were all she had.

How long would they need to provide for Ellie? What was going on with Thelma?

Kate had barely finished making a pot of coffee for her father the next morning when someone clattered into the waiting room and hollered, "Doc, are you there?"

She was used to the doctor being called away any time of the day or night, so she quickly filled a cup of coffee for her father. "Eat something while I go see what it is." She'd delay the caller long enough to allow Father to have breakfast. A few minutes to eat leisurely would go a long way to preventing any problems with his memory.

She went into the waiting room. A man she recognized from the community stood before her.

"My mother fell getting out of bed this morning and is hurting. Could the doctor come and see her?" His mother was a frail elderly woman.

Father appeared behind her. "I'll go immediately." He reached for his black doctor's bag.

"I'll go with you." Kate untied her apron and hung it on a hook.

She had barely finished speaking when one of the young cowboys she recognized from the Marshall ranch burst through the door.

The cowboy grabbed the hat off his head. "Miss Kate, Conner says would you please come immediately? The baby isn't eating. He says she's really weak."

Kate's hands clenched. She'd hoped and prayed for a better report. She wanted nothing more than to hurry to the baby's side and will her to be strong, but her father was needed elsewhere. She had accompanied him on almost every call since their arrival. Often she had guided him through a task or reminded him of a medical fact as he struggled to regain full use of his memory. Lately, she'd needed to help less and less, but she wasn't yet confident he was completely better. But she couldn't be in two places.

Father saw her concern. "I'll be okay on my own. You go take care of that baby, nurse it back to health and strength."

She hesitated a moment longer before making up her mind. By the sound of it, the baby required medical care. Kate would give her that and more. She'd pour love into that little girl until she grew strong. Only for the sake of her health, of course. She knew better than to let her emotions get involved.

"Let me get a few things." The supplies she needed

were in the office, but she turned back to their living quarters and slipped into her bedroom, where she sat on the edge of the bed and leaned over, her face to her knees. She needed to be calm and collected. She needed wisdom to guide them through dealing with the weak baby.

Oh, God, You are my friend and my strength. The Lord is my light and my salvation; whom shall I fear? The Lord is the strength of my life; of whom shall I be afraid?

Her soul calmed and her courage renewed, she joined the cowboy and hurried toward the buggy.

As she settled herself on the bench, she glanced around. To her left was the newly constructed schoolhouse. To her right, the new barbershop. Past that were other new buildings taking shape, replacing those that had been destroyed in a fire a few months ago.

Bella Creek, Montana, was a town Grandfather Marshall had built to provide an alternative to the wild mining town of Wolf Hollow. He took the welfare of the town very seriously and was largely responsible, with the help of his sons and grandsons, for the rebuilding after the fire of last winter. The Marshalls had located a doctor and teacher as well, to replace the ones who left following the disaster.

She would miss the small town when she left. She'd already been accepted at a medical school in St. Louis, Missouri, but had delayed her entrance to care for Father.

They reached the ranch and the cowboy helped her down. Kate hurried through to the sitting room. One look at the baby, her eyes unfocused, her breathing shallow, and Kate's mind kicked into a gallop.

"You should have sent for help earlier."

"I kept thinking she would improve." Conner scrubbed his hand over his hair, turning it into a blond tangle and bringing a fleeting smile to Kate's mouth.

She lifted the baby, cradling her close. Normally a baby was warm. This one was not. "Did she drink any milk at all?"

"She wouldn't swallow. Most of the time she won't even meet my eyes. What's wrong with her?"

Kate knew his frustration came from concern for the life of this little one. There was no point in her saying anything to allay his worries. If the baby didn't begin to eat… She couldn't bring herself to finish the thought and instead closed her eyes and breathed a prayer. The baby needed fluids immediately. Did her body even have the strength to digest milk? There was an alternative.

"I'll start her on sugar water."

Wanting to preserve what body heat the little one had, she swaddled her in the soft, white blanket from the basket, then handed her to Conner. "Hold her close. She needs to be warm."

Conner pressed the baby to his chest. Kate plucked the hand-knit blanket from the back of the brown couch and draped it over his arms, covering the baby until only her eyes showed—eyes that showed no interest in life. Kate met Conner's gaze, saw her concern echoed. Something shifted inside her, knowing they were united in caring for this baby.

She jerked her gaze away. She must not cross the line between a patient and a doctor's assistant. And that included the patient's family. *Don't let your emotions get involved. You do what you can and leave the family to pull together.*

She hurried to the kitchen to prepare the water mixture for the baby. A few minutes later, she had everything ready and returned to the sitting room.

Conner shifted to make room for her at his side on the couch.

She eased the tip of the syringe into the little mouth and squeezed out a drop, then massaged the thin neck. "Come on, Ellie, swallow." A sigh escaped her when the baby did so. "Thank you," she whispered.

She met Conner's look, found there a sense of accord in shared concern for this wee bit of struggling humanity. It warmed her cheeks and heart to feel united with him in this.

Turning her attention back to the baby, she squeezed out another drop and then another. After a few swallows, little Ellie refused any more no matter how much Kate rubbed her face and neck and begged her to take more.

With no desire to drown the wee thing, Kate withdrew the syringe. "I'll feed her every few minutes."

Conner's blue eyes filled with worry.

She patted his arm. "We aren't solely responsible for the outcome here. God has a bigger part in healing than any mere man can play." She needed the reminder for herself as much as for Conner. She was often frustrated by the limitations of medical science.

He nodded and she again felt as if they shared equal concern and responsibility for providing what this baby needed. He bent his head over his daughter and whispered her name.

She wondered if Conner watched the rise and fall of the tiny chest as desperately as she did.

In a bit, Ellie made a mewling sound.

"Hand me that whatever it's called and I'll see if

Ellie will drink some more. I'm no doctor, but I know she needs something in her stomach if she's to survive."

Kate gave him the syringe of sugar water. He eased the tip between Ellie's lips and squeezed out a shot.

Ellie choked. Her face grew red.

Conner's face blanched. "What do I do?"

Rather than explain it to the distraught man, Kate took Ellie, turned her over and patted her back. She bent over the baby, watching her face. "Come on, little one, take a breath."

The baby calmed.

Kate's heart took slightly longer to return to a normal pace.

She turned Ellie about to look in her face. "You gave us quite a scare." Solemn eyes focused on her for a brief moment before losing interest.

Conner let out a long sigh. "I almost killed her." His voice shook. His gaze met hers. She couldn't say if it was gratitude or caution she saw in his eyes or something else entirely. Nor could she explain why the look made her ache inside.

She struggled to adjust her thinking about this man. She'd always thought him noble and honorable. To learn he had fathered a child left her wondering what sort of man he really was.

She placed the baby back in his arms and looked at the syringe. "Just a little at a time."

Conner studied her for a moment, then turned to the baby. "Swallow for me, little Ellie. Please don't choke."

Water dribbled from the baby's mouth.

Conner watched the baby for a moment, then lifted his gaze to Kate's. "I can't do this by myself. Will you stay and help?"

How could she stay? Father needed her.

"Please?" Conner's eyes filled with kindness and something she wasn't able to identify. Was it determination or regret? Fear or warning?

She brought her attention back to the baby. She had to do what she could to ensure little Ellie lived. A baby's life hung in the balance.

"I'll stay until she's doing better." Father would have to get along without her for a few hours. After that? Conner would need to find someone to tend his baby, but he had lots of people to choose from—his sister and his sisters-in-law.

Conner smiled. "Thank you. This baby needs a family, but right now she needs more. She needs what you can give her."

Family. The word caught at her heart. Why did it trouble her? She could think of no reason and dismissed the thought. It wasn't like she longed for something more. Medical care was what she offered. It was the focus of her life.

She'd once thought things might be different. As an eager seventeen-year-old, she'd loved the attention given to her by Edward Sabin over a six-month period. Her eyes full of starry dreams, she'd told him of her plan to become a doctor. He'd said she would have to choose between him and her dreams because he didn't intend to share her with every Tom, Dick and Harry, or even every Mary, Alice and Harriet.

She'd said it wasn't that easy and told him of her promise to Grammie. Grammie, who had raised her since her birth parents died when Kate was four until her own death six years later, said she had the gift of healing and made her promise not to waste the gift. Besides, she liked taking care of people.

Edward had stopped calling, but he'd made her acknowledge the impossibility of trying to be both a doctor and a wife and mother. Her own childhood after the Bakers had adopted her provided further proof. How many times had her sleep been interrupted as she was taken next door so her parents could attend some medical need? How often had she missed a social event for the same reason? But in exchange, she'd learned much about caring for others.

Kate went to the kitchen. Grandfather sat outside on the veranda, rocking in the sun and watching the activities in the yard. She glimpsed one of the cowhands riding by the garden.

It was all so ordinary and peaceful. Unlike her own home, where every ordinary moment ended with a call for the doctor's services, where there was often a flurry of activity as they faced a medical crisis. It was just her father and her now. Mother had died eight years ago when Kate was fourteen.

Kate was a willing, eager participant in dealing with the frequent illnesses, accidents and childbirths, but as she waited for the water to boil, she leaned on the windowsill, taking in the calm scene.

The kettle steamed and the moment passed. She prepared Ellie's feeding and returned to the sitting room and drew to a halt at the sight before her. Conner leaned back on the couch, his mouth open as he snored softly. The poor man must have been up most of the night. Ellie slept peacefully on his chest. A beautiful picture of fatherly love and care.

It triggered an ache hidden deep within her heart. One she must deny.

This man had a daughter and thus belonged to another woman. Not that it mattered to her. She had plans that would take her away from here. But for today, she would enjoy the feeling of warmth that being with the Marshall family gave. She would enjoy caring for a baby who needed her.

Surely it was possible to do so without struggling with secret longings.

Wasn't it?

Chapter Two

Conner snorted at the sound of someone clearing a throat, opened his eyes and looked up at Kate.

"I think I fell asleep." He bent his head to check on Ellie. She slept. Her cheekbones pushed against her skin. Such a frail baby. His resolve tightened his chest. She needed him. He would do everything possible for her.

"It's time to feed her again." Kate leaned over him and gently shook Ellie to waken her. The baby's eyelids came up slowly. Her pupils remained unfocused. She stared past Kate as if unaware of her.

He shifted the baby so Kate could feed her. But Ellie's mouth hung slack and the liquid ran down her neck.

Kate's face filled with purpose. "Did anything you tried last night get her attention?"

"She seemed to like to hear me sing." Heat swept over his chest at how foolish he felt admitting it.

"Well, then, I suggest you sing to her."

"No one but Ellie listened last night." He could barely squeak the words out as embarrassment clogged his throat.

She chuckled. "I'll assume she is a good judge of your singing ability. Now sing."

"Can't. My throat's too dry."

"I can fix that." She hurried to the kitchen and returned with a glass of cold water. "Drink."

Seemed she wasn't prepared to accept any excuses from him. "You're bossy. Did you know that?" It was his turn to chuckle as pink blossomed in her cheeks.

She gave a little toss of her head. "I'm simply speaking with authority. You did ask me to stay and help. I assumed you wanted my medical assistance."

No mistaking the challenge in her voice.

"Your medical assistance, yes, of course." He humbled his voice and did his best to look contrite.

"You sing to her and I'll try to get more sugar water into her."

He cleared his throat. "Sleep, my love, and peace attend thee. All through the night; Guardian angels God will lend thee, All through the night." The first few notes caught in his throat and then he focused his eyes on Ellie at the words of the familiar lullaby.

Ellie blinked and brought her gaze to him.

"Excellent," Kate whispered and leaned over Conner's arm to ease the syringe between Ellie's lips. The baby swallowed three times and then her eyes closed.

"Sleep is good, too," Kate murmured, leaning back. "I think she likes your voice."

He couldn't stop himself from meeting Kate's eyes. Warmth filled them and he allowed himself a little glow of victory. "Thelma hated my singing." He hadn't meant to say that. Certainly not aloud.

Kate's eyes cooled considerably. "You're referring to Ellie's mother?"

"That's right." No need to say more.

"Do you mind me asking where she is?"

"'Fraid I can't answer that."

She waited.

"I don't know. I haven't seen her in over a year."

"I see."

Only, it was obvious she didn't. But he wasn't going to explain. Not until he figured out what Thelma was up to.

Kate pushed to her feet.

The side where she'd been sitting next to him on the couch grew instantly cold.

"How long before we wake her to feed her again?"

"Fifteen minutes. You hold her and rest. I don't suppose you got much sleep last night."

There she was, being bossy and authoritative again. Not that he truly minded. It was nice to know someone cared how tired he was and also knew how to deal with Ellie.

The fifteen minutes passed quickly and Kate wakened the baby.

"She's weaker." His voice cracked. "Wasn't she supposed to be getting better by now?"

"It's a fine balance between getting fluid into her and not overtaxing her strength." She tried to get the baby to swallow, but her head lolled and her eyes had a distant unfocused look to them.

"Sing to her again," Kate said. "It makes her more responsive."

"I find it hard to believe you don't beg me not to, but if it helps Ellie, I'll do it." He again sang the words of the lullaby.

The baby turned her eyes toward Conner. Kate leaned

close to feed her some sugar water. Ellie swallowed without urging.

"My grandmother used to sing that to me," Kate said.

Conner stopped. "I remember my ma singing it to Annie and then Mattie. I expect she sang it to me, but I don't remember." He thought of the number of times he'd heard her crooning to his little sister and his niece. Memories of his ma and her steadfast love almost choked him.

"I don't recall my mother singing to me either, but then I was young when she passed away."

The baby stopped swallowing as soon as Conner stopped singing. Kate pointed it out to him and he turned back to Ellie and sang again the same lullaby. Only, he added his own words to the tune. "Didn't I hear that your mother died when you were fourteen? Did I misunderstand?" he asked Kate in a singsongy voice. He was curious about this woman and wanted to know more about her.

She didn't normally talk to patients or their parents about herself, but she rather found she wanted to tell him about her parents.

"My birth parents died from a fever when I was four. I went to live with my Grammie, but she wasn't well. Dr. and Mrs. Baker cared for her until she died when I was ten. She asked them to adopt me and they did. Grammie said I had a gift for healing and helping and wanted the Bakers to help me follow that path." Why had she said that? He surely wasn't interested in why she'd chosen this goal. "Mother died four years later. It's just been me and Father since."

He squeezed her hand. "I'm sorry."

The knot in her chest disappeared at the comfort of his warm palm.

He shifted his attention back to the baby, removing his hand from Kate's for her to squeeze out a drop of sugar water.

"So you're following your grandmother's and your parents' dreams."

"Their dreams? No, I'm following my dream."

He nodded, though she couldn't say if he was satisfied with her answer or not. Nor did it matter. She knew what she must do. What she *wanted* to do.

"You're an only child?" he asked.

"I am." Why did the answer trouble her? It wasn't as if she'd minded having no siblings.

"Were you ever lonely?"

"My mother often accompanied my father as his assistant. When I was younger, I was left with the Bramfords next door. There were eight children in their family. Two girls about my age. Younger brothers and sisters and an older brother and sister. I was not lonely at their place." She told him more of the big, rambunctious family.

"There wasn't time for games or parties at our house. Most of my parents' time and activities involved taking care of the sick and injured and reading the latest medical journals."

Conner's expression grew serious.

Kate realized he might have misunderstood the way she described her parents. "I loved being involved with their work."

"I can't imagine being an only child," Conner said. "When we moved out here, my brothers and sister were my only playmates and companions. When Ma died, we helped each other through it. We've been through a lot—the death of Mattie's ma and—" He broke off.

She wondered if he'd been about to mention Thelma, but he did not continue.

Instead, he turned back to Ellie, singing a familiar hymn.

Kate slowly brought her gaze to his. Her head was only inches from him. She could make out the flecks of silver in his blue eyes. She could see his pupils narrow. Could hear the sharp intake of his breath.

She forced her gaze to shift and concentrated on the baby. "Were her dreams more important than giving Ellie a home?"

She couldn't imagine letting a child of hers out of her sight. How many times had she watched her mother and father leave on a medical call and felt so alone? Even when she was surrounded by the large family next door, whom she stayed with in their absence. It was the reason she had made the decision not to try to combine being a doctor with being a wife and mother. That, and realizing that men weren't willing to share her. After Edward, other men had as quickly stopped calling on her when they learned of her plans. She agreed with their evaluation. She knew it was fooling herself to think she could be a wife, a mother and also a doctor.

Conner's singing stopped and his voice flattened as he answered her question. "It would appear Thelma's dreams were more important than caring for Ellie, though for all I know she has married someone else."

"Then why…?" She broke off. If Thelma had married before the baby was born, her husband would be the legal father of the child, even if Ellie was Conner's offspring. It was not—she reminded herself—her business.

"Then why would she send the baby to me?" He shrugged. "That's something I aim to find out."

The baby had stopped eating and her eyes had closed.

Kate sat back on the chair that she'd dragged next to the couch. "She did well this time."

"You sound hopeful."

"I am. Why don't I take her and you can take a break? Maybe get a drink, stretch your legs."

He hesitated as if he didn't want to leave the baby. She understood his concern. Ellie was so fragile. "I'll watch her carefully."

Conner nodded and she lifted the baby from his warm arms, wrapped the blankets about her and cuddled her close. The feel of a baby in her arms tugged at her lonely heart. If only she could believe she could follow her dream *and* enjoy a family.

But she knew the cost would be too high both for her children and herself. To leave them to tend others...

She shook her head, ignoring the ache behind her eyes.

She must stick to her convictions.

"I need to take care of my horses." Conner bolted for the door. He had chores to do. But more than that, he needed to get outside where he could think.

Yesterday, he'd been breaking horses and making plans to sell them to the right owners, making money to buy more animals. Soon, he hoped to be the best horse dealer in the country. That would make him a valuable part of the Marshall Five Ranch. Not, he argued with himself, that he wasn't now. But it would make him *more* important. Able to contribute more.

How had he gone from there yesterday to here

today, holding a tiny baby in his arms and neglecting his horses?

And watching Kate hold Ellie and croon over her. Kate's brown hair was almost a match for Ellie's. They had similar brown eyes. They could have passed for mother and child. The thought made him break his stride. He knew of her plans to be a doctor. Did becoming a wife and mother fit into those plans? Not that it mattered to him one way or the other.

He yanked off his hat and rubbed his head. How had things gotten so mixed up? Had Thelma married? If so, why had she sent the baby to him? And why was the little one doing so poorly? They needed to find her and get some answers from her. He'd send a message to his friend Sheriff Jesse Hill as soon as he could. How long would it take for Jesse to locate her?

He fed and watered the horses, then walked around them one at a time. Two were already spoken for and he'd promised they'd be ready within the week. It didn't appear that would happen now if he was stuck inside looking after the baby. When would his sister and sisters-in-law return? He was counting on them to take over Ellie's care. Though he was most grateful for Kate's expertise at the moment.

Thinking of Kate brought his thoughts back to his newfound responsibility. He jerked to a halt and stared toward the house. Was everything okay? He bolted from the pen and crossed the yard in double time, clattered across the kitchen and dining room to grind to a halt in the doorway to the sitting room.

Kate held the baby, stroking her pale cheek and murmuring to her. She glanced up at Conner's noisy entrance and smiled. Something in his heart tipped a little to the side and remained so for several seconds. Then things righted and he entered the room.

"How is she?"

"Taking a few drops at a time."

"That's all?" He settled by her side and pressed his hands to the baby. "I wish we could do more."

"I'm doing all I know to do."

"I couldn't manage without you." Her face was inches from his. Conner watched a play of emotions in Kate's eyes and longed to be able to read them. Then her gaze dropped to Ellie. She caught the little hand and rubbed it. She looked at him again, her eyes full of determination.

"I will do everything in my power to see this little one grow strong."

He had made the same vow and felt as if he and Kate stepped across some invisible threshold, united in heart and purpose.

He was not alone in fighting for this baby and found immense comfort in the thought. He couldn't think of the little one not getting better. Even though she wasn't his, his heart had laid claim to her.

Kate hummed as she tried to feed the baby, but Ellie pressed her lips together and turned away.

"Give her to me," Conner said. His voice was rough, but he couldn't help it. Ellie needed to drink. When Kate shifted the baby into his arms, he cradled the little bundle to his chest.

"It's like she has almost given up trying." Her eyes filled with regret. "I'm sorry. I shouldn't have said that."

"You haven't told me anything I can't see on my own. Have you seen this before?" He meant, *did people give up the desire to live?*

"Only in discouraged and ill adults." Her voice broke and she turned away. With a choked sound, she hurried to the window to stare out. Her shoulders heaved.

Was she crying? Fighting her fears? He couldn't say, but he wanted to ease her obvious strain. "Come here." He kept his voice soft even though his insides felt as if they'd been sliced with a thousand dull blades.

She didn't move. "Give me a moment." She sucked in air.

He waited.

Slowly she turned. Her face a careful mask as if she had pushed all her feelings behind a wall. She crossed to the couch.

"Sit down." He indicated the chair at his side and she sat. "Give me your hand."

She hesitated, then put her hand in his.

He brought it to the baby and placed it over the tiny chest and covered her hand with his. "Feel that?"

"It's her heart beating."

"Yes. You said the outcome is in God's hands."

She nodded.

"Then we will pray for His healing." He bowed his head and prayed. "God, You love Ellie. You have a plan and a purpose for her life. She's so young. So needy. We're doing all we can to help her. But only You can heal her. We humbly ask that You would see fit to touch her little body and make her strong." He paused, wanting so much more, answers to questions about Thelma, a caring home, loving parents for the baby, but he could say none of those aloud. He simply had to trust God for all of it. "Amen."

"Amen," Kate echoed.

Conner expected she would pull away, but she stayed

as they were, their heads almost touching, their hands on Ellie's chest feeling her heart beat and the rise and fall of her breathing. "Thank you."

"For what?"

"For reminding me that it's in God's hands, not mine."

The afternoon became a continual round of waking, feeding and hovering over the baby. But each time the baby took a little more.

"It's good, isn't it?" He was ready to rejoice.

"Yes, it's very good. Maybe she'll take some milk now." She hurried to the kitchen to prepare it.

Conner leaned back, shifting the baby so they were face-to-face. Ellie's eyes met his. "Who are you, little one? Why are you here? Where's your mother? I need to find her, don't I? Did she forget to take care of you? Is that why you're so weak? Or have you been sick?" So many questions. "And you aren't giving me any of the answers, are you?"

The sound of approaching footsteps warned him of Kate's return and he stopped questioning the baby and chuckled at the silliness of doing so.

Ellie's eyes widened at his laugh.

Kate pressed to his side so she could feed the baby. She eased the rubber nipple into the tiny mouth. Ellie gagged but then closed her mouth about the contraption and sucked. Her eyes widened as she tasted the milk. She drank eagerly for a moment or two.

Kate leaned over them both and Conner was so full of gratitude over the improvement that he wrapped his arm about her shoulders and drew her against his chest, next to the baby. His heart felt ready to burst.

She stiffened and pulled away, sat upright in the chair

by the couch, folded her hands in her lap and studied him with a solemn expression.

"Forgive me. I was rejoicing over her improvement."

Kate nodded. "Of course."

He reached for her hands and clasped them to his chest. "We're doing all we can, aren't we?"

She curled her fingers into the fabric of his shirt. "I believe so."

He understood then that the baby was still not out of the woods.

Chapter Three

She should not have revealed her worry about the baby. A doctor or nurse did not frighten family members with either words or expressions, but she could not put a serene mask over her features. All she could do was cling to the fact Ellie was improving.

Conner lifted one hand and cupped her shoulder. "Kate, you're doing a good job if Ellie's present condition means anything."

Ellie opened her eyes and found Kate's face.

"See, even the baby knows it. She likes you. She knows you're helping her."

Kate smiled at the baby and stroked a finger along the tiny cheek. "She is certainly a sweetie. So beautiful." A fierce protectiveness crowded all else from her mind. "Ellie, you are going to eat and fight and get strong. You hear me?"

The baby considered her solemnly, then smiled. The smile disappeared so quickly Kate wondered if she'd imagined it. "Did you see that? She smiled."

Conner chuckled. "I told you, she likes you."

"We're going to do this." She looked deep into Conner's eyes. "We are going to save this baby, so help me God." She meant it as a prayer and a vow, and when Conner nodded, she felt as if they had joined hands in mutual agreement.

There welled up within her a sense of something sweet and powerful. She tried to tell herself it was the same sensation she got whenever she helped her father, saw a baby or a child or an adult improving and knowing she had a hand in it. Only, the feeling was unlike any she'd ever before experienced and she could not dismiss it so easily nor fit it into a tidy slot in her brain.

She knew of one sure way to bring her thoughts into order and she concentrated on feeding Ellie. When she was satisfied the baby had taken all she would, she hurried to the kitchen…in need of an escape from the intensity prevailing in her thoughts while sitting so close to Conner, feeling the rise and fall of his chest, hearing his deep voice murmur to the baby. And knowing all the while that Thelma belonged where Kate now sat.

She found food in the pantry that Annie had prepared earlier and served them a simple dinner. She wished she had time to do more. Cooking and baking were pleasures for her. And wonderful diversions. Grandfather joined them to eat.

They all retired to the sitting room again. She needed to get back to her father. As she had done all morning, she prayed he would be handling things well on his own.

She was about to say she must leave when the sound of approaching horses drew their attention to the window. She was holding Ellie, who dozed after another decent feed. Conner hurried to look out. "Pa, Logan and Dawson are back." His father and two brothers. Conner scrubbed his hand back and forth over his head, as if anxious over their reaction to discovering a baby in the house.

Grandfather made a disapproving sound. "You hoping to frighten them with a scarecrow look by doing that?"

He smoothed his hair into some semblance of order and jammed his hands into his front pockets.

Grandfather continued, "You'll have to tell them the truth."

"Yeah. I guess so."

Kate could almost feel sorry for him, but having fathered a child, he must face up to his responsibilities. Still, she didn't envy him having to confront his brothers and father.

They all turned to listen to the outer door open and shut, booted feet stomp off the trail dust and then a parade of thuds across the floor toward the sitting room.

Conner's pa entered, followed by his two sons.

She studied them, wondering how they would react to Conner's predicament. Bud, the father, was tall, blond and blue-eyed as were all the Marshalls. A man used to working hard and expecting those around him to work equally hard. Dawson, the eldest brother, was now married to Kate's best friend, Isabelle. Logan, the youngest, was married to Sadie, the schoolteacher.

Bud's gaze rested on the baby in Kate's arms. "What do we have here?"

Kate rose, eased the baby into Conner's hold. "I'll let you explain." She walked from the room and into the kitchen, where she couldn't overhear a conversation she expected would be difficult.

Kate heard no angry sounds as she waited in the kitchen. What sort of reaction would Conner be facing?

How would he be feeling? Shame? Regret? She twisted her hands together, wishing she could offer him the same comfort and encouragement he had offered her.

Which was rather silly. All she could offer him was help with Ellie and that only for a few more hours at most.

Logan and Dawson hurried through the kitchen saying they were going to hitch up a wagon. She expected they were going to see their wives. In the men's absence, Dawson's six-year-old daughter, Mattie, and his wife, Isabelle, had gone to town to visit Sadie and the children she and Logan had adopted.

She stared at the doorway to the dining room. She couldn't see the sitting room door beyond. What had taken place in her absence?

Bud strode through the room, muttering under his breath. Grandfather shuffled out to sit on the veranda and she waited. Should she return?

"Kate?" Conner's voice came to her and she needed no more invitation to hurry back. Perhaps he would tell her what had transpired. She drew to a halt, facing Conner.

"That went as well as could be expected." Conner sat with Ellie cradled close to his chest, wariness in his eyes. "Dawson is going to ask Sheriff Jesse to come out and see me. I'll ask him to find Thelma. Dawson said he could easily give Jesse all the needed information, but I'd like to see him myself." He shrugged. "Maybe I can explain a few things and hope he'll understand."

She kept her attention on the baby. How did he hope to explain away a baby daughter? There was simply no way. Thelma must be found. He must marry her. Kate would no longer be needed. But who was she fooling?

Once Conner's sisters-in-law returned, Kate would have no reason to stay. Yes, the baby was weak still, her condition fragile, but she was eating. Anyone could take care of her now.

"I can't imagine going through another night like last night," he said.

"You will manage just fine. Just make sure she eats often."

His mouth drew back. His eyes widened. He wore the expression of a fearful man.

She almost laughed. "She's getting stronger with every feeding."

He shook his head. "What if something happens? What if she takes a turn for the worse? Or—" His mouth worked before he finished. "What if she chokes again? Can't you at least stay overnight?"

She assessed her choices. Ellie likely needed her more than Father did. And she truly wanted to tend the baby a little longer…to hold her, feel her chest rise and fall with each breath, listen to her suck the bottle and catch a fleeting smile or two. "I'll stay, but I must get word to my father and ask him to send a few things for me."

"Here, hold Ellie. I'll go let Logan and Dawson know they need to stop by before they leave. There's paper and pencil in the desk that you can use to write a note to your father." He pointed to the rolltop desk in the corner. "Help yourself."

"Thanks." But he was gone before she finished. She smiled at Ellie. "I'm glad I get to enjoy you for a few more hours." She cradled the baby in one arm as she quickly wrote a note explaining the situation and asking Father to send out a few items of clothing. She finished with, *Are you doing okay? If you need me, I will come back.*

She folded the paper just as Dawson came to the door and handed him the note. "This is for my father. He'll want to send a bag back with you."

"I'll take care of it. Kate, I'm glad you're staying." His footsteps rang across the kitchen floor, and seconds later, the rattle of a wagon signaled his departure to town.

Kate stared toward the sound. She'd been away all morning and into the afternoon. Was Father managing okay or was he suffering memory lapses? What if he had one while tending a patient? If something happened, it would be her fault for leaving him.

She turned back to Ellie. But if she left the baby, how would Conner manage on his own?

How would she live with herself if things went wrong?

Conner returned and took the baby while Kate prepared a bottle.

He chuckled as he fed Ellie. "Logan was in a mighty big hurry to get to town."

"I suppose he misses his family."

"It was good of Sadie to give up teaching to be a mother." He referred to the fact that Logan and Sadie had adopted three orphans. "Is there anything nobler than providing a home for a family?"

"Isn't it nobler to serve a bigger cause, help more than those in a family circle?" She'd been taught so since the Bakers had adopted her at age ten. Even Grammie, before her death, had asked Katie, as she was then called, to use her gift wisely. Kate knew she referred to her ability to help those ill and suffering. She'd been doing so for Grammie for over a year as she'd grown weaker. "I thought it was too bad she gave up teaching." She laughed a little in an attempt to hide her defensiveness.

Ellie blinked and her eyes focused.

"Do it again," Conner said. "She likes it."

"Do what?"

"Laugh. It got her attention."

"I can't laugh unless I'm amused." And at the moment she wasn't feeling very amused at Conner's opinion about Sadie giving up teaching. It seemed to her she could do both. After all, Sadie was an exceptionally good teacher and there were far too few of them out in western Montana.

Conner brought his gaze to her and studied her a moment. "How many men are willing to live with sharing a wife with the whole world?"

"Probably none, which is why I don't intend to combine doctoring with marriage or raising a family." She'd made a promise to Grammie, but besides that, she liked taking care of people. It went a long way toward filling her heart.

"I think I hear someone riding in." She rushed to the window. "Yes, it's Dawson and he's got Isabelle and Mattie with him." Unable to stop her rush of words, she recited every detail of the man's approach. "I hear him talking to Grandfather." And then the outer door opened and booted feet crossed the floor.

"Howdy," Dawson said. He handed a satchel to Kate. "Your father put a note in there for you."

"Thanks." She took the bag and reached in for the paper her father had written on.

"Jesse is on his way?" Conner asked.

"'Fraid not. There was a note on the door saying he

had gone to Great Falls with a prisoner. He'll be back in the morning. Now I'm going home to enjoy some time with my wife and child." He strode from the room.

Kate unfolded the message and read, *Dear Kate, you must indeed stay and tend that baby. I am coping admirably though I haven't been able to find the carbolic acid. Stay as long as you are needed. As you ask, I will send for you if I think it necessary. Blessings, your father.*

She folded the page carefully and returned it to the satchel. She'd put the carbolic acid on the shelf where it belonged. Was Father having a forgetful spell? They had grown infrequent in the past few weeks, but having her away, not pointing toward the things he needed, not reminding him what he meant to do would surely be a test of his recovery. She shivered. If he should fail while she wasn't there to direct him, it could prove disastrous. *Father God, please keep his mind clear. Don't let him make a mistake.*

She lifted her head to discover Conner watching her.

"Is everything all right with your father?"

"What do you mean? What could be wrong?" She'd done her best to cover her father's momentary lapses as he mended.

Conner's eyes narrowed. "I wasn't suggesting there was. But I saw the little worry frown in your forehead and wondered what caused it."

"My forehead?" She rubbed the spot that she knew furrowed when she worried overly much. "You're imagining things."

He laughed. "Not that line across your forehead and don't think you can rub it away."

She covered her forehead with her hand and tried

to look as if it didn't matter a bit. But heat stole up her neck and she knew her blush would reveal how much his words flustered her. Wanting to divert him, she went to the baby, forgetting how close it would bring her to Conner. Thankfully he was too interested in Ellie to notice her warm cheeks and she slowly backed away.

The rest of the afternoon passed quickly with repeatedly feeding Ellie. Knowing Conner and his family must learn to care for the baby on their own, Kate purposely spent as much time in the kitchen as she could. Annie was a good housekeeper, so there wasn't a lot to do. Kate washed up the dishes that had accumulated throughout the day, scrubbed the few items of clothing that had accompanied Ellie and hung them to dry. For a moment, she considered making a batch of cookies. But this wasn't her house. She didn't have the right.

However, they had to eat and she prepared another meal from the food Annie had left. Conner held the baby in one arm, just like he'd been born to be a father, as he joined the others at the table.

Kate sat on the chair that Bud indicated, across from Conner. Grandfather and Bud sat across from each other. It was Grandfather who offered the grace.

"We're grateful for the food, Lord, but right now we're concerned with little Ellie and we beseech You to make her strong. Amen."

Grandfather concentrated on dishing up food for a moment or two, then turned to Kate. "Conner says you are staying overnight. I have to say I'm glad you're here. Don't mind telling you I was worried about that little one in there last night."

"Can't see the boy managing on his own," Bud

added. "He thinks because he fed an orphaned calf, he knows about babies."

Kate laughed at Bud's woeful tone and wondered how Conner felt about being referred to as "the boy."

"You, my dear, are an answer to prayer." Grandfather's gratitude was a balm to Kate's soul. "Though we acknowledge that the results are in God's hands. We humans do what we can. No one should ask any more than that from us. Or us of ourselves."

She promised herself to keep in mind that gentle reminder to do her job and leave the results in God's control.

The conversation shifted to talk about the cows Bud and the others had checked on. He brought a good report.

"Sure wish I could go see for myself," Grandfather said. Then he brightened. "But then I wouldn't have been here when the baby was dropped off on the doorstep." He chuckled. "Sure glad I was here to see the look on Conner's face." He tipped his head back and roared with laughter.

Conner shook his head and gave a half smile. "It was the last thing I expected." His gaze came to Kate. His eyes warmed as if to remind her how they had shared that moment of surprise and concern.

For the briefest of moments, she allowed herself to think he enjoyed having her at his side during those first awkward, tension-filled hours. Then she reminded herself she was simply a medical person, appreciated for her ability to help Ellie and teach Conner how to care for his little daughter.

No doubt the sheriff would soon locate Thelma and there would be a wedding for Ellie's parents.

That was as it should be and she promised herself

she would rejoice that Ellie would have a permanent home with a father and mother.

While Kate continued with her own plans...ones that left no room for babies and family. Her decision had been made, based on the facts she understood and accepted.

The men pushed back from the table and Conner took the bottle Kate prepared for Ellie. He remained in the kitchen while she cleaned up. She told herself his only reason for staying had nothing to do with keeping her company and was to have her nearby to coach him, but in truth, he needed no guidance from her. And despite all her arguments against the idea, she enjoyed him being nearby as she worked.

Later, the others went to their rooms, leaving Kate and Conner in the sitting room, caring for the baby.

"You might as well relax in Grandfather's chair. He often sleeps in it, so I can only assume it's suitable for a nap," Conner said.

She sank into the deep armchair, surprised at how weary she was. "It's very comfortable."

"Feel free to close your eyes and rest."

"Just for a few minutes, then I'll take her and feed her while you sleep for a bit."

She had no intention of sleeping. Her role there was to provide medical care.

She leaned back, watching Conner from beneath her half-lowered eyelids. He stroked the baby's face and hummed a lullaby. Little Ellie watched him, slowly drinking from the bottle of milk. Such adoration in Conner's face. He would be an excellent father.

She must have dozed for she jerked awake, suddenly alert with the sense of someone watching her, and she met Conner's steady gaze. It must be sleep clouding her mind to think his look was warm. Heat crawled up her neck and pooled in her cheeks. Why was she so aware of this man especially given the circumstances? A father of a baby. And somewhere, a woman who would claim his name. She broke from the intensity of his look and turned toward the baby sleeping contentedly in his arms.

Why was it that, after years of schooling herself to be professional and detached, she continually failed to do so in this situation? What was wrong with her?

Conner had studied Kate as she slept through the lengthening night hours. She was a beautiful woman with a serenity about her that intensified her beauty.

Familiar sounds of the house settled for the night and the little sleeping noises Ellie made were all that broke the silence. The quiet gave him time to review the events of the day. Like how Pa had reacted when he saw Ellie.

Conner, hoping to delay the questions in his pa's face, had cradled Ellie in one arm and faced his father and brothers. "Pa, Dawson, Logan, meet Ellie."

"Howdy," Pa said and his brothers had each touched the baby's hands, tenderness in their eyes and curiosity on their faces.

"Why are you holding her like you own her?" Pa asked.

"Yeah, Conner, you can't bring babies home and keep them," Logan said. "They aren't like puppies."

"Where'd you find her?" Dawson asked.

Conner had plucked Thelma's note from his back pocket and handed it to Pa. Logan and Dawson read it over Pa's shoulder. Then three pairs of shocked, disbelieving eyes came to him.

"She's yours?" Pa's voice rang sharp enough to make Conner cringe inside. He'd never let anyone see him cringe on the outside.

"No." It took a minute to convince them Ellie was not his daughter.

"Then why?"

Conner repeated his worry that the baby was in danger. "It's best if no one knows the truth until we can find Thelma and know why she did this."

"In the meantime, who is going to look after her?" Pa asked. "Is Annie back?"

Grandfather grunted. "He knows nothing about babies. Thinks they're like calves. If not for Kate..." He shook his head.

Conner's confidence in caring for Ellie grew with each feeding, thanks to Kate. Like Grandfather said... if not for Kate. A rod of tension had eased when she agreed to stay the night.

He didn't know how long he'd been watching her when her eyes opened and their gazes connected. She blinked away her sleep and she sat up, instantly awake. Her gaze darted away from him. Likely she wondered why he watched her so intently.

"You deserve to marry and have a family of your own." He blamed the fact that they were alone, the room lit only by a lamp, for his rash words.

She jerked her wide-eyed gaze back to him. "That will never be. I am going to become a doctor." She bolted to her feet.

He caught her hand before she could escape. "You could also be a wife and mother."

She shook her head. "I know I couldn't do justice to both roles. Doctors can't count on being there for family events. I should know."

The truth hit him like a sledgehammer. "Did you feel you were less important to your parents than their work?"

She tugged at her hand, but he wouldn't let her get free. She shook her head and turned away.

He knew as surely as he breathed that her life had been full of loneliness and uncertainty. "Oh, Kate." He felt her pain and confusion as if it were his own and his voice cracked with emotion.

He could not stand to see her so distressed and pulled her close, pressed her face to his shoulder, Kate in one arm, Ellie in the other. His throat tightened. His chest clamped tight so that it hurt to breathe. Why must people be wounded and suffer such pain? Little Ellie so weak because of neglect or illness. Kate feeling neglected by her parents if even for a noble cause.

She shuddered and tried to sit up, but he pressed her back, not ready to let her leave his arms. "I want to hear all about it."

"They were only doing their job and I understood that. Their dedication was why Grammie sent me to them. 'You've the gift of caring,' she said to me. 'Promise me you won't waste it.' And I won't."

She pulled away and Conner, feeling the depth of her resolve, let her go even though he longed to persuade her that she could make other choices. A promise given to her grandmother when she was a young child should not control her into adulthood. Surely her grandmother would want her to choose what suited Kate best.

"We all must do what we must do." Her tone was

flat as if the final word had been spoken on the subject. "Just as you must marry Thelma."

"Thelma?" He'd forgotten about her. It was on the tip of his tongue to say he didn't love her. Perhaps he never had, though it had devastated him for her to walk away without a backward look. It no longer hurt.

He tried not to think of the many reasons she would have sent the baby to him and said it was his—none of them reassuring. A cruel husband and father, choosing her profession over her own baby, or worst—she had died and just before her death arranged for the baby to be taken to Conner. If she was alive and unmarried, would he marry her to give the baby a home? He studied wee Ellie. She certainly deserved a loving, supportive family.

But he could not tell Kate the truth about her or the baby until he found Thelma and straightened things out.

"Time to feed her again." With a great deal of dignity in every step and in the way she held her head, Kate went to the kitchen.

Conner leaned back. He must tell her the truth about Ellie…that he wasn't the father. How would she react? Would she welcome the news? He closed his eyes and forced himself to think sensibly. Why would it matter to her? She'd been clear that she had no interest in anything but pursuing her plans to become a doctor.

From Grandfather's room came a rumbling snore. Bedsprings creaked upstairs as someone rolled over. Outside a horse whinnied softly. From a nearby hill came the yipping of several coyotes. The moon shone through the window, giving a silvery glow to the room. So calm and peaceful. Unfortunately the feeling did not reach his heart. His thoughts tangled with questions about Thelma and why she had sent Ellie to him and a yearning from deep within.

He sat up and met Ellie's gaze. This tiny little girl was the reminder he needed. He was not going to allow himself to care for a woman who didn't put him and family life ahead of dreams of what some might see as bigger, better things…like being a singer. Or a doctor. How had Kate put it? She saw it as being nobler.

He had a baby who needed him. And then there was Thelma. Whatever Thelma's situation, she had done the right thing and sent Ellie to him, no doubt knowing Conner and the entire Marshall family would see that this little one was well taken care of. His life was quite complicated enough at the moment.

Kate returned and gingerly took Ellie from him. Her movements were stiff and unnatural and he couldn't deny it hurt a little to know she tried not to touch him.

She returned to the armchair and spoke softly to the baby.

Conner caught only a few words…enough to know that Kate informed the baby she was going to eat well and get strong and healthy.

Ellie seemed fascinated with all the things Kate saw for her in the future and drank steadily. Finally, she turned away and smacked her lips.

Kate held the feeding bottle toward the lamplight and gasped. "It's half gone." She sprang to her feet. "Conner, Conner. She took half a bottle of milk."

"She did?" Conner grabbed Kate by her upper arms. "Really and truly?"

"Really and truly." Kate laughed. "She's taken a turn for the better."

"That's wonderful." Conner's voice caught. The

good news filled him with an overwhelming sense that the world was a good place. "God has answered our prayers." He pulled Kate close, the baby between them.

Kate tipped her head back to smile at him. Her smile dipped into his heart. For the moment, all that mattered was the joy over Ellie's improvement and gratitude toward this woman who had been instrumental in that improvement.

Her gaze held his, searching for what he could not say. But he longed to be the one to give her what she sought.

He trailed the back of his hand along Kate's cheek. His fingers lingered at the corner of her mouth and his gaze dipped and then he caught her lips in a gentle-as-dawn kiss. If not for the baby between them, he would have held her close.

She pushed away. "How can you kiss me when you belong to Thelma?"

"Kate, it's not what you think." He pulled the baby closer as if it would anchor his thoughts.

It failed to do so. He wanted to explain about Thelma.

"I'm not interested in dillydallying with a man. I will be pursuing my studies in medical school as soon as it can be arranged."

He wasn't interested in dillydallying either. Nor was he interested in a relationship of any sort with a woman whose plans left no room for him.

But if she knew the truth about the baby and Thelma, would she be willing to consider a different option than the one she seemed committed to? He'd heard loneliness in her voice when she talked about the difference between the family next door and her own. Kate, he knew, wanted and needed family. But she fought it. He wanted her to see that even if there remained no room for him in her heart. But before he could say anything, Grandfather shuffled from his bedroom. "How is the patient this morning?"

Conner realized with a start that the night had flown by. Holding the baby, he told the older man of the improvement.

Grandfather patted her cheek.

Suddenly Conner held the baby away from him. "I believe our little girl's kidneys are working just fine."

Kate burst out laughing.

He narrowed his eyes. "You think it's funny?"

"The look on your face is priceless." She seemed to try to muffle her amusement as she found a dry diaper in the basket, then took the baby from his arms.

He was glad to have lightened the tension between them. He watched as she changed Ellie's diaper.

Conner saw her spindly legs and thin thighs. "She's gaunt." He blurted out the words without thinking.

Kate finished pinning the dry diaper in place, then turned her serious gaze to him. "She's been ill or neglected for a long time."

Conner's jaw muscles tightened. "I will find Thelma and get an answer as to why this baby is like this." His heart thudded. Finding Thelma was likely going to make his life even more complicated than it was now.

Grandfather had gone to the kitchen.

Kate faced him. "I know you belong to another woman. We should not have kissed. It must not happen again."

He had no response. What could he say?

Kate laid the baby in her basket and hurried away without a backward look.

Conner took his time going to the kitchen. How could he explain to Kate he didn't belong to Thelma in any way? He looked at the baby snuggled in her blankets looking more content than she had since she'd arrived on his doorstep. It was more important to protect Ellie than anything else that he might want to do.

He joined the others for breakfast. Kate sat across the table from him and kept her attention on her plate. Would it make a difference to her to know Ellie wasn't his daughter? He failed to see how it would. She had made it crystal clear that she would soon be going to medical school with plans to never marry. Imagine not wanting a family. He couldn't understand it.

Would anything make her change her mind?

Someone banged on the outside door and Pa hurried to open it. He led the sheriff into the kitchen.

"Jesse. Good." The man was practically a brother and would have helped even if his job didn't require it.

Jesse greeted everyone.

"Did you get your business tended to?" Pa asked.

Jesse grabbed one of the hard chairs and plunked down, his hat dangling from his hands. "Turned my prisoner over to the marshal and rode home again. But what can I do for you?" He looked at Conner.

Before Conner could answer, Annie clattered into the house. She saw Jesse and Kate. "What's going on? What did I miss?"

Conner got to his feet. "I'll show you." He led the way into the sitting room. Everyone followed. Conner scooped the baby from her basket.

"Ahh," Annie said, her eyes full of tenderness toward the baby.

Jesse's mouth fell open. He closed it, swallowed hard and stared. "It's yours?"

Conner didn't answer. Let his friend draw his own conclusions.

Jesse tried again. "You have a baby?"

"Thelma does." He wondered if Kate would notice the distinction he made.

"Thelma is back?" Jesse glanced around. "Where is she?"

"She's not here." Everyone waited for him to continue. "I need you to find her for me."

"Where do you suggest I look?"

"She was with the traveling show last I heard from her. But that was a year and a half ago."

"I know the show you mean. I'll make some inquiries," Jesse said. "So this is your baby? A boy or girl?"

"Little girl. Elspeth, but we call her Ellie."

Jesse watched the baby for several minutes, shook his head as if he still didn't believe what he saw. "You sure you want me to find Thelma?"

Conner opened his mouth but could not utter a word. What did Jesse mean?

Jesse continued, "She could take the baby away and it's obvious you're very fond of her."

Conner wondered how Jesse had come to that conclusion. From the look on Conner's face, the way he held the baby close to his heart or had he seen some other indication?

Kate crowded to Conner's side and stroked Ellie's head. "Doesn't he have as much right to keep the baby and care for her as Thelma?"

Grandfather harrumphed. Pa gave Conner a very pointed look.

"Not if I'm not the father." He spoke quietly, knowing his news would shock her.

Silence followed his admission.

Jesse broke the silence. "Then why is the baby here?"

"I don't know, and until we learn the reason, would you keep the fact she isn't mine a secret?"

"Of course." Jesse headed for the door. "I'll start inquiries about Thelma."

The others quietly slipped away, leaving Conner and Kate.

Kate came round to face Conner. "You're not the father? Why would you lead me to think otherwise?"

"I didn't know why Thelma sent her to me. I still don't."

Kate kept her head down so he couldn't see her face. It left him floundering to guess how his announcement had affected her. "Does it make a difference?"

"It changes nothing." Her head high, she returned to the kitchen, not once looking his direction.

He had his answer as to whether or not she would reconsider her decision regarding a family.

There was no reason he should feel a weight of disappointment pressing on his heart.

She'd never given him reason to think otherwise.

Nor had he changed his mind about protecting his heart against a woman like her.

Except could he really think she was the least bit like Thelma?

Chapter Four

$\sim$

He wasn't Ellie's father.

The words echoed in Kate's head. It left him free of obligation to marry Thelma. Not that it changed anything for her. Her plans were the same as ever: see that Father was well enough to manage on his own and then go to medical school.

Another thought interrupted her insistence. Conner had grown very fond of Ellie. Would he marry Thelma in order to keep the baby?

She knew it was a possibility.

Annie started washing the breakfast dishes.

Kate grabbed a towel and began to dry them.

"You don't need to do that," Annie said. "I fully expected to have a mess to clean up when I returned. Instead, I find the kitchen clean except for a few breakfast things. Not that I mind the work. It's worth it to have a good visit with Carly."

"I've always found it soothing to do housework." No drama, no fears, no obligations.

"Pa said you didn't know the baby wasn't Conner's. I'm guessing it surprised you to learn the truth."

Kate nodded, her resolve returning. "It restores my belief that he is an honorable man, but apart from that, it changes very little for me. This is something he and your family have to sort out." Her job here was about done. And none too soon. Several times she'd found herself forgetting her goal, attracted to a man in a way she could not allow.

They finished cleaning the kitchen. "Now that you're home, I will show you how to feed Ellie."

Looking apprehensive and eager at the same time, Annie accompanied her to the sitting room. Kate explained her plan to Conner. "The baby is going to need lots of care. Until you find Ellie's mother, you're going to need help. I'll show Annie and your grandfather how to feed her." Though the baby would soon need nothing more than someone to prepare a bottle for her.

Annie settled into a chair and Kate put the baby in her arms, noting that Annie seemed at ease with holding Ellie. No doubt she had held lots of babies, including her niece Mattie. "Okay, little Ellie, it's time to eat. Show your auntie Annie what you can do." Except Annie wasn't her auntie. Kate needed to readjust her thinking.

Ellie looked at Annie, then found Kate. Her expression brightened with recognition and she started to drink the milk. Pleasure at knowing the baby sought her was laced with resolve to walk away from the situation. She had come as a medical person to help. Success meant she would no longer be needed.

Kate watched, satisfied the baby was doing well. "Excellent job. Now let's give Grandfather a turn." Kate placed the baby in the old man's arms. "Sweetie, everyone calls this man Grandfather."

Grandfather sighed. "It's been far too long since I've had the pleasure of holding a little one."

Kate bent over the baby. "Did you hear that? He likes you."

But it was Kate the baby looked at as she sucked her milk. And it was Kate's arms that ached to hold her close. She glanced toward Conner. He was watching her and smiled…a gentle, sad sort of smile as if he regretted the way she'd learned the truth. Or perhaps he'd guessed at her confused feelings. She tried to look away, to convince herself she handled this situation very well, but she couldn't. Not any more than she could stop the sting of tears that she blinked away.

The smile in Conner's eyes deepened as if he understood. How could he? He was surrounded by his family, all ready and willing to support him in caring for Ellie, while Kate would return home with empty arms.

And an empty heart?

No. Her thinking was clouded. She was returning to resume her own plans.

She forced her mind back to her rightful role.

"She's stopped eating," Grandfather said, and Kate turned back to Ellie. She checked the bottle.

"A good feeding. Excellent." She was no longer needed here. She took the baby. There was no reason she couldn't put the baby in her basket or give her to Conner, who watched her closely. But she wanted to hold her as long as she could.

The baby didn't sleep but watched Kate with wide, deep brown eyes.

Ellie rumbled her lips. Her eyes widened. She did it again.

Kate laughed and shifted closer to Conner. "Look at this. Do it again, Ellie."

Ellie looked at Conner, rumbled her lips and gave Conner a look that seemed to say, "Your turn."

"I think she wants to play." Conner rumbled his lips and waited. Ellie did it again. Back and forth they went until Kate started laughing.

They played with the baby until it was time to feed her again and then she slept. Kate put her in her basket. She smiled down at the sleeping baby, then turned to Conner.

Kate had promised herself she would leave the baby for the Marshalls to tend, but here she was, alone with Conner, sharing the care of Ellie and enjoying every minute of it.

She hurried into the kitchen, where Annie was busy cooking. "Can I help?"

"You could prepare the vegetables in the basin for dinner. I'm running late. It seems I always have more work than time." She sighed. "But I suppose that's what most women say."

Kate washed the potatoes and carrots in the sink and put them on the stove to cook, watching them until they boiled.

Together, they prepared a meal.

"It's nice having another woman in the kitchen with me," Annie said.

"You're very efficient."

"I've had lots of practice."

"I know." She wondered if Annie ever wished she wasn't responsible for her father, grandfather and brothers. Though only one brother remained at home.

Perhaps soon Conner would establish his own home with Thelma and Ellie.

No matter what Conner's future held, it would not include Kate.

Pain grabbed at her chest and she paused, her hands curled into fists, waiting for it to pass.

Grandfather and Bud came in from outside.

"Dinner will be ready shortly," Annie said, and the men sat down to look at the newspaper they had gotten in town.

With a guilty start, Kate realized how long she'd been absent from the sitting room and hurried back to check on Ellie and Conner.

Conner held the baby. "I was about to call and see if she should eat again."

"I'll prepare a feed immediately." She returned to the kitchen to do so.

She came back and handed him the bottle. "You and your family will soon be able to take care of her without my help."

He got Ellie eating, then turned back to her. "You're anxious to leave?"

It should have been easy to agree with him, but she could not be untruthful. "Leaving her is going to be difficult."

Their gazes caught and held. The air seemed awash with liquid sunshine. A jolt of something both sweet and sad rushed through her. How had she allowed this to happen? To be drawn to a man and child when she knew they could never be hers. Even if Conner was free, Kate had plans that made it impossible to picture herself in their lives. And yet she did. In full, vibrant color, every detail bright with joy.

She ripped her attention from Conner. Remembered he'd asked a question. "My father needs my help." And when he didn't, she would head back east for medical school. That was her plan. Her purpose. Her calling.

Ellie ate well for Conner. Kate didn't need to hover nearby and yet she did. Conner's attention was on the baby, allowing Kate to study the pair. Conner's face revealed love for Ellie. She shivered, thinking of what the future might hold for this pair. *Please, God, protect them from pain and sorrow.*

He put the baby in her basket to sleep, then he and Kate joined the others in the kitchen. Kate remained in the kitchen after the meal and helped Annie with the dishes and swept the floor for her, finding, as always, a comfort in doing routine things.

"I'm going outside for a bit," Annie said. "Do you want to come with me?"

"I'd like that." It would give her time to get her thoughts back to normal. "Let me tell Conner." She hurried to the sitting room. Ellie slept in Conner's arms. He looked up at Kate's approach and smiled.

"Look at her sleeping so peacefully."

She faltered, took a deep breath. That look of tenderness in his eyes was meant for Ellie, but for a heartbeat, she'd thought it included her. She folded her hands at her waist. "I'm going outside with Annie for a few minutes." But she didn't immediately return to the kitchen, held in the spot by a longing to prolong this moment, make this feeling last, allow herself just a moment or two of filling her heart with—

She jerked away and forced herself to keep her pace reasonable as she left the room, even though everything in her wanted to run.

But did she want to race from the house or back to the pair in the sitting room?

She continued to the kitchen, where Annie waited, and they stepped out into the bright sunshine, which immediately warmed her skin. She sucked in the summer-laden air and looked about.

The mountains rose to the west, greens of every hue filling the woods and covering the hills. Here and there, bright patches of wildflowers dotted the lush landscape. The air carried a hundred different scents…smells of grass, horses, wildflowers and pine from the mountains.

"It's a beautiful country," she said, knowing she would miss it when she went east to study. City activity could never outshine the offerings of nature.

"Wild and beautiful," Annie said as they walked along the path to the garden, then turned toward the barn.

They wandered past the buildings along the trail to a grassy slope. Annie pointed out many things, including the horses in the pen. "Conner is breaking them. He'll sell them."

"Does he have special plans?"

"You mean like having a place of his own?" Annie chuckled. "I don't think so. He's the only one of my brothers still living at home and he says someone has to stay and help take care of us. He means Grandfather." She paused. "I think."

The farther they got from the house, the more Kate's insides tightened. What if Ellie needed something? She stared at the distant mountains and forced herself to think rationally. Ellie's needs were not what bothered her, she admitted. It was knowing she would soon no longer be needed. Life for the Marshalls would go on with the addition of Ellie until her future was resolved.

Kate would go back to Bella Creek. She'd help her father, and once she could be assured he was well enough to be on his own, she would leave. St. Louis and medical school awaited her. Nevertheless, she was not comfortable being away from Ellie too long. "I should get back."

Annie sighed. "I know. Me, too." They returned to the house at a quicker rate than they had left.

Kate hurried through the kitchen to the sitting room, where Conner held Ellie.

"How is she?" Kate asked.

The baby's eyes shifted to Kate and she brightened.

"See that? She recognizes you." Conner's smile was warm. She was drowning in his approval, floating in the sky of his eyes, forgetting the boundaries she had in her role as her father's assistant.

Annie followed and stood watching her brother and the baby. "You look pretty comfortable caring for her."

"I've had a good teacher." His smile was like warm honey to Kate's insides.

She had taught them what they needed to know. The family would now be responsible for making arrangements for Ellie's care, she reminded herself. They did not need her help in doing so.

Accepting the situation for what it was, she pulled herself together and turned to the brother and sister. "Ellie no longer needs my care." *Please ask me to stay.* But what about Father? What about her decision to follow her dream to become a doctor? To not get overly involved with a family again? And especially one with a baby girl?

Kate ducked her head, not wanting Annie or Conner to see her feelings as they stung her eyes.

Conner could hardly swallow past the tightness in his throat. He didn't want to make other arrangements for Ellie's care.

"I'll help all I can," Annie said, "but my days are already full."

He nodded. Would Kate see how much she was needed here? Wanted here? Because she offered something that no one else could and he didn't mean her expertise. He enjoyed her company, found her presence reassuring, and even with his inexperienced eyes, he could see that Ellie responded to Kate like she didn't to anyone else.

But it would be wrong to ask Kate to stay. She'd made it clear she planned to devote her life to medicine. He'd hoped she'd show some kind of relief or give him a bright smile when she learned he wasn't Ellie's father. But her response had been cold. Enough to inform him she wasn't interested in accepting any attention from him.

Not that he felt he could offer such. Ellie's future held so many unknowns. Would Thelma return alone and seeking his help or with a husband in tow? A husband would leave Conner with no right to decide what was best for Ellie.

He was reluctant to leave Ellie in someone else's care, but he couldn't continue to hang around the house. He had to pull his share of the workload on the ranch plus work on breaking his horses. Nor could Kate stay much longer. She had her own plans.

God in heaven, send us Your answer. Send us help.

Trust calmed his heart. It was strengthened as he remembered it was an oft-repeated prayer of his mother's.

He glanced past Kate. Annie had slipped away and they were alone, leaving him free to speak his heart. "Kate, you are more than a doctor's assistant. You do realize that, don't you?"

She shook her head, her eyes cooling.

"You admit you love this baby. Just as I do."

She started to turn away, but he caught her by the shoulder and her gaze returned to him.

His heart stalled at the hungry, desperate look in her eyes.

She stood upright and backed away. "I'll see if Annie needs any help." She walked through the door, crossed the dining room and went to the kitchen.

She'd explained her reasons for choosing to be a doctor and denying herself a family. On one hand, they seemed noble and good. On the other…well, it sent regret pulsing through every part of his body. It was too great a sacrifice.

Someone came to the door. He recognized Isabelle's voice. Of course. The answer to his prayer. Why hadn't he thought of her? She could help with the baby.

The three young women visited in the kitchen. He couldn't hear what was said but knew Annie and Kate would be bringing Isabelle up to date on recent events. Isabelle had popped over for a quick visit last night but didn't linger, anxious to be back in her own home.

He smiled at Ellie and whispered, "We'll ask Isabelle to help with your care." Even as he rejoiced in the answer to his prayer, his insides twisted. Isabelle would take the baby to her house. Conner wouldn't be able to see her as often as he liked.

The three ladies entered the room.

Isabelle crossed to Conner's side and squeezed one of his hands. "They said Jesse has called. I hope he can find Thelma quickly."

His jaw muscles twitched. "Ellie is going to stay here." He knew he didn't have the right to make such a claim, but his heart had spoken. He would do all he could to keep the baby.

Isabelle looked from Kate to Conner and back again. "You're going to stay here as well?" she asked Kate.

"For a few more hours only."

"Then what happens to Ellie?"

This was Conner's opening. "I hoped you would agree to help."

"Me?" She drew back. "But I know nothing about babies. Not even how to feed them."

"Kate would show you, wouldn't you?"

Kate nodded, though she didn't appear overjoyed about it. Dare he believe it meant she was reconsidering her decision? Conner hoped she would look at him. If she did, could he communicate his wish that she could be a more permanent part of Ellie's care?

Now hold on one minute, he warned himself. It was premature to be making future plans for the baby. Nothing could be decided about her until Jesse found Thelma. Besides, he knew Kate's plans and they didn't include a baby.

Isabelle had turned to Kate. "Do you really think I could learn to look after her?"

Kate chuckled. "If I've said it once, I've said it a hundred times or more. You can do just about anything you set your mind to."

Isabelle laughed softly. "You've certainly said it a

number of times. But that doesn't mean you're always right."

Kate smiled serenely. "But I am this time."

Isabelle looked at Ellie, who watched Conner as if trying to understand how this conversation would affect her.

"She is very sweet. Yes, I'll check with Dawson, and if he has no objections, I will help with the baby." She grinned as if pleased with her decision.

"Good." Conner was pleased, too.

"There you go. Things have a way of working out, don't they?" Kate's words, no doubt meant to sound encouraging, carried a note of regret. At least that was what Conner allowed himself to believe.

Things were working out. But was it the way he wanted? Was it the way Kate truly wanted? He told himself to let it go. Kate had convinced herself this was what she wanted and he couldn't foresee her changing her mind. "Could you stay one more night?" He was both reluctant to be alone with the baby and equally reluctant to bid Kate goodbye.

She hesitated, then nodded. "This will be my last evening. I must get back."

After a bit, the ladies went back to the kitchen. Kate returned with another feeding for Ellie and hurriedly rejoined the others in the kitchen.

"Well, little bitty one, it looks like we have things worked out for the next little while. Until Jesse locates your mother." His satisfaction ended on that note.

Even after Isabelle left, Kate stayed in the kitchen helping Annie prepare supper. Conner wondered if she stayed there to avoid confronting him. Or did she struggle with second thoughts about her decision?

* * *

Turning the care of Ellie over to someone else was a sign of Kate's success as a medical person…cause for rejoicing. She had saved this baby from dying. Yes, Ellie would require a good deal of attentive care yet, but it was nothing Isabelle, with Annie and Conner and the entire Marshall family, couldn't handle until Thelma was located.

A shiver crossed Kate's shoulders. If Ellie's condition indicated how Thelma had taken care of her, finding Thelma could signal more problems for the baby.

Surely Conner would see that the baby wasn't neglected in the future.

The rest of the day passed peaceably. The baby continued eating well. Not as much as a child her age should take, but a vast improvement over the first two days. Ellie slept while Conner and Kate joined the others at the kitchen table for supper.

The conversation grew more general as they finished the washing up. Kate prepared another feeding and took it into the sitting room.

"I'll try feeding her again," Grandfather offered, and Conner shifted the baby to his arms. Kate waited until the older man looked comfortable, then spoke to Ellie, got her attention so she would eat.

A contented silence filled the room, broken only by the sound of Ellie sucking until the opening of the outer door drew them all from the peaceful state.

Isabelle rushed into the room. "Dawson says he approves of me helping with the baby. I can start tomorrow."

Conner crossed the room and squeezed his sister-in-law's shoulders. "So glad to hear it."

Kate smiled at her announcement. "I'm very glad.

She's eating better with each feeding and perking up more all the time."

Isabelle studied the baby. "I haven't seen enough of her to be able to judge that, but I'm glad you think so." She straightened. "I can't stay. I promised Mattie I would be right back to read to her."

"The child could come and say hello to her grandfather," the older man said. Mattie usually ran in to talk to her great-grandfather after she got home from school.

"She would have, but she was rather naughty and Dawson said her punishment was to stay in the house."

Grandfather harrumphed. "Seems as much punishment for me as for the child."

Isabelle bent to plant a kiss on his weathered cheek. "I'll be sure to point that out to Dawson." Calling good-night to them all, she left.

Conner turned toward Kate. "Can you stay another night? I don't think I can manage on my own."

Kate looked at the family gathered in the room. Grandfather holding the baby, his face wreathed in pleasure. Conner hanging over the older man's shoulder, smiling at the baby. Annie in a chair next to her grandfather, also watching the baby.

Bud sat across from his father, a pleased look on his face as he studied his family.

A loving, caring family.

A faded memory floated through her mind. Something lingered there that contained both joy and sorrow. She'd been aware of it off and on in the past. She stared at the opposite wall and waited for the shadows in her head to take shape, but nothing more came. Perhaps it was nothing more than something she had seen years ago. She shook her head and returned her attention to the people in the room.

She was here only to provide medical help.

When she left, they would continue on as usual. With the addition of little Ellie and, perhaps soon, Thelma as well. She could see them pulling her into their family in order to keep Ellie safe and in their midst. But they needed Kate tonight and that had to be enough for her.

Ellie slept and, one by one, the others slipped out. Annie told Kate she was welcome to use the bedroom next to hers.

Kate and Conner remained alone with Ellie.

The baby slept sweetly in her basket.

Kate got to her feet. "I'll sleep a bit while the baby is sleeping. You should, too." She escaped up the stairs before Conner could say anything.

Used as she was to falling asleep whenever the opportunity arose, she lay awake a long time shepherding her wayward thoughts back into order. She ached at the thought of leaving. But it was the only thing she could do. If she had listened to her conscience, she would have left as soon as Isabelle said she would help with the baby. Telling herself it was too late in the day was not believable.

Poor Father. She'd left him to manage on his own with hardly a thought to how he was doing. If he should have a memory lapse that caused him to make a mistake, she would forever bear the guilt. As soon as Isabelle came to get the baby in the morning, Kate would go home. Where she belonged. Her eyes closed and sleep came.

She bolted awake. How long had she slept? She tiptoed down the stairs expecting to find Conner asleep, but he sat in the armchair, the baby basket pulled close so he could watch Ellie sleep. He lifted his face to her as she stepped into the room.

The light from the low-burning lamp caught his features, making one side sharp and strong, the other soft and gentle.

She stared. It was as if she saw two sides of him— the tough and the tender. A smile tugged at her lips. Could she think of a better way to describe this man?

He beckoned for her to join him and she sat in the chair next to his. "She's making little sounds in her sleep."

She bent to listen. "I hear it," she whispered and turned to meet Conner's smiling eyes. "Little sounds of contentment."

He reached for her hand and squeezed it. "Do you realize we've achieved that? When she came here, she was frightened, on death's door, and now she lies here sleeping and content." He pulled Kate closer until mere inches kept their foreheads from touching.

She tried to resist, but sleep had left her weak and needy.

He caught her chin and tipped it upward. "I'm grateful for all you've done. But more than that—" He studied her eyes, let his gaze drift down her cheeks and come to rest on her mouth. "More than that—" His voice had a husky tone that made her wish for the stars and moon. "More than that, I'm glad you truly care about her. What you give is more than medical attention."

Ellie snuffled louder and woke herself up.

Kate jerked away from Conner's touch and his look. "It's time to feed her again. I can do it if you want to get some rest."

"Harder to rest than you would think."

She wondered if he struggled with the same confusing thoughts she did. "Conner, get some sleep. If you plan to take care of her at night, you will have to learn to sleep when she does."

"I suppose you're right." He made his way upstairs.

Kate prepared the milk and held the baby while she ate. She changed the damp diaper and rocked Ellie, humming softly until she slept again, then laid her in the basket.

She could take the basket upstairs and put it by her bed so she could waken if Ellie needed anything, but instead she sat awake, watching the baby sleep.

Kate jerked awake to a soft noise. Her first thought was of Ellie and she checked the basket. Blinked. Pulled the lamp closer so it threw light into the basket. But the baby was gone.

"Conner?" Her whisper choked from her throat.

She remembered Conner had gone upstairs.

She drew in a breath. Tried to calm her racing heart. The golden glow of lamplight drew her to the kitchen. She rushed into the room. Conner sat at the table. Her steps didn't slow until she reached his side and pressed her hand to the warm bundle in his arms. "Is she okay?" Her voice trembled.

"Fine as could be. I woke up and saw you were asleep, so we tiptoed out here. I'm getting ready to feed her."

"When I woke up and she was gone..." She shuddered.

"Sorry. I didn't mean to alarm you."

"I know and my reaction was completely out of the ordinary." She yawned. "How long did I sleep?"

They both glanced at the big clock over the doorway. "Three o'clock! She's slept all this time and not a peep."

"Is everything okay?" Grandfather called from his bedroom.

"Everything is fine," Conner replied. "We're just feeding the baby."

Ellie ate well. "Each feeding she takes a bit more." It was cause for rejoicing and yet Kate felt a tiny, thin thread of regret. Kate no longer was required to be there.

Already she felt the wrench of loss.

How had she allowed herself to open her heart to the warm longings she had grown so adept at ignoring?

That didn't make sense. She didn't ignore anything. She simply had other goals than family and babies of her own.

As soon as she got back to Bella Creek, her life would settle back into her long-established routines and plans.

Conner sat at the table eating breakfast with the others when Isabelle hurried into the house. He grinned. She was eager to learn how to take care of Ellie. But she looked slightly frazzled. Isabelle never looked frazzled.

"Kate, Mattie is sick. Can you come look at her?"

"Of course." Kate pushed from the table. "Let me get my bag." She slipped into the sitting room to retrieve it.

"It's not serious, is it?" Pa asked. As his only grand-child for six years, Mattie held a special place in his heart. In the hearts of all the family. She had lived with them for several years before Dawson and Isabelle married. Now, of course, there were the three children Logan and Sadie had adopted, but they lived in town at present and so weren't in and out of the house like Mattie.

"She's running a fever and vomiting. The poor child is miserable." Isabelle wrung her hands. "I hope it's not serious. It couldn't be measles again, could it?"

Kate rejoined them in time to hear. "You only get measles once. Let's go have a look at her."

Conner and his family stared after the departing pair. The air in the room grew thin and hard to breathe. She was only going across the yard to Dawson's house, but this strange feeling made him realize what life would feel like when she left.

Nonsense, he informed his foolish brain. She'd been here only a few days. Nothing had changed. Except he had a baby girl to take care of and Thelma to find and get answers from and—he paused as the truth rose to the surface—a growing fondness for a woman whom he knew would walk away and seek her own goals, follow a path to the profession of her choice.

Conversation flowed around him as the others discussed the possibilities of Mattie's illness.

They finished breakfast and Kate still did not return.

Conner began to wonder if she needed help. But he couldn't imagine a situation where she would require it. Especially given that Dawson and Isabelle were there as well.

Annie put Kate's plate of uneaten food in the warming oven and began to clean the kitchen.

Ellie would soon need feeding. Of course, he could prepare the bottle on his own. Wouldn't they soon have to manage Ellie's care without Kate's guiding hand? It was not a cheering thought.

"When does Ellie need to eat again?" Annie asked.

"Soon. But don't worry. I can manage it." He hoped he sounded more certain than he felt.

"Good. Because I mean to start some baking."

He prepared the next feeding and went to the sitting room. The little girl watched him with a glint of recognition that she normally reserved for Kate. His heart squeezed out a protectiveness that burned along his veins. "Elspeth—whatever your last name is—you are safe with me. No one is going to hurt you or neglect you."

He ground his teeth together. If Thelma had a husband, they were both responsible for neglecting this baby. They had sent Ellie to him. Didn't that give him some rights? He cradled Ellie in his arms and got her to start taking the milk. She ate slowly. Was that normal? He simply didn't know.

The outer door opened. He recognized Kate's voice as she spoke to Annie. Would she eat breakfast before she told him about Mattie? But she hurried through and stood before him, her hands folded at her waist.

"How is Mattie?"

"She has an upset stomach. I gave her something to help settle it, but she's miserable." She paused. "I told Isabelle that Ellie must stay away from Mattie until Mattie is no longer sick. Ellie is much too weak to withstand a bout of vomiting and diarrhea."

"Of course. That makes sense. Why do you look so troubled?" Was she more concerned about Mattie than her words led him to believe?

She sat on the chair facing him, perched on the edge of the seat. "It means Isabelle won't be able to look after Ellie until Mattie is better."

His breath eased past his teeth. "That's not a problem, is it? I know I'll feel a little better if you can stay a few more days." Then it hit him. "You aren't comfortable staying longer, are you?"

"It's not that. But I am concerned about Father." She looked past Conner.

"There's more. What is it?"

She sprang to her feet and went to the window. "I've let myself grow too fond of Ellie. It's going to be a wrench when I leave." Her words were soft, almost lost against the pane of glass.

Then stay. But there were far too many reasons he couldn't offer the invitation. She had her plans for the future. He had Ellie's future to take care of in whatever way he could. And there was Thelma to consider.

Grandfather and Pa came through the door, Annie at their heels. "What's the news on Mattie?" Pa asked.

Kate relayed the information. Grandfather and Pa both looked relieved to know the child had only an upset stomach.

Pa studied him. "What about the baby? Who is going to look after her? Isabelle has a sick child to take care of. Annie is too busy. Sadie is in town looking after three children. You can't keep Kate here forever."

"It's only until Thelma comes."

"Son, if Thelma was interested in caring for that baby, she would be here now. And I hasten to say, the baby wouldn't be in the condition she's in."

He didn't need his father to point out that fact. It was obvious to everyone. All the more reason to hope Kate would stay.

As if reading his mind, Kate spoke. "I will stay until Isabelle is able to help."

"Thank you." Conner was more than grateful at her offer.

Later that afternoon, Kate sat holding Ellie, talking to her as if she understood every word. The baby focused on Kate with such intensity it brought a chuckle from her. At the sound of Kate's amusement, the baby's eye's widened.

Conner, sitting at Kate's elbow, laughed. "She is certainly learning to trust you."

"And you." Kate turned to him, a smile still lingering on her lips. The air between them shimmered with promise and possibility.

"I almost wish we could stay as we are right now."

She jerked her gaze from his. "That's not possible."

"I know."

She wouldn't look at him again.

He wanted to assure her that he understood this was a temporary situation, that he knew her goal would take her far away.

"I wonder how long it will take Jesse to track down Thelma." Kate meant the reminder for both of them. She rose, handed Ellie to Conner and joined Annie in the kitchen to help prepare the evening meal.

How was he to let her go when the time came? But how could he think anything else was possible? He must protect his heart from destruction and the only way he knew to do that was to let her go with no regrets.

Chapter Five

Sunday morning arrived, calm and serene. The mood was helped along by the fact Ellie had eaten so well and wakened in the night for only one feeding. She was doing so much better that Kate mentioned going home and leaving them to manage.

"Father will be needing me."

Conner knew she also wanted to escape. She'd done her best to avoid him the last twenty-four hours. Of course, he'd done the same, spending a great deal of time outdoors working with his horses. Being in the house with Kate was bittersweet agony. He wanted her to smile at him, but when she did, her eyes remained guarded. The only time they were both honest with each other was when they smiled at something Ellie did. Those moments were fleeting as butterflies.

Sunday morning meant church.

"I think I'll stay home with Ellie," Conner said.

Every eye at the table turned toward him. Refusing to go to church was tantamount in Grandfather's sight to robbing the bank.

"That might be best," Kate said. "She needs a few more days to get truly stable."

Later, as they tended the baby, he thanked her for backing him up.

"You'll have to face the public curiosity at some point."

His chuckle was mirthless. "It isn't their curiosity that concerns me. It's the fact everyone will have an opinion." He knew the slanted looks he'd get if he walked in carrying a baby. Not that he could avoid the situation for very long. Maybe by next week Ellie would be stronger and he'd have some answer as to why Thelma had sent the baby to him.

Kate had bathed the baby and dressed her in a new little flannel gown Annie had unearthed. "So long as you let them believe the baby is yours, people are going to be upset that you haven't married Thelma."

"I realize that, but at this point, I don't even know if she's still unmarried." He scrubbed his hand over his hair, not caring that it would end up looking like a windblown haystack. "I don't even know if she's alive."

Kate finished getting Ellie comfortable and came round to face him, the baby hooked on one hip. "What will happen to Ellie if that's the case?"

"Do you have to ask?"

She nodded. "Yes."

"She'll become mine, of course."

"Good to know. I can't think of anything better than for her to be part of the Marshall family. I know you all stand by each other."

"Family comes first. That's been drilled into us all our lives."

"You're fortunate."

"You have a good family." He'd seen the affection between Kate and her father. "Though I understand you went through a lot of losses to get to where you are. I'm sorry."

"I've grown used to it."

"You're going to church, aren't you?" He couldn't ask her to stay and keep him company. That would be plum foolish on his part.

"I am and I better hurry and get ready. I'll spend the day with Father."

"You'll come back, won't you?" Mattie was still feeling sick, so Isabelle couldn't help.

"Annie is adamant she can't manage on her own. I'll stay until Mattie is well enough for Isabelle to take over Ellie's care." Kate was about to head upstairs to prepare for church.

"Kate?" He couldn't let her go without saying how he felt.

She paused and turned. "Yes?"

"Thank you for everything. I don't know how we would have managed without you."

Kate touched Ellie's face as she lay in her basket watching them. "I'm glad I was able to help. This little one is worth every bit of effort." She bent over and kissed Ellie's forehead.

As she straightened, Conner caught a glimpse of her eyes and was almost certain they glistened with unshed tears.

She loved Ellie every bit as much as he did. But it wasn't enough to make her give up her plan to become a doctor. And he wasn't even sure he would have asked it of her. Like she said, her gift of caring and healing should be shared with many.

After the others left, Conner paced about the house. He watched the horses from the kitchen window, aching to be working with them.

His gaze went beyond to the rolling hills. It hadn't been that long since he'd ridden out to check the cows with Pa, but it seemed an age. This must be how Grandfather felt every day as he watched the others go about the ranch business. Conner promised himself to be more deliberate about taking the poor man out in the buggy along the trails that were passable for such a conveyance.

He fed Ellie and sat outside on Grandfather's chair with the baby perched on his knee and told her all about the ranch and the cows and the horses. "I hope you'll be able to stay with us. I'll buy you a little pony as soon as you're big enough and we'll go riding together."

But he could not make plans until he discovered what had happened to Thelma.

He heard the buggy approaching and slipped inside lest someone get the idea he waited for them to return. Kate wouldn't be with them.

He sat at the table, an empty coffee cup before him.

Grandfather entered and turned to speak to someone. A jolt rattled Conner's teeth. That sounded like Kate. He was on his feet headed for the door when she stepped into the kitchen. Their gazes met with such force he leaned back on his heels. The air between them shone like sunshine had poked a hole in the roof and poured itself into the moment.

Had she realized how easily she fit into this home, this family? How much he and Ellie needed her? Perhaps she had missed them and found they satisfied something in her life.

Or perhaps it was all his imagination.

Grandfather eased by Kate, Dr. Baker at his side. "Least you could do is say hello," he said to Conner.

Conner nodded. He would if he could find his voice.

"I asked Kate and her father to join us for dinner," Annie said.

"Thank you." Kate's voice seemed to come from the distant meadows, carried on the scent of wildflowers. "How's Ellie?" She nodded toward the other room.

"Sleeping," he managed to say.

"I'd like Father to take a look at her."

"Of course." Though he saw no need. He trusted Kate completely.

He followed Kate and Dr. Baker into the sitting room. Pa, Grandfather and Annie were right on his heels.

"Hello, little one." Kate bent over and spoke to the baby.

Ellie cooed a greeting.

She lifted Ellie out and laid her on the couch.

Dr. Baker stepped forward. He listened to the baby's heart and lungs. He felt along her jaw and behind her ears. He pulled up her gown and thumped gently on her chest and tummy. He bent her legs, bringing her knees to her chest. He lifted her, turned her tummy to his palm and ran his finger along her spine.

"What I see here is a baby who needs some good feeding and lots of loving. Other than that, she's a normal baby of about six months of age."

Conner didn't realize he'd been holding his breath until it whooshed out.

Grandfather chortled. "I knew she was okay, but it's good to hear it from you, Doc."

Kate tidied up the baby's clothing and picked her up. When she would have perched the baby on her hip and carried her to the dining room, where Annie was setting the table for a large family gathering, Conner stopped her.

"I'd like to take her."

"Of course."

He heard the reluctant note in her voice. "I don't mean to be selfish, but I want to make everyone see that she's a part of the family." He swallowed hard. "At least for now."

Kate met his gaze, her eyes brimming with sorrow and sympathy. "It will be nice when you can be settled about her future."

It would be even nicer if Kate could be part of that future.

She must have read his regret. "My job here is about done."

Your job here will never be done. The words vibrated inside his head. "I'm glad you are staying until Isabelle can take her. According to Dawson, Mattie is feeling much better."

"That's good to hear."

"Yes." He didn't want to see his niece sick, but once she was well, Kate would leave. He didn't look forward to that…a purely selfish desire. Time to man up, as Pa would say.

A wagon rattled into the yard and childish voices filled the air.

"I believe Sadie and Logan are here."

He and Kate returned to the kitchen to greet his younger brother and new sister-in-law and the three children they'd adopted. Kate and Sadie hugged.

Dawson joined them. "Isabelle says Mattie should stay away from the other children today. Mattie isn't happy about it." He chuckled. "Isabelle promised to do something special with her. She was getting out pretty paper and scissors when I left."

They crowded around the table for the meal. Kate ended up at Conner's side, which seemed only right. He glanced around the table. His brothers and sister were there. His pa and grandfather. His sister-in-law and the children. Mattie and Isabelle were across the yard. His gaze lingered at the end of the table where Ma had once sat and now Annie did. What would she think of the growing family? What would she think of Ellie? Of Kate?

He smiled to himself and hoped no one would notice. Somehow he knew Ma would approve of Kate—a perfect balance of practical and caring. And Ellie? Why, Ma would love that little girl even if she wasn't Conner's. That reminded him. He lifted the baby forward. "Ellie, meet the rest of the family."

"She's darling," Sadie said. "What do you think, Beth?"

Thirteen-year-old Beth studied the baby. "Mama told us the baby had been sick. That's why she's thin, isn't it?" She touched Ellie's hand. The baby curled her fingers around Beth's. The older girl smiled. "She's very sweet."

As usual, conversation held more importance than the food. The talk turned to community events. The buildings that had been destroyed by the fire of last winter had almost all been rebuilt.

Then there was a discussion about the sermon. The new preacher, Hugh Arness, had impressed them all.

Annie looked troubled. "It must be hard for Preacher

Hugh to know his wife is dead and not be able to find his son."

A sobering topic. Hugh had come to Bella Creek to search for his missing wife and child. A week ago, he had discovered his wife was deceased but his son had disappeared.

"He won't give up until he locates the boy," Grandfather said. "He's a very determined man."

The main course over, Annie, with assistance from Kate and Sadie, served coffee and chocolate pudding for dessert.

Kate finished her pudding quickly. "When did you last feed Ellie?" she asked Conner quietly.

"It's time to feed her again."

Beth crowded to his side as Kate prepared the bottle. "She sure is sweet."

"Do you want to feed her?"

She nodded and Conner shifted Ellie to Beth's arms. Beth sat on the nearest chair and smiled at the baby. "It reminds me of Jeannie. I mostly looked after her after our real ma got sick."

Three-year-old Jeannie leaned against her big sister. "Was I as sweet as Ellie?"

Beth leaned her head against her little sister's. "I thought you were the sweetest baby in the world. Now I think you're the sweetest little sister."

Jeannie looked pleased.

Beth crooned to the baby and Ellie locked gazes with her.

Conner and Kate exchanged glances. He couldn't say for sure what she thought, but it felt like she agreed with him… Ellie was learning to trust people.

Ellie took her usual feeding.

Beth looked at the bottle when Ellie stopped drinking. "Is that all she eats?"

"She's not very strong yet," Kate explained. "But soon she'll be taking a full feed."

Beth sat the baby up to face Jeannie. Jeannie smiled. "You're a nice baby."

Ellie smiled and gurgled.

Kate had returned to Conner's side, and under the table, he slipped his hand over and cupped hers. He might have imagined she leaned closer to him until their shoulders brushed, but then she straightened and withdrew her hand.

Seven-year-old Sammy edged forward on his chair. "I got a question."

Everyone turned to him.

"Where does a chicken have the most feathers?"

"Under their wings," Annie said.

"On their head," Pa said.

Sammy chuckled. "Nope. On the outside. Get it?"

He looked pleased with himself when everyone laughed.

"On that note…" Dawson got to his feet. "I told Isabelle I would go home and let her come visit."

"May we be excused?" Sammy asked.

Sadie gave permission for the two younger children to go outside. "Mind you stay out of trouble."

Isabelle entered the house to visit her two friends. She, Sadie and Kate had come in on the same stagecoach in response to an advertisement for a new teacher and new doctor after the previous ones left following the fire. Only Isabelle wasn't either. She was Kate's friend and a rich heiress—a secret she kept from everyone until she fell in love with Dawson and had to confess the truth. And then she'd given away the bulk of her money so she could know that people liked her for herself.

Conner grinned. If his brothers had taught him anything, it was that the road to love tended to be rocky.

The ladies cleaned the kitchen and the men moved outdoors. Grandfather and Dr. Baker settled on two chairs on the veranda. Pa, Logan and Conner wandered to the corrals, where they leaned on the top rail of the fence and watched Conner's horses.

Sammy joined them and climbed up to sit on the top rail. After a bit, Pa and Logan returned to the house, but Conner and Sammy remained, watching the horses and talking softly. It didn't take long for Conner to realize the youngster had a rich imagination as he invented long complicated stories for each of the horses.

Sammy grew restless. "I'm hungry."

"You just ate."

"No, I didn't. Dinner was hours ago." He eased to his feet, conscious of the watching horses. "You think Aunt Annie has any cookies in the house?"

"Why don't we go find out?" It would give him an excuse to see what Kate and the others were doing.

"I'm hungry," Sammy announced as he burst into the house.

"You're always hungry," Sadie said.

"No, I'm not. I'm not hungry when I'm sleeping." He sidled up to Annie. "You are the bestest cookie maker."

"I thought I was." Sadie sounded hurt though her eyes flashed with amusement.

"You are in our house." Sammy managed to look completely sincere, which brought a chuckle from the adults.

Annie pulled a tin from the shelf and took off the lid. "You want one of these?"

Sammy's hand went to the tin. He paused. "Only one?"

"You can have two."

His shoulders fell and he looked desperate.

"All right, you can have three."

He brightened and took the cookies. "Thanks. I'm going outside to talk to Grandfather. Maybe I'll go see what Grandpa Bud is doing."

Annie passed the cookies around. Soon they were crowded about the table again, chatting. Ellie slept in Beth's arms, but when Kate offered to put the baby in her bed, Beth begged to be allowed to hold her. Jeannie leaned against her big sister, watching the baby.

"Kate, isn't it something to be part of a big, warmhearted family?" Isabelle turned to explain to the others. "We're both only children and grew up lonely for this kind of belonging and connection. Isn't that right, Kate?"

But Kate got a startled look on her face, bolted from the table and out the door.

Isabelle's question slammed into Kate with the force of a winter blizzard. Her face felt hot and then cold. Her chest muscles refused to work. Her stomach churned. Her wooden legs carried her from the house.

She didn't slow her steps until she reached a tree. She leaned her head against it, panting for breath. The rough bark dug into the skin of her forehead. She pressed harder into the trunk, welcoming the pain. Wishing it would erase all else, make it impossible to think...to remember...to feel. But the memory circled again and again, each time increasing in strength and clarity. Each time bringing a fresh wave of pain.

Needing something to anchor her, she grasped the solid tree with both hands.

"Please, God, make it stop."

But she couldn't forget. Didn't want to forget. She wanted the memory to stay and the pain to go.

"Kate." A warm hand touched her shoulder. "What's wrong?" Concern filled Conner's voice. "Are you ill?"

She shuddered, tried to calm her ragged breathing. She couldn't speak. Could only rock her head back and forth.

He caught her by the shoulders and eased her away from the tree. "Talk to me."

Her gaze went past him to the distance. An invisible distance existing only in her mind.

She had no ability to make her feet obey her, yet he got her to move a few steps to a fallen tree. He turned her and pulled her down to sit beside him. He put his arm about her shoulders and pulled her tight to his side.

She clung to his hand and pressed her face to the hollow at his shoulder. He was an anchor. A solid rock.

"Tell me what's going on."

His voice rumbled beneath her ear, settling into her trembling heart, encouraging her to speak. But how could she? How could she admit this awful thing? How could she bare her fickle heart?

"Whatever is wrong, I want to help you."

His gentle voice, the thought of how he cradled Ellie so tenderly, his loyalty to the baby even though she wasn't his daughter, tugged at her resistance.

But tugging equally hard in the opposite direction

was his loyalty to his family. "You would never understand," she whispered hoarsely.

His arm tightened about her. "I don't think it's fair to judge me without giving me a chance."

"Family means so much to you."

He paused a moment before he continued. "I can't deny that, but it doesn't mean I don't care about anyone outside the family."

She couldn't miss the hurt note in his voice.

He added, "I should think taking care of Ellie has proved that to you."

It was true. Only more reason to feel he wouldn't understand how she could have—

"I had two brothers."

"I see."

"I don't think you do." She would have pulled away, but he held her tight and she subsided. "You must wonder why I've never mentioned them before now."

"I expect you have your reasons."

She jerked from his grasp and leaned over her knees. "I forgot about them." A sob caught in the back of her throat. She coughed to clear it. "How is it possible to forget them? They were older than me. I guess I saw them as a little distant. It was Mama who filled my days. And Papa who caught me and tossed me into the air. Who tucked me into bed at night. Still, to completely forget them." She shuddered.

"Tell me about them."

"Johnny and Martin. They were thirteen and fourteen. Almost as big as Papa. They both worked with him." She lifted her head and stared into the blue sky, seeing back into her memories. "They used to have races and Johnny always won even though he was younger. I stood at the sidelines cheering them on." The gate unlocked now, words poured forth. The memories overwhelmed her and she had to give them voice. She told of playing hide-and-seek with them. Of games of tag. Of being taken to the barn to see the newborn kittens or the unsteady new foal. She told of trips to town and attending church as a family. And then she couldn't go on.

He had pulled her back into his arms and held her tight.

She clung to the fabric of his shirt, warm from his body.

He rubbed her back and thankfully said nothing.

Slowly the rest of it came. "It was sitting around the table, laughing, telling jokes, listening to each other that made me remember." She eased back to look into his face. "We used to do that. We were like your family. Happy, noisy, funny." She sighed and rested her cheek against his shoulder. "The Bakers aren't. It wasn't until I took over the household chores that we even sat down together. Before that, it was dish up our plate from the stove and eat on the run. Conversations centered around patients, plans, medical findings." She paused. "I don't mean to speak critically of my family."

He pressed his hand to the back of her head, warm, strong, protective.

She let the feeling soothe her pain.

"You must miss your birth parents and your brothers so much."

She jerked back. "How could I forget Johnny and Martin? It doesn't make sense."

He held her hand. "Kate, maybe your memories were too painful, so you shut them out."

"For eighteen years? That seems a little excessive."

He lifted one shoulder as if to say he didn't have any answers. Not that she expected him to.

She bolted to her feet and took three steps away, then turned and stared at him. "I don't remember seeing them when Mama and Papa were so sick. Where were they? Were they there and I don't remember it?" She shook her head, but it did nothing to clear her thoughts.

Conner rose and closed the distance between them, taking her in his arms. "Kate, you were so young."

She remained stiff in his arms. "How can I be so… so…unnatural." She pushed back. "You'd never forget anyone in your family."

"I'm not four and have not just lost everyone." His smile was gentle, forgiving. "Your world had turned upside down."

"That's no excuse." Her harsh words ended on a wail. "But where were they? Why can't I see them with Mama and Papa?"

She left his arms, left his shelter and strength. She didn't deserve any of it. "Where were they?" she repeated.

Her memories faded and twisted, fleeting images of her brothers and her parents. The house they'd lived in. The table they'd gathered round. The church they'd attended. The barn. Her bedroom. Her parents' room, where they had lain burning up with a fever that couldn't be cured. Her room was next to theirs. Her brothers shared a room on the other side.

Their room was empty.

With a cry of pain, she sank to the ground. "They were already gone."

Conner sat beside her and held her tight, her back to him as he rocked her back and forth.

"They got sick first. I can't remember how much earlier than Mama and Papa. But they were already gone. Their room was empty. All that mattered to me was seeing my parents grow weaker. Grammie came and stayed until the end."

He drew her to her feet and led her back to the log, where they sat side by side, his arms cradling her.

She shuddered. "I miss them. I miss having family. I loved the Bakers and I love Father, but it's not the same." Her voice caught. "It will never be the same. There's no point in wishing for it. My life is different now. I will become a doctor and serve others."

"Will that be enough?" His gentle voice raced through her thoughts.

"I can't undo the past."

He tipped his head against hers. "But you can seek a future that meets your needs."

She wanted to look into his eyes, try to judge what he meant, but she didn't want to end the pressure of his arms nor withdraw from the warmth of his chest. "I will honor my parents and Grammie and my family by helping those who are sick." It made sense. "Perhaps I can do something to spare another family the pain I've known."

"It's noble."

She heard the doubt in his voice and leaned back to watch his expression. "But?"

His smile was tender, his blue eyes full of caring. "Will it be enough? Will it fill the hole in your heart?"

The question unsettled her enough to bring her to her feet and away from his comfort. "It's what I am meant to do." But for the first time since she'd gone to live with the Bakers and become their daughter with the express purpose of learning to be a doctor, she wondered if—

No, she would allow no doubts.

"I'm sorry for taking you from your family. I must go and apologize. And I'll need to feed Ellie again." Her words tumbled out…a tangle of excuses.

He caught her hand and stopped her from rushing away. "You didn't take me from anything. I came because I was concerned." He looked deep into her eyes. "I'm still concerned. I think remembering your brothers and realizing they are gone must feel like losing them all over again."

At the truth of his words, she burst into tears.

Chapter Six

Conner held Kate gently as she sobbed into his shirt. She was so fragile, he feared to tighten his arms about her. He could not fathom the pain of remembering two brothers just to realize they were gone. His insides were raw, torn by the stories she had told. Stories of a warm, loving, noisy family similar to his and a marked contrast to the Baker home though he'd always felt the kindness and caring of the Bakers' home.

It was plain that she missed her family. He couldn't help wondering if her desire to become a doctor was fueled in part by a desire to avoid more pain. By closing herself off to family, she perhaps hoped to protect her heart. Of course, there were more noble reasons as well. Promises to her grandmother and her adoptive parents and a desire to help those in a situation similar to what she'd endured.

Her sobbing subsided and she rested in his arms.

He longed for words of comfort and wished he could offer more…wisdom and insight that would enable her to look at her decision with open honesty.

He could let it go. Offer her nothing but sympathy,

but would that be fair to their friendship? Didn't friends speak the truth to one another in love?

"Kate, I think you owe it to yourself to honestly examine your reasons for wanting to become a doctor." She stiffened and he tightened his arms about her, wanting her to hear him. "I know it's noble and serves mankind. Just be sure your decision isn't made out of guilt. Or the hope you can escape more pain."

She pushed free of his arms. "What are you talking about?" Her gaze shafted through him, accusing him of being unsympathetic.

He told her his thoughts on avoiding family, not because she couldn't combine that with a medical career, but because she didn't want to risk the pain.

"Conner, you are sadly mistaken. Please, don't give me your opinion on the matter again and I'd appreciate it if you didn't tell anyone what I've revealed to you." Her head high, every step a sharp scolding, she marched toward the house.

He kept pace with her but had nothing to say. He had done his best, intending to help, and instead had made her angry. He didn't regret telling her what he thought, but still, he wished for a different outcome.

Her anger would make it awkward to be together as they cared for Ellie.

She paused before she reached the house and slowly came round to face him. "I'll check on Mattie. If she's well enough, Isabelle can care for Ellie. There will be no need for me to stay here."

His thoughts crashed to a halt. She couldn't leave. How would he manage? "Kate, I'm sorry if I've offended you. Please don't let it drive you away."

She considered him. Then her eyebrows went up.

"No doubt you'll interpret my leaving as another in-dication that I am running from something. But you would be wrong. I need to do what I need to do." Her eyes narrowed. "I *am* going to medical school. It's what my parents—both sets—would want me to do. It's what Grammie wanted me to do. It's what *I* want to do." She went into the house.

He followed more slowly, regretting every angry mo-ment. Just when he had begun to think she might care for him. And he'd let himself care for her. Why hadn't he kept his mouth shut?

He might say it was out of concern for her future. That would be true, but he couldn't deny there also ex-isted a touch of selfish desire. He wanted her to see how lonely her future would be if she insisted on denying she needed or wanted a family of her own. He wanted her to see him as a part of her future.

Grandfather and Dr. Baker sat on tipped-back chairs on the veranda, watching as they approached.

"Everything okay?" the doctor asked, eyeing Kate.

"Everything is fine." She smiled. "I just had a mo-ment of upset. Nothing to be concerned about."

"Good."

"Glad it wasn't anything serious," Grandfather said as he lowered his chair to all fours. "Doc and I have been talking. He mentioned that we might have saved some of the buildings in the fire if we'd had some kind of warning system. You know, a way to alert everyone. It took far too long to get enough help on the scene. We've come up with a solution. A church bell." He looked pleased with himself. "We'll have a fund-raiser for the bell and you two are in charge."

"Us?" Conner and Kate spoke in unison, shock in both voices.

Conner swallowed. Work together with Kate when she was angry at him? That did not seem appealing. "We can pass the hat at church."

Grandfather gave him a look meant to quell any further dissention. "We could, but how much fun would that be? Boy, I'm in need of some fun and socializing and I'm expecting you and Kate to come up with something that will involve the community more than dropping a few coins into a hat."

"Father?" Kate's voice dripped with appeal.

"It's an excellent idea. It will give you something to do while you wait to go to medical school."

"I don't need anything to do," she protested.

"Except let me manage on my own so you'll be comfortable leaving me when the time comes."

Out of the corners of his eyes, Conner watched her squeeze her hands into little balls.

"I don't see how we can plan anything," he said, keeping his voice calm in the hopes of convincing everyone they should listen to him. "Kate is returning to town."

"As soon as possible," she added. "In fact, I'll go check on Mattie and see if she's well enough for Isabelle to take over Ellie's care."

"I've already examined her," Dr. Baker said. "She's fine and Isabelle is with the baby as we speak."

Conner let out his pent-up breath. "Well, that solves it. We don't have time to plan anything. I'll pass the hat next Sunday."

Grandfather favored him with a bushy-browed scowl.

"Dear boy. You ever heard of riding into town to see her? Do I have to tell you every little thing?"

It was on the tip of his tongue to say this wasn't little at all, but at Grandfather's deepening scowl Conner thought better of the idea. He brought up one more argument. "What about Ellie?"

"What about her? Isn't Isabelle going to be looking after her? Or take her to town with you. People take babies to town all the time. Or hadn't you noticed?" Grandfather tipped his chair back with a grunt.

Then he dropped his chair to all fours again and banged one of his canes on the floor. "I know just the thing. We'll have a county fair. The ladies can bring in their sewing and baking and have it judged. The men can show off samples of their hay. There can be food booths and stuff like that."

"An excellent plan," Dr. Baker said, beaming his approval.

"There you go." Grandfather waved his hand in a benevolent gesture. "Now all you have to do is make the arrangements."

Oh, yes, that was all they had to do. Practically a mere nothing.

Tossing her hands upward in a sign of frustration, Kate hurried past the older men and into the house.

Conner stayed long enough to give his grandfather a disbelieving look, then followed her inside.

"You're doing very well." Her voice came from the sitting room and he went through.

Isabelle held Ellie as the baby drank the milk from the bottle. Isabelle had a look of adoration on her face.

Kate looked at Conner. Their gazes caught and held.

Hers a mixture of accusation and frustration that rapidly disappeared into peace.

He knew his likely showed the same. They might disagree on some things, but in the matter of little Ellie they were agreed.

Ellie pushed the bottle from her mouth and turned to smile at Kate. She gurgled her happiness at seeing her.

She patted Ellie's head. "You're doing fine, Isabelle." And she walked slowly from the room and outdoors.

Kate eased past her father and Grandfather Marshall, not slowing to let them engage her in conversation. How many times would she run from this house as pain tore at her? She kept a steady pace until she reached the corrals and leaned against the top rail as if watching the horses.

It was time to say goodbye to little Ellie and the Marshall family. Oh, she'd see them from time to time. But she wouldn't be part of the family.

She never had been.

The fact that she even thought about it proved she was letting Conner's accusation get to her.

It was not guilt or fear that guided her desire to become a doctor. It was concern for those ill and suffering.

But she'd allowed herself to grow much too fond of little Ellie. One of the things Mother Baker had warned her about. "You must guard your heart from getting too involved. It will only cloud your judgment."

And Conner? a mocking voice called. *Have you grown too fond of him?*

No, she denied vehemently.

"Kate?"

Conner speaking her name so close behind her sent a shock through her body.

He came to her side and leaned against the fence, his elbow brushing hers.

She did not move if only to prove to herself she wasn't affected by his closeness or his touch.

"We need to talk about the fund-raiser." He rumbled his lips. "A county fair. What is Grandfather thinking? We don't have time to organize such an event."

Grateful to discuss something that didn't strike at the depths of her heart, she gave a mirthless chuckle. "Seems he thinks you can work wonders."

"I wish I could. There's many things I'd change."

His words felt like warning flags suspended before her. What things would he change? Ellie's condition, without question. Perhaps he'd bring Thelma back and create a home for the baby with her.

"For you." The words were so soft she thought her imagination had created them.

She faced him. "What did you say?"

"Nothing. It was only a slip of my tongue." But he held her gaze with a firmness that provided the truth without need of words.

She turned away. She would not ask what things he'd change. He'd already said enough to give her cause to think he thought she should abandon her plans to become a doctor.

No. He hadn't said that. Hadn't even suggested it. Why had she put those words in his mouth?

It was getting too complicated. The sooner she got back to Bella Creek, the sooner she could think clearly again.

But unless she and Conner set out the plans for the fair right now, she'd have to see him again.

"I don't know much about county fairs. How are they run?"

He shrugged. "I have only attended one and I was just a kid, so all I remember is the many food booths, especially the one selling pies." He thought a moment. "Seems Ma entered a pie to be judged and was so proud to come home with a blue ribbon. But as to how one is run…well, I suppose you just announce there is going to be one."

She snorted. "And it simply happens? This I have to see."

"You think there's more to it than that?" He gave her a wide-eyed look.

She squinted. "Conner Marshall, I do believe you are joshing me."

He grinned. "I do believe you are right. But it would be nice if it just happened. How do we plan this?"

"Your grandfather said judging of sewing and baking. That would require a place for entries and judges, I suppose."

"And people who would sell coffee and candies and baked goods."

"And some form of entertainment."

They looked at each other as the truth grew clear.

"It sounds like a lot of work," Conner said.

"How long do we have to do this?"

"I don't know. How long would it take?"

They turned to stare at Grandfather. He was obviously watching them as he waved, a broad smile upon his face.

"Why, the crafty old man."

Kate jerked toward Conner at his remark. "What do you mean?"

"Nothing." But Conner's jaw set hard as he strode across the yard to face his grandfather.

Kate scurried to catch up. She meant to hear what Conner had on his mind.

He stopped at the edge of the porch. "I have you figured out, Grandfather. And it's not going to work."

"Boy, the fund-raiser had better work. I suggest you get the plans laid out and put up announcements in all the local businesses. You can announce it next Sunday as well. You want to have it when the gardens are at their best."

"Gardens?" Kate was as surprised as Conner. What did gardens have to do with it?

"Certainly. There's to be a section for judging garden produce, won't there?"

Kate recognized it as a statement, not a question. It appeared there was a lot more to a county fair than a few booths and some judges. She wasn't sure she wanted to hear anything more.

"Let's say the first weekend in August. That should give you lots of time to get things organized." The old man sat back with things—in his mind—settled, but a sense of panic gripped Kate's insides.

She sent a help-me look to Father, but he nodded and smiled, completely unaware of how impossible this was.

"That's three weeks away. How are we to get it organized in that length of time?" Conner asked.

"Not by standing here jawing with me." Grandfather waved them away.

Conner grabbed Kate's hand and hurried her into

the kitchen. He held a chair for her and, after she sat, he plopped down next to her.

"This is crazy. No way we can get a fair organized in less than three weeks and hope for it to be a success."

"I agree. You go tell your grandfather."

He stared at her, then laughed. "No, it will be easier to put on a fair."

"Then let's get at it."

"I'll get paper." He brought a piece from the sitting room and they started a list of categories to be judged, entertainment, food, races. The list grew and grew.

Kate stared at it. "I don't know where to begin."

Annie stepped into the room and began pulling out pots and putting them on the stove.

Father called from the veranda. "Kate, it's time to go home."

Seemed it had been decided her stay here was over. She couldn't argue with the facts—the baby was strong enough not to need medical attention. Isabelle would do fine with her. It was time to move on. As soon as she got back to town, she would write to the medical college and inform them she was ready to pursue her studies. She'd already been accepted but had postponed her start date due to Father's accident.

Only one thing stood in the way of her leaving Conner Marshall behind—the fact her father and his grandfather had foisted this event upon them.

"We are far from done with this." She pointed to the list.

"I know. Guess I'll have to come to town and we can work on it some more."

Nice of him to sound so eager.

She recognized his sarcasm, but she was no more

eager to spend time with him, especially given his opinion of her. "Seems we have no choice."

"Given the time frame, I better come in tomorrow evening. Is that okay?"

"That will be fine." She told herself it was annoyance that she felt at being forced into this position, but it felt strangely like anticipation.

On Monday evening right after supper, Conner rode the four miles into town. He kept his horse at a steady trot if only to prove to himself that he wasn't anxious to get there. He knew Grandfather was at it again. Playing matchmaker. Conner wanted nothing to do with such foolishness.

The road became Mineral Avenue and he slowed to a walk. He passed his uncle's mercantile store, where Sadie had held school for a number of weeks. He stopped in front of Miss Daisy's Eatery and turned left to the doctor's house. He knew that the office and waiting room were on one side. The living room faced the street, with the kitchen and bedrooms at the back of the house. It was too light for lamps to be lit, but the sun's rays slanted through from the kitchen window and made the inside of the living room bright. From what he could see, the room was empty.

He swallowed back disappointment. Perhaps she had gone out on a call with her father.

He tied his big bay to the hitching post. Copper lifted one foot and prepared to wait.

Conner clattered up to the door to the left of the waiting room door, knocked and held his breath to listen for footsteps. Somewhere he thought he heard a noise and then nothing. He was about to knock again when Kate opened the door.

"You're here. Come on in. Let's get this business taken care of." She led him into the kitchen, where two pies cooled on the table.

She didn't sound at all eager to see him, but he wasn't about to comment on the fact. A tempting aroma of sweetness and spices pulled at him. "You've been baking." A completely unnecessary observation.

Pink stained her cheeks. "Mrs. Bramford taught me to bake. I thought I might enter the pie-making contest."

He tried to fit this bit of information into what he knew of Kate but failed.

"You needn't look so surprised."

"Don't mind confessing I am. They sure look good."

"I'll let you sample them after we tend to our business."

He sent his hat sailing to the hook by the door, grabbed a chair and sat down. "Let's get at it."

She chuckled. "Nothing like a bribe, is there?"

"Nope. Especially one that smells so good." He leaned over the pies and inhaled. "What other secrets have you been keeping from me?"

The amusement in her face fled. "You know more of my secrets than anyone else."

He met her intent gaze. Felt her look go deep as if seeking something. Perhaps reassurance. Or perhaps she was recalling the way he'd held her. He half rose, wanting to hold her again. Wanting to ease her worries. But the table stood between them and he sat back down before he'd even gotten up.

"Kate, your secrets are safe with me."

Relief filled her eyes.

"Though once people see how you bake…" He shook his head. "I don't know if I'll be able to keep it a secret."

A sweet smile replaced her worry. "You best wait until you taste them before you pass judgment." She sat facing him. "I've been doing a lot of thinking about this."

"So have I." He understood that she referred to the fair.

Within minutes, it was clear they had been thinking along the same lines. He'd asked Annie for suggestions on categories and they soon had a list for baking, sewing, preserves and gardening. They came up with a few categories for grain and hay.

Because she lived in town, she agreed to make posters and have them put in each business establishment.

"I'll ask Uncle George to recommend people for judging," Conner said.

"It's an honor to be a judge, I suppose. Why not ask prominent persons, like the lawyer, the preacher—"

"Your father."

She nodded. "He'd like that."

It took a bit of time to decide how many judges they would need. Even using prominent persons, they came up short, so it was agreed he would ask his uncle for suggestions.

"What about food booths?" he asked.

"And games?" she added. "From what I've learned, games and entertainment are essentials."

He pushed the lists aside. "I can't think of this anymore with the aroma of your baking filling my nostrils."

She gathered their notes into a neat pile. "We need to ask around and see what others are willing to do. Perhaps on Sunday we can present a list of our needs and ask for volunteers."

"Good idea." He eyed the pies.

With a little chuckle, she brought out a knife, two forks and two plates. "This one is rhubarb." She cut him a generous portion and a sliver for herself.

Rhubarb was not his favorite, but he took a bite. And surprise widened his eyes. He chewed and swallowed. "That is without a doubt the best rhubarb pie I have ever tasted. What did you do to make it so good?"

She planted her elbows on the table and signaled for him to lean toward her.

He did so.

She glanced over her shoulders, then whispered, "Mrs. Bramford swore me to secrecy. If I told, I think she would know and hunt me down." She gave an exaggerated shiver. "I don't want to think what kind of punishment she would exact."

Conner leaned back and laughed. He liked this teasing side of Kate and wished he saw it more often.

"I suppose it's all right for me to guess."

"You can try." She ate a bite of her pie and looked unconcerned.

"Go ahead and look smug. I have no idea. I just know it's very, very good." He finished his portion and looked toward the other pie. "What kind would that be?"

"That is another secret recipe from Mrs. Bramford— apple and raisin."

"Sounds intriguing."

She laughed. "I think what you mean is it sounds unusual, but fear not, your taste buds are in for a surprise." She again cut him a generous portion and a thin slice for herself.

Half eager, half wary, he took a bite and the flavor exploded in his mouth. He didn't need to say anything. She read his enjoyment in his face and gave a pleased little laugh.

She sobered. "How is Ellie doing? I've worried about her all day."

"Isabelle took her this morning. I confess I detoured to the house several times throughout the day to assure myself she was okay. Isabelle is managing well, which is a relief."

Kate nodded. "I didn't doubt she would. So the baby is eating well and all?"

"She seemed pleased to see me every time I popped in but looked past me. I think she was looking for you."

Kate gave her empty plate a great deal of study. "I'm sure you're mistaken. She's likely missing her mama."

Conner didn't need to point out that if Thelma had been doing a good job of mothering the baby, Ellie wouldn't have been in such poor condition when she was delivered to his doorstep. Though he had no right to judge Thelma until she was located. There could be a reasonable explanation, though he would be hard-pressed to accept any excuses. "Thelma better have a good reason for why Ellie was so neglected."

"And if she doesn't?"

He had no answer. "Where is she? Why did she send Ellie to me?"

"She knew the baby would be safe if she was seen as a Marshall. You're a firm believer in family."

He wondered where Kate was going with that observation. "I've made no secret of it."

"Then when you find Thelma—"

"If we do." He admitted he wondered if something had befallen the woman.

Kate acknowledged his statement with the flicker of her eyelid. "When you do, what will become of Ellie?"

It was a question he didn't want to confront. He had no claim on the baby, but he wasn't prepared to let her return to whatever situation had brought her to such a precarious state.

Chapter Seven

All day, Kate had been troubled by the question she asked Conner. What would become of Ellie once they found Thelma? Would Conner marry her to provide the baby a home? It seemed like the sort of thing he would do. *Lord, guide me, guard me, help me keep my eyes focused on the path set before me.* She had prayed the same prayer many times throughout the day.

"I wrote to the medical school this morning, letting them know I was ready to start classes. I'm waiting for confirmation as to when I can begin school."

"Then you have made up your mind."

She knew he referred to his suggestion that her reasons for pursuing medicine were in part about avoiding risk. She had already had a taste of those risks. Leaving Ellie, knowing she would not be part of the child's future nor would she be part of Conner's, had brought on another level of pain. She didn't know how much more she could endure. Pain of losing her family, remembering her lost brothers, seeing big happy families and not being a part of one consumed her. Medical studies would fill her mind with facts and figures…not emotions. "I've never planned otherwise."

"I see. Forgive me if I thought deep down you might desire something more." His gaze held hers. She couldn't break free of the silent demand any more than she could deny that his words stirred a longing.

He looked away first, leaving her breathless and confused, then turned to the notes they'd made. "It would seem we have things under control for now. Thanks for the pie." He got to his feet. "On Sunday, I'll make an announcement regarding the fair."

She followed him to the door. "I'll see to the posters and other things."

He stood in the open doorway, his back to the street. The light from the kitchen window flooded his face. He smiled, though it did not reach his eyes. "Kate, I wish you nothing but success and happiness in the future."

It felt like he was saying a final goodbye. Shouldn't that provide relief rather than panic? She took a deep breath and willed herself to be calm. But surely they would see each other again while they completed plans for the fair. She didn't feel at all like they were ready for the event. He'd have to come back to finalize things.

But she could find no words that didn't sound needy and she didn't want him to get the wrong idea.

"Until Sunday, then." He smiled and strode to his horse, swung into the saddle and rode away.

She didn't close the door until he disappeared from sight.

Sunday was a long time off. Conner and Ellie would be together. She would be alone.

She hurried back to the kitchen, intent on putting

aside her troublesome thoughts. She gathered together paper and pens and drew up posters announcing the fair.

That night, she tossed and turned, unable to sleep as her thoughts circled round and round. Now that she'd remembered Johnny and Martin, she couldn't stop thinking of them.

The games they'd played with her. The outings they'd gone on. The family tradition of counting wildflowers on their summer picnics. Johnny was a great one for jokes and had them alternately laughing and groaning. Martin was a little more serious, more studious. He often brought a book with him on their outings. His favorite was one identifying the various plants and animals. The Latin names rolled off his tongue with such ease. She smiled. Having heard Latin at such a young age had helped her learn anatomy.

The next morning, she went from store to store with the posters. And at every one she was given more advice.

"I have a cousin who plays the fiddle."

"My sister would be a good judge."

She noted all the offers of help.

It was the lawyer's question that filled her with anxiety. "Where do you plan to hold the fair?"

How had location never been considered? She needed to talk to Conner about it, but how was she to do that?

The answer—go to the ranch—was simple enough.

The way her heart rejoiced and at the same time tightened with anxiety left her unsettled.

Father had gone to Wolf Hollow to take care of an accident victim. She had asked to accompany him, but he had refused. "You need to let me do this. Besides, you know I don't think Wolf Hollow is a safe place for you even in my company."

She didn't expect him home any time soon. The house echoed with emptiness. She wandered from room to room, her heart filled with such loneliness it hurt to breathe.

She couldn't stay there and hurried outside and across the streets until she reached the house where Sadie and Logan lived with their children. Logan had gone to the ranch as he did every day.

Sadie sat on the back step shelling peas. She smiled at Kate's greeting. "Just what I need. A visitor. Sit—" she pointed to the chair next to hers "—while I make tea."

Kate sat and began to shell peas. Beth, on a low stool, also shelled. Sadie's two younger children were watching ants at the corner of the yard.

Sadie returned with cups of tea. "Beth, will you take Sammy and Jeannie for a walk?"

Katie knew then that she wore a troubled look.

As soon as the children left the yard, Sadie spoke. "Tell me everything."

A flood of words broke forth. Kate told about the baby. "She's doing much better now and Isabelle is caring for her during the day. Conner keeps her at night." She told about remembering her brothers.

Sadie squeezed Kate's hands. "I'm so sorry."

She told about the fair. "Grandfather and Father insisted we had to plan it."

Sadie chuckled. "He's playing matchmaker again."

"What? Surely not. Everyone knows I am going to medical school very soon."

"Grandfather has never let little details get in the way of his scheming."

Kate drank the rest of her tea and resumed shelling peas. "I suppose he has nothing else to do, but he's going to be disappointed."

Sadie smiled and nodded.

They sat in silence except for the snap of pea pods opening and the plunk of peas added to the bowl.

Kate sighed. "Won't you miss being a teacher?"

"I will still be a teacher. My students will be our children."

"But what about the needs of the other children in the community?"

"There will be a new teacher."

Her calm answers did nothing to ease Kate's muddled thoughts. "Don't you feel guilty at confining your teaching to three children?"

Sadie's smile was so serene it made Kate's eyes sting.

"I can't think of anything more noble or satisfying than teaching my children the values I cherish, in using everyday moments as opportunities and in watching them grow into responsible, caring adults, knowing I had a hand in doing that. It's like I am working hand in hand with God."

A lump the size of an orange lodged in the back of Kate's throat. Sadie made it sound so wonderful to be a mother. "Why don't you both teach and mother?" She knew the local school board, made up mostly of Marshalls, had offered her the choice to continue as a teacher after she married.

"Because I don't feel I could do justice to both."

Kate nodded. "Exactly how I feel. A doctor's time is too uncertain to allow him or her to be a full-time parent." Being in the Baker family had taught her that family life did not exist for the doctor's family.

"Your father is."

"I suppose it's different if the doctor is the father." But he was often missing from family meals and events. In fact, both her parents had been. She'd spent a good deal of time at the Bramford house and, as she'd grown older, alone in her own house.

Sadie studied Kate with her gentle eyes. "I suppose in the end, every person must decide what it is he or she wants and whether or not they are prepared to make the necessary sacrifices." Her expression grew dreamy. "For me, I couldn't bear the thought of missing any of the ordinary events of everyday life. I want to share every little discovery with the children. I want to bake them cookies and take them on picnics. I want to wash their clothes and see them drying on the line. I want to be available when Logan rides home in the middle of the day simply because he misses me or he wants to show me something. I know I could do most of that and still teach, but I simply didn't want to." She leaned back. "Being part of the Marshall family is the best thing I could ask for, apart from being Logan's wife and mother to the children. There is something about a big, happy family that I wouldn't trade for anything."

Kate's mind filled with flashes of herself and her brothers with their parents. Joyous, happy, noisy moments. "I had that once."

"No reason you can't have it again."

"I can't imagine regaining what I've lost."

Sadie squeezed her hand. "I didn't mean you could replace your family, but you can enjoy a new family. Like the Bible says, 'beauty for ashes, the oil of joy for mourning, the garment of praise for the spirit of heaviness.' Our past is not our future."

Kate tucked Sadie's words into her heart. Grammie had taught Kate to read the Bible and find answers there and to speak to God frequently, taking to Him every concern. She would trust Him to keep her steady.

"Now tell me more about this fair you and Conner are planning."

Kate told her what they had done so far. "I thought we had it under control until someone asked where we were holding it." She gave a mocking laugh. "If Conner has a place in mind, he hasn't told me. Perhaps you can get Logan to ask him."

Sadie chuckled. "I could ask him, but he'd likely forget. You best go out there and speak to Conner yourself."

"But—"

Sadie's eyes narrowed. "You've been out plenty of times before. Why all of a sudden are you reluctant?" She grinned. "It's Conner, isn't it? Perhaps Grandfather knows what's going on after all."

"It's nothing of the sort. I just wonder if they aren't getting tired of seeing me. But I need to take care of this little detail." Though having a place to hold the fair would be a huge detail if they didn't find one. "I'll go out after supper and speak to him." At the same time, she would prove to one and all that she and Conner were only working together out of necessity.

Father had not returned by supper time and she ate a lonely meal, then went to the livery stable and rented a buggy. Soon she was on her way to the Marshall Five Ranch.

The evening was cool, the breeze refreshing, and wildflowers bloomed in abundance. Martin would have been overjoyed to see so many and would have soon known the name of each. Sadness pulled at her heart. How she missed her brothers, her parents...her family.

The ranch came into sight and she studied the place. Annie was in the garden. Bud was walking toward the barn. She saw no one else and drove to the house and put on the brake.

Conner stepped from Dawson's house, the baby in his arms, and Kate jumped down and hurried toward him.

"Is something wrong?" she asked, wondering why he was taking Ellie from Isabelle's care.

Ellie cooed and bounced with excitement at seeing Kate.

"Nothing's wrong. She's sure happy to see you." Conner shifted the baby into Kate's arms and Kate nuzzled the sweet-smelling baby.

"I thought when I saw you..." Well, it was obvious she'd overreacted.

"I miss the little sweetheart, so I am bringing her home for the night."

They reached the house. Annie saw that Kate and Conner were together and waved, then returned to her work.

Grandfather was in the sitting room. "Wondered how long it would take for you to come and visit."

Kate's cheeks warmed as she realized that he thought she had come to see Conner. "We have overlooked a slight detail in our plans."

Grandfather looked from one to the other. "Not surprised to hear that."

Conner seemed more interested in the way Ellie pulled at Kate's collar than at her announcement.

"Yes, we haven't said where the fair will be held."

Grandfather pushed to his feet. "I'll let you two figure that one out." Leaning heavily on his canes, he went to his room.

The baby pulled herself upward, trying to get the collar in her mouth. Kate turned her toward Conner. She arched her back and whined in protest.

"Looks like she's developing a mind of her own." Kate smiled, knowing Ellie's actions indicated her growing strength.

"Yup. She's beginning to let us know what she wants."

They chuckled as Ellie was diverted with a yarn ball Conner offered. "Annie resurrected some toys from a trunk in the attic."

"I can't believe how much she's improved in two days. It's good to see her so much more active."

"She's eating much better. Your father said if she was taking a full feed that she didn't need to be wakened to eat. She sleeps six hours at night."

Ellie squirmed around to look at Kate, reaching out to pat her face.

"She remembers you." His gaze came to her, steady, searching, wanting.

She didn't know what he sought. Didn't want to think about it. "Do you have a place in mind for the fair?"

He blinked as if the fair was the last thing on his mind.

She wouldn't allow herself to think she might be the first.

"I really haven't thought of it. There's an open area west of town toward the river, but I don't know if it's big enough. I've never looked at it with the idea of holding a fair."

"How much room do we need?"

He lifted a hand in defeat. "I don't know. Why did Grandfather put us in this position? It's like he wants us to fail."

She held back her reply that if Sadie was right, Grandfather had something else in mind.

Ellie wrinkled her face and began to fuss.

"It's time for her to eat." Conner went to the kitchen to prepare a bottle. It was heartening to watch him. He was careful to see everything was clean. The baby was in good hands with him to care for her.

Kate jostled the baby. "Hush, sweetie. It will be ready in a minute."

He warmed the bottle, tested it and offered it to her. "Do you want to feed her?"

"I'd love to." She sat in Grandfather's armchair. Conner sat nearby, watching the baby eat.

Ellie's eyes drifted shut. She jerked awake to drink a bit more. She repeated the performance several times until the bottle was empty.

Kate set the bottle aside and smiled at Ellie. Was there anything better than a baby asleep in her arms?

Pain sliced through her. Her plans did not include a baby. They did not include a family.

Conner leaned over to wipe Ellie's chin. His shoulder brushed against Kate's. She breathed in the scent of grass and leather and soap. Her heart kicked into a gallop as memories of moments spent together tending the baby flashed through her head.

He turned without sitting back. His face was inches from hers. She saw the way his irises were a lighter blue toward the center. Saw something more that made it impossible to breathe or to think. An invitation, a wish.

"Kate." Her name whispered from his lips.

"Conner." She echoed the call.

"Do you know how sweet it is to see a baby sleeping in your arms?"

She gave a barely there shake of her head, unable, unwilling to break free of the powerful look between them. Was this where she belonged?

Somewhere a door slammed. A voice called out.

She looked past him, felt his disappointment as he sat back. What did he want from her? Something she couldn't give.

"I need to look at that place by the river." His voice was cool. "I'll come to town tomorrow. Do you want to come with me to see it?"

He surely didn't need her opinion on the matter. "I'd like to see what we are dealing with."

"I'll take the baby upstairs and put her in the crib."

"She has a crib now?"

Conner chuckled. "Annie found it. Come on, you better see for yourself."

Still holding the sleeping baby, she followed him upstairs to one of the bedrooms. Conner's? She glanced about and saw a cowboy hat and leather vest hanging from hooks on the wall. A brush sat on top of a chest of drawers along with a framed picture.

He saw her look at it. "My mother."

A crib had been set up against one wall and she tucked the baby under the covers. She and Conner stood side by side watching Ellie sleep.

"She's beautiful," Kate whispered.

He draped an arm about her shoulders and tipped his head against hers. "She is. I wish she really was mine."

There was one way he could make the baby his—marry Thelma.

She could imagine him doing so.

Perhaps his choices weren't all that different than hers. She was prepared to give up having a family in order to pursue medicine. He might well be prepared to give up a chance at finding the sort of woman he deserved in order to have the child he wanted.

Her heart went out to him. It was a huge sacrifice. Thelma had proved her fickleness already. Conner deserved more. A woman who would welcome being part of the Marshall family, who would be true and faithful. A woman who would love him enough to put him above every other pursuit.

It was all Conner could do not to pull Kate closer, hold her tight and beg her to reconsider her goal. But it wasn't like he could offer her something better. He could offer her nothing until he found Thelma and learned the truth. He had fallen hopelessly in love with tiny Ellie and would do everything in his power to help her, to be a part of her life.

Including marrying Thelma?

He didn't love Thelma. Perhaps never had.

Instead of pulling Kate into his arms, he dropped his arm from around her shoulders and took her hand. "We'll let her sleep." They tiptoed from the room. As they reached the stairs, Kate freed her hand from his.

He told himself it was for the best. Tried to convince himself he didn't feel as if a part of his insides had been wrenched away at the same time.

Pa and Annie greeted them as they reached the main floor. They clustered about the kitchen table, chatting about the daily events of their lives and the plans for the fair.

"I'm going to enter Ma's chocolate cake," Annie said. "And some of the garden produce."

"Pa, do you think the area by the river is big enough to hold the fair?"

His pa considered the question. "It might. I suppose it depends how many booths and tents you'll have."

Booths and tents? This was far more involved than he'd anticipated.

Kate pushed back from the table. "I should get home."

He escorted Kate to her buggy.

She turned toward him. "What was your father talking about? Booths and tents? I thought we'd just have tables or something." Her voice trailed off. "I honestly hadn't given it that much thought."

He glanced over his shoulder to make sure no one overheard. "Nor have I. I'll be in tomorrow and we'll get this sorted out."

"I hope so. I would not like to be remembered as the woman who planned a fiasco." She shuddered.

He helped her up to the seat and patted her hand. "Kate, you'll be remembered for far better than that."

"Oh, really. Do tell."

He had to tip his head back to meet her gaze and was instantly trapped by the teasing light in her eyes. "I'll remember how you saved Ellie. And how—" How she clung to him as she wept in his arms. The gentle kiss he had helped himself to after a worried night with the baby. He couldn't tell her that. "How good your pies taste." He glanced over his shoulder and then leaned closer as if sharing a guilty secret. "Best I ever tasted.

Even better than Ma's or Annie's. I think you'll win the blue ribbon for sure."

She chuckled. "Conner, what would your mother think to hear those words? Or Annie for that matter?"

"Oh, Annie would be okay. She knows she's the best cake baker around."

Something in Kate's gaze held him immobile. Unable to think beyond this moment. Sharing something sweet and private with her.

"I best be on my way." She turned her gaze forward, leaving him dizzy.

"I'll see you tomorrow." He stepped back so she could drive away.

She flicked the reins and headed down the trail. At the top of the rise, she turned and waved.

He gave a little salute and stood there until the last whiff of her dust had settled. Only then did he turn toward the house.

Grandfather leaned against his canes, an all-knowing grin on his face. "Good to see you've finally gotten over that Thelma girl."

"I was over her long ago." He couldn't keep aggravation out of his voice. "I thought you'd gone to bed."

"Nope. Just trying to give you young folks some privacy." He chortled as if pleased with himself.

The old man took liberties with his comments. "We were taking care of Ellie. Don't need privacy for that."

Grandfather banged one of his canes on the wooden floor. "Sure hope I ain't gonna have to show you how to treat a girl special-like."

"If it ever comes to the place I need your help…" He shook his head as if deeply saddened by the thought.

But as they went into the house, Conner wondered

how Grandfather would handle someone like Kate. A woman who closed her heart to family.

That effectively left no room in her life for Conner. When would that knowledge become easy to bear?

Chapter Eight

Father had not returned when Kate got up the next morning. "God," she murmured aloud, "keep him safe. Help him care for the injured." She made herself breakfast, and as she ate, she read her Bible. Grammie had given it to her and elicited a promise to read it, seeking God's will in her life.

Kate read the verse she had underlined years ago. *No man, having put his hand to the plough and looking back, is fit for the kingdom of God.*

She looked out the window into the distance as she recalled when she had taken her pencil and a straightedge and drew a line under those words. She'd been seventeen and Edward had been calling. She'd fancied his attention would soon bring an offer of marriage. Instead, he had delivered an ultimatum. She'd have to choose between him and a medical career.

It had been tempting to choose him. He was a pleasant young man and had treated her kindly. Made her feel valued. Reading this verse had enabled her to make her choice. She'd put her hand to the plough when she was ten and promised Grammie she would not waste the gift God had given her. She'd renewed the promise when Mother Baker was dying and reminded Kate of the Bakers' agreement to give Kate the opportunity to follow in Father's footsteps.

Kate returned her attention to the printed page before her. She would use her skills and abilities to serve others.

Sadie's words echoed in Kate's mind. *I can't think of anything nobler or more satisfying than teaching my children the values I cherish... It's like I am working hand in hand with God.*

She'd made it sound as if serving her family was enough.

Troubled by her thoughts, Kate hurriedly cleaned the kitchen. She dusted the entire house. She tidied the examining room and the waiting room, then looked around. There was nothing more to consume her attention in the house and she hurried outside to tend the tiny garden at the back of the lot.

Unfortunately, the work gave her plenty of time to think and every thought returned to Conner and Ellie. She yanked out weeds and tossed them aside. She pulled some baby carrots and took them to the house.

A glance at the clock said it was lunchtime. She made a sandwich and ate it standing at the window, looking out at the backyard.

As soon as she finished, she pulled out a big mixing bowl. She'd make cookies. They would be nice to nibble on when she and Conner went to look at the place by the river. Hopefully it would be suitable for the fair.

Sadie had told of a romantic picnic with Logan by the river. Kate could see herself sitting by Conner's side, watching the lowering sun drip pink and orange into the water.

She beat the batter with unusual energy. The trip was about the fair. Nothing else. The only reason for Conner to come to town was the need to investigate the site.

A smile caught at her mouth as she recalled Ellie's happiness at seeing her. It had felt right to stand side by side with Conner as they watched the baby sleep.

Her arms formed a cradle. Sweet baby. It had felt good to hold her again.

"Enough." She plopped mounds of cookie batter onto the baking sheet. She would bake the cookies and enjoy them, but it had nothing to do with babies or family or Conner. She shoved the tray into the oven.

Father entered the kitchen. "Did I hear you talking to yourself?"

"You're back. I didn't hear you return."

"I came through the office." He sank to a chair with a heavy sigh.

"Are you okay?"

"Tired but otherwise fine." He looked past her. "Is there coffee?"

"I'll have it in a minute." She spun around to grind the beans and fill the coffeepot with water. "How is everything at Wolf Hollow?" she asked over her shoulder.

"Two injured men. One pretty serious, but he made it through the night and should recover. I left his wife tending him."

By the time the coffee boiled, the first tray of cookies was ready and she slid a half-dozen gingery-smelling cookies to a plate and put them before her father.

"Lovely. You are such a good housekeeper and I truly appreciate it."

It was not the first time he had commented on her housekeeping. But this time, it seemed to mean more. She liked keeping the house running smoothly, liked preparing meals and sharing them around the table. She enjoyed seeing that Father's needs were met.

Not that it meant anything of significance. She had Sadie and Conner to blame for making her second-guess her every action.

Father drank coffee and ate a cookie, then brought his attention to Kate. "You sounded frustrated." He referred to the way she had scolded herself aloud as he entered.

She sighed. "It's this fair that you and Grandfather Marshall have us planning. It's going to be a disaster. We don't know what we're doing. We need a place to hold it. We need tents." She explained all the things that a fair required.

"Rather than a bunch of small tents, you could use one big tent."

"But where would we get one?"

"I know a man at Wolf Hollow who has one."

"Father! Really? And you think that will suffice?"

"I think it would."

She leaned over and hugged him. "You've lifted a load from my mind. I can't wait to tell Conner. He'll be as relieved as I."

The outer door opened. Someone needing the doctor and her father slipped away.

Kate sang as she finished making cookies and cleaned the kitchen. She returned to the garden and picked the peas and sat in the shade as she shelled them. She tried to think of her upcoming departure to St.

Louis for medical school. How would Father manage? Perhaps he should hire a housekeeper.

Would Conner marry Thelma? Why did she allow the idea to hurt so much? Why did her heart leap unexpectedly when she thought of him coming this evening?

She shook her head. They would make sure the fair was a success. That was all that concerned her.

She and Father had barely finished supper when a knock sounded on the door.

"I'll get it," Father said before Kate could get to her feet. Not that she was anxious to see if it was Conner, but how did she explain the way her breath rushed in and out when she heard his voice?

She forced herself to remain seated as Father brought him through to the kitchen.

He greeted her with a warm smile and sat across from her. "I see there's pie left."

She could not bring herself to admit she had purposely saved some for him. "Would you like a piece?"

"I have been drooling all day thinking of your pies." He swallowed loudly. "That's yes in case you didn't understand."

She chuckled and served him a generous portion. "Coffee?" At his nod, she poured him a cup. "I have some good news."

He glanced at her.

"Father knows where we can find a big tent." She explained it.

"That's great." He finished the pie and leaned back. "But nothing is as great as your pie making." He sighed expansively.

His praise brought a glow of pleasure.

"Are you ready to go?"

"Give me a minute." She hurriedly cleaned the table, put the dishes in the basin and poured hot water over them. She'd wash and put them away later. A little sack held cookies and she took it in hand. "I'm ready."

He held the door and they went out into the warm summer evening.

A young boy ran by and bumped Kate. She stumbled.

Conner took her hand and pulled it to the crook of his arm. "Wouldn't want you to be knocked off your feet."

"Thank you." She let herself believe there was nothing more to it than that.

"Let's go talk to Uncle George and ask his advice about the fair."

Kate didn't point out that she'd talked to George Marshall twice about that very thing. He'd helped her consider a variety of categories.

George and his wife, Mary, lived above the store and Conner led Kate up the steps. She had never been in the living quarters before and looked around. The rooms were small and crowded with furniture and ornaments, and yet they had a warm, welcoming feeling to them. Perhaps because Mary rushed forward.

"My, this is nice. We don't often have company during the week. Come right in. I'll make tea. You can taste my cinnamon rolls. I'm going to enter them in the fair."

Conner gave Kate a questioning look.

She shrugged. How could they refuse the invitation? "I'd love to sample them."

With an eager smile, Mary served tea and handed each of them a dessert plate holding a large cinnamon roll covered in golden thick syrup.

Kate took a bite. "These are superb."

Mary beamed. "Thank you. This fair is a wonderful idea."

Conner spoke up. "Uncle George, we need help getting this organized."

George seemed guarded. "Did Grandfather give you this task?"

"Yeah." Conner sounded glum.

"Then I'm not about to interfere."

"What? You're a grown man and still afraid of your father?"

Kate wondered how George would respond to the mocking question, but he laughed.

"You're pretty much a grown man, too. Don't see you refusing his orders."

Conner shuddered. "And you won't any time soon. But can't you at least give us some advice?"

"I think I can do that without incurring any wrath. What can I do for you?"

Conner laid out their concerns. Was a big tent enough? Would the clearing by the river serve as a site? How did they arrange food and entertainment?

"A big tent will work. People selling food, the games and entertainment can take place outside. You better pray for good weather."

"Thanks." Conner pushed back and escorted Kate back outside. "Did you hear that? Now there are to be games."

"I'll add it to the list of things we need volunteers for." She took his arm again, needing his strength. This whole thing was exploding into something that required months to plan and they had three weeks. Two and a half now, she corrected.

They made their way to the town square, where two

men visited. They passed by with only a wave and continued down Silver Street in the direction of the river.

The business area of Bella Creek was small and soon behind them. They passed houses with tidy yards. Children called to each other. From one of the houses came the sound of a baby crying.

"How is Ellie?" Kate asked. The question had been on the tip of her tongue since Conner stepped into the house, but she didn't want to appear too eager and so hadn't voiced it. Hearing the nearby baby gave her the perfect reason to ask.

"She's doing so well. Today she put her arms out to me when I went to see her at noon. She babbled away like she had a long story to tell me." He sighed. "I wish her future was more certain."

"No word of Thelma?"

"No. I stopped to see Jesse. He said he'd notified a wide range of towns. Several knew of the traveling show but hadn't seen it in months." He paused. "Sooner or later we will find her. I wish it to be sooner rather than later."

"I pray for the same thing."

He patted her hand where it lay on his arm. "I know you care as much as I do."

She couldn't deny it.

They left the town behind, reached the clearing and stopped to look around.

"This will work," Conner said. "There's room for a big tent there. Wagons and horses can be corralled there. Smaller tents or booths can go along the edge along the trees and there's still lots of room for people to gather."

"And play games."

He laughed. "I feel better knowing this will work."

They walked around the perimeter, assessing and approving. They reached a break in the trees. "Shall we?" Conner indicated the path leading to the river.

"I'd love to." It was not a romantic interlude. But seeing as they were so close, they might as well go to the river.

The path was narrow, requiring they go single file. She followed him. He broke through to the wide, grassy bank and stopped and held out his hand.

It wasn't as if she needed help. The ground was level. It wasn't as if she longed for this contact and yet she took his hand readily enough. He drew her forward. The low murmur of the moving water, the call of marsh birds and the warning, protesting quack of several ducks provided a musical backdrop.

They wandered a hundred yards upstream to a slightly wooded area. He indicated a fallen log and they sat.

Almost like the day she'd remembered her brothers and cried in his arms.

Her cheeks warmed at the memory. He knew more about her than anyone else. That forged a bond she couldn't deny. Nor was she prepared to think it meant anything special.

Conner was beginning to feel better about the fair. It might not be a total flop after all. Grandfather and Dr. Baker just might get the bell they wanted.

With no reason to hurry back to town, he sat beside Kate, wishing he could prolong the moment.

She lifted the sack she had carried with her. "I brought cookies. I had thought we might be wanting a little snack about now, but between the pie and your aunt's cinnamon rolls, I don't suppose you're a bit interested."

He couldn't think of anything he'd sooner do than linger here with Kate at his side. "Cookies? Why, I'd love some." Thankfully, as Grandfather, Pa, Annie and Ma had often pointed out, when it came to eating, Conner was a bottomless pit.

She opened the drawstring and held the sack toward him.

He dug in and pulled out two ginger cookies. He bit into one. Moist and chewy with enough ginger to send his taste buds into full gallop. "These are good." He spoke without waiting to empty his mouth.

She favored him with a pleased smile. "Good." She nibbled at one as well. The way she ate, he decided she wasn't in the least hungry, but perhaps she wanted to keep him company. Maybe, even, she wanted to make this evening last.

For the moment he would ignore the truth that this was only temporary. She wasn't staying. He wasn't leaving. She didn't want family. He could think of nothing he wanted more…except for Ellie to be his child.

Kate stared at the water. "I remember when I was very young our family had a picnic by a river. I don't know where it was, but I suppose where we used to live." She smiled at him. "We had a farm near St. Louis." Her gaze returned to the rippling water. "Johnny wanted to see if he could catch a fish by hand and stood on a rock in the river and tried to catch one. I remember Martin kept saying he couldn't do it. But Johnny managed to grab the tail of a trout. It wiggled and fought and Johnny ended up in the water. He wouldn't let the fish go even though it meant he had his face in the river.

I was jumping up and down, worried he was going to drown. Mama and Papa were on their feet watching. I knew Papa would jump in and rescue him if necessary. Finally, Johnny got up holding the fish. He crowed that he had proved Martin wrong. Martin laughed so hard he had to sit down." She chuckled. "It was a happy moment in my life." She turned to him. "It's because of you and your family that I remembered my brothers."

"Really?" He couldn't imagine what they had done.

"Yes. I began to have flashes when I was around your family, but I couldn't identify the memory. But then Sammy told that silly joke and it reminded me of the jokes Johnny told. It took only a little longer for me to realize what I was remembering." Her laugh was low and throaty.

He curled his finger against her chin. "I'm glad we helped you remember those pleasant times."

Her eyes darkened. He felt her surprised waiting. Could she tell how much he longed to pull her into his arms? Keep her close?

Even more, pull her into his family?

She lowered her eyes and eased away. "One cookie left. Do you want it?"

His bottomless pit was about full, but if it gave them a reason to linger...

"Can't turn that offer down." He took his time eating that last reason for delay. In fact, he could make it last a long time if he held it in his hand and told her about the time he and his brothers had gone to the waterfalls. "Dawson said he read somewhere that there is always a hollow behind waterfalls. I said I didn't see how that could be with our falls. They are really a series of falls rushing into each other. But Dawson was sure it was so. He pointed out a particular place where the water could have pounded out a hole. Logan and I wanted him to prove it, so we tied a rope around his waist and he jumped into the stream." He laughed at the memory. "The river caught him and tore him downstream. Logan and I had our hands full pulling him back. Somehow he managed to get directly into the falls. But all he found was a solid rock wall. He was soaking wet and bruised when we finally pulled him out. Ma wanted to know how he managed to get so wet. But we had sworn not to tell. We said he jumped into the river because he thought he saw something. It was a good day."

Kate's eyes were wide. She shook her head. "Was it good for Dawson?"

He shrugged. "He never complained." A beat of contemplation. "Never again insisted there was a hollow behind the falls either."

"Your poor mother."

"I know." He shook his head sorrowfully as he purposely misunderstood her. "Imagine being married to Pa and having Grandfather for a father-in-law. I don't know how she endured it. And then to have a son like Dawson." He brightened. "Good thing I came along when I did."

She stared in disbelief and then, understanding his teasing, burst out laughing. "How fortunate for her," she said when she could speak.

"I know." He sobered. "I wish you could have met her. She was a special woman." He took the last bite of his cookie.

"She must have been to survive you…" She let the sentence drag. "And your brothers."

The smile she gave him made him swallow his

cookie half chewed. He put on a mock frown and caught her shoulders. "Kate, those are fighting words." He pulled her to her feet and stared down at her wide, waiting eyes.

"And how do you fight?"

He could not mistake the invitation in her voice. "I'm not much of a fighter." He studied her mouth, thought of kissing her. He pulled her closer, then thought better of it. A kiss had to mean something. Yes, sometimes it was offered out of joy or gratitude. But mostly, for him, it meant mutual affection. And more.

There might be a degree of regard between them, but not enough for him to open his heart. He shifted away and took her hand. "Best get you home before your father comes looking for you."

"Yes, of course."

He allowed himself to think she conveyed regret.

Could it be she was beginning to entertain the possibility of staying in Bella Creek, of becoming part of a big, happy family?

Or was he being foolish in hoping that was the case?

Chapter Nine

Kate checked her reflection in the mirror. She was ready for church, but it was too early to leave. Father still nursed a cup of coffee. He gave Kate a considering look. "You in a hurry?"

"I guess not." She stirred the pot of stew she had made and pushed it to the back of the stove so it would simmer slowly while they were gone.

He chuckled and she knew she hadn't convinced him. "You've been restless the last couple of days."

"I'm anxious to hear back from the medical school."

"Yes, I suppose so. Or perhaps see a certain young man."

She suddenly found a spot on the cupboard that she needed to scrub. It was on the tip of her tongue to argue his suggestion, but she couldn't find it in her heart to do so. Conner had not been back since the evening they had gone to the river. They'd parted with a list of things each of them would do regarding the fair. Somehow she'd expected him to return, if only to discuss the plans. But he hadn't.

Had he decided she wasn't worth his time?

Oh, what was she thinking? It wasn't as if she wanted him to court her. Of course not. But still, would it hurt for him to let her know how Ellie was doing? But even that wasn't excuse enough for her eagerness to see him as Annie had come to town and brought news that Ellie was getting stronger every day. And Logan daily brought news to Sadie and Sadie repeated it to Kate. She was simply feeling out of sorts for no reason.

"It's time to leave," Father said.

Finally! She grabbed her drawstring handbag, put on her Sunday hat, and they headed down the street toward the church. Buggies and wagons trundled past them. Horses and riders trotted by. And if she glanced up at each one, it was only to call a friendly greeting.

And then she saw the Marshalls already in front of the church. Hatless, the three brothers' hair glistened golden in the sunlight. Grandfather and Bud were behind the boys. Sadie and Isabelle and the children clustered together.

Kate's steps slowed. She had never before realized or perhaps hadn't acknowledged how solitary she was with only her father for family.

More foolishness. She dismissed the thought.

Conner saw her and stepped away. Ellie perched happily in his arms.

Her heart beat a rapid tattoo against her ribs as he approached her. She stopped and waited while Father continued on, speaking to those he encountered.

Conner reached her side.

She stroked Ellie's cheek. "Aren't you looking as sweet as pie?" Her cheeks had begun to fill out. Her skin was flawless. She wore a white cotton dress with eyelet lace along the hem and a pair of white knitted bootees. Her brown eyes shone from under a lacy cotton bonnet. Wisps of light brown hair peeked out around the edges of the bonnet.

Kate's throat closed off. The baby was beautiful. Obviously she was being well taken care of at the Marshalls'. Why would she think otherwise?

Ellie chortled and bounced so hard Conner had to tighten his hold on her. "She's that happy to see you." But he shifted the baby and kept her in his arms.

Kate understood that he wanted those in attendance to see the baby with him. She glanced around. Already people had noticed and whispered together, no doubt wondering where Conner had found a baby. They'd be speculating if it was his and who was the mother.

Unless he told the truth, once they learned Thelma was the mother, they would assume he was the father and expect him to marry her.

He leaned close to whisper. "I'm not going to try to convince anyone the baby isn't mine until I know for sure she isn't in some kind of danger."

She nodded. "The secret is safe with me."

"Thanks. I'm going to announce the fair today. Are you ready? Not that it's news to anyone who has been in town during the week."

"I prepared the list of volunteers we need." She handed it to him. Her fingers brushed his and she had to force herself not to jerk back. She had to stop acting like a silly schoolgirl. It was like she'd been with Edward—too aware of every touch, reading things into every glance, dreaming and wishing and hoping. Remembering how that had turned out, her insides settled.

Conner glanced over the list. "It looks like you've got everything covered."

"I wasn't sure about asking for volunteers for entertainment. What if one of the elderly ladies wants to sing hymns in a quavering voice? Wouldn't that put a damper on the festivities?"

He grinned at her. "The only thing that could be worse would be rain."

She acknowledged his smile with her own. It felt good to be with him, working together on this project and sharing the same sense of humor. "We'll pray that neither happens."

"If the volunteers speak to you, you can always say you'll take it under consideration until both of us have a chance to finalize plans."

"That will work." And give them a reason to visit.

They joined the others entering the church. She slipped in beside Father. Conner usually sat with his father and grandfather, but today he followed her into the pew and sat beside her. He shifted the baby to the arm closer to Kate. His elbow pressed into hers and she welcomed the touch. The two of them protecting Ellie.

Preacher Hugh Arness took the pulpit. "Please pray for me. I am still trying to locate my son. I trust God to lead me to him, but sometimes my faith falters." He looked around the congregation, his dark eyes seeming to see everything. "In all this, I know God has not changed. Let us worship Him and rejoice in His love." He announced a hymn.

Conner took up the hymnal and passed it to Kate. She found the number and held it between them. Little Ellie reached for the book and Kate had to move it out of her reach. She smiled at the baby trying to squirm from Conner's grasp in order to get to the book and she stole a glance at Conner. They grinned at each other, then turned toward the front before anyone could accuse them of not paying attention. Kate's smile lingered in her heart throughout the service.

Preacher Hugh closed his sermon. "Conner Marshall has an announcement. Come on up."

"You hold her." He shifted the baby to her lap and strode to the front.

Ellie babbled a protest.

"Hush, sweetie," Kate whispered, keeping her attention on Conner.

He announced the planned fair. From the startled murmur, she knew there were some who hadn't heard the news yet. "It's to raise money for a church bell." He explained the reasons and many nodded their heads in agreement. "It's short notice, but I have no doubt that we, as a community, can make it work. However, we'll need some volunteers." He read off the list. "Miss Baker will take the names of each volunteer, then she and I will make a plan. Is that acceptable to everyone?"

Again, most of those present nodded their heads.

Mr. Grieves stood to his feet, looking somewhat uncomfortable.

Mrs. Grieves elbowed him. "Ask him." Her whisper carried across the room.

"Conner, whose baby is that?" He plunked down, his face a brilliant red.

Conner walked down and took Ellie. He carried her to the front.

Kate held her breath. How was he going to explain this?

He faced the congregation, a proud smile on his face. She wanted to warn him that he presented the picture of a proud papa, but it was too late.

"Folks, this is Elspeth, better known as Ellie. At the present, she is living with us."

Murmurs greeted his announcement. Kate tried to hear what people were saying.

"Is she yours?" Mr. Grieves asked.

"Where's the mother?" Kate couldn't see who asked the question. "Who's the mother?"

The murmurs increased in volume.

Preacher Hugh stood at Conner's side. "Jesus placed a child in their midst and said, 'Who so shall receive one such little child in my name receiveth me.' I think what matters here is that little Ellie is welcomed." He placed his hand on her head in blessing.

The murmurs subsided.

"Thank you."

Kate wasn't sure if Conner thanked Hugh or those gathered together in the church and it didn't matter. Hugh's words had ensured that Ellie would be welcome even if there were questions about her parentage. Ellie was an innocent child and shouldn't be judged by the actions of her parents, but sadly Kate knew it was not always so.

Conner returned to Kate's side and sat down. "That went well, I think," he whispered.

Preacher Hugh dismissed the service and they rose. Before they could escape, they were surrounded by a crowd. Some wanted to get more details about the fair. Many volunteered to help and Kate was kept busy writing down names. However, more than a handful came by simply to have a closer look at Ellie.

No one spoke out again about Ellie's mother, but Kate would have to be blind not to see the speculative look in most of those who came around. She knew they hesitated to say anything with the entire Marshall family gathered behind Conner.

It took several minutes for them to make it outside.

Kate remained at Conner's side. Would he now return to the ranch? The afternoon stretched long and boring.

Annie paused at Conner's side. "Like I said, I'm spending the day with Carly."

Conner's shoulders sank. "I'm going to starve."

"Maybe someone will find it in her heart to invite you to share a meal." Annie winked at Kate.

Kate stared at the younger girl. Did she mean to suggest Kate should invite Conner to join her and Father for dinner? It would be different to sit across from him in her own home as they shared a meal. It would feel— her pulse pounded behind her eyes—as though he belonged in her life. She swallowed hard in an attempt to push the foolish thought away and grew aware that he watched her with expectation in his eyes.

Her breathing was too fast, making her words airy. "There's a pot of stew on the stove if you care to join us for dinner."

He grinned. "I accept. Do you, by any chance, have pie as well?"

"I just might." Boredom and restlessness had turned into several afternoons of baking. "Father and I won't be able to eat all I've baked before it spoils. We welcome your help."

"And I'm most grateful to give it."

They looked at each other and laughed.

"There you go," Annie said. "Pa and Grandfather are going to Uncle George's, so I can leave without being accused of trying to starve any of you." She joined Carly and they hurried away.

"Are you ready to go home?" Father asked.

"Conner and Ellie are joining us."

"Good. That will put an end to your moping about." He walked away.

Kate's cheeks burned. "I wasn't moping," she protested to Conner. "But he refuses to let me accompany him on calls. Says I'll soon be gone and he'll be on his own. Says he prefers I stay at home in case someone comes to the house. Though what he plans to do when I leave, I can't say. I suppose he needs to find an assistant." She knew she babbled, but she couldn't stop herself.

Conner tucked the baby into the crook of his arm on one side and caught her elbow with his other hand. "I'm about to starve into a shadow. And my taste buds keep thinking of your pie."

"Of course." She fell into step beside him, all the while telling herself she was an intelligent woman, trained to be unaffected by drama, change or uncertainty. So why did she struggle to think straight?

Several people spoke to them as they made their way home, mostly wanting a closer look at the baby.

The aroma of meat, onions and other vegetables greeted them as they entered the house.

Conner paused to sniff. "My stomach is kissing my backbone."

She laughed. "What? Did you forget to eat breakfast?"

He looked shocked. "I have never in my life forgotten to eat a meal. But breakfast was long ago. Hours and hours and hours."

Ellie fussed a little.

"Even Ellie is complaining. I better feed her."

As he prepared a bottle, Kate got dishes from the cupboard. She turned around and Conner stood before her, his large body blocking her. Her gaze went to his. She couldn't be certain what she saw, or thought she saw, in his eyes. But it made everything else fade away as he searched her thoughts. She felt exposed by his look. Mentally she hesitated, undecided as to whether she should close herself to his look or let him see her deepest secrets.

Ellie fussed, impatient with waiting for her bottle, and Kate realized the baby perched on Conner's hip and Kate's father as he sat at the table were both anxious for dinner.

She sidestepped Conner and, with arms that seemed too long and unwieldy for the task, set the table.

Conner pulled out a chair and sat feeding the baby.

Why was it he seemed to take up so much space in the kitchen? It wasn't as though he'd parked in the middle of the room, and yet when she took bread and butter to the table, his presence almost overwhelmed her.

She returned to the stove and counted in and out four deep breaths before she lifted the hot pot from the stove and set it on a trivet in the middle of the table.

"Can I dish you up?" She nodded toward Conner's plate.

"Thank you."

Pleased with how steady both her voice and hand were, she served him a generous portion and then put stew on Father's plate and her own.

She sat.

"I'll ask the blessing." Father bowed his head and said a short grace. "Amen."

Conner held the baby on one side, holding the bottle with the same hand. "You're getting to be quite an expert," Kate said. Seeing his ease with Ellie brought a sting of tears to her eyes.

"No word on the mother yet?" Father asked.

"Jesse was able to locate the traveling show and learned that Thelma left it several months ago."

Kate heard the concern in his voice. The baby's future would remain unsettled until Thelma was found.

Conner continued, "Jesse has someone following up on that, but it's like looking for a needle in a haystack."

If they'd been alone, she would have reached for his hand and offered encouragement. Instead, she had to limit herself to words. "I will continue to pray she is located." Except wouldn't it then mean Conner might marry the woman? His love for Ellie grew more evident, stronger, every day.

The subject was dropped as they concentrated on their meal. Seeing how Conner struggled to manage with one hand, Kate went to his side. "Let me hold her while you eat."

"I appreciate that."

She sat with the baby on her knee. Ellie had finished her bottle and reached for the objects on the table. Kate gave her a spoon and let her bang the tabletop with it.

The spoon fell to Kate's lap as Ellie's head drooped. "Why, the little darling has fallen asleep," Kate said. She shifted Ellie to a more comfortable position.

"I'll make a bed for her on the floor." Conner rose. "Do you have a blanket?"

"There's a quilt hanging over the back of the chair in the front room."

He prepared a pad on the floor by the sofa and eased Ellie from Kate's arms. Of necessity, his arms practically held hers. She lifted her gaze to his. He looked at her and again she felt as though he sought something she normally kept hidden from view.

Ellie stirred and he laid her down. Side by side they stood watching her to see if she would settle.

"She'll sleep like a baby," he whispered, grinning to indicate he meant to tease, and then he caught her hand and led her back to the kitchen.

She eased her hand free of his grasp, hoping Father wouldn't notice. She did not want to cause him concern that she might change her mind about following in his footsteps or give him any more reason to think she held special feelings toward Conner.

They returned to eating the meal. After a second helping of stew and three slices of bread, Conner said he'd had enough and glanced around.

Kate chuckled when she saw the disappointment in his face. "Do you think I got you here under false pretense?"

"The stew was mighty good and I appreciate it."

"You're welcome." She let the moment hang between them, enjoying how he struggled to ask where she'd hidden the pie.

He glanced toward the door beside the stove. "Is that a pantry?"

"It is."

He darted a glance toward her as if to suggest she should stop stalling. "You store food in there?"

"I do believe that is one purpose of a pantry."

Father cleared his throat. "Kate, I'd like some pie for dessert. I'm sure Conner would, too."

She laughed as Conner let out a gusty breath. "I was going to make him ask."

"You were enjoying my misery."

"Not at all. Simply enjoying a little fun."

"At my expense."

"Perhaps." Their gazes crashed together as she admitted how much she enjoyed the give-and-take she felt free to participate in with him.

"Pie?" Father reminded her and she hurried to the pantry.

"What kind?" Conner said, his eyes glued to the pie as she prepared to cut it.

"Bumbleberry."

"Huh? Never heard of such a fruit."

She laughed. "It refers to a mixed-fruit pie. This one contains rhubarb, raspberries and serviceberries." She put a generous slice before him. "I hope you'll enjoy it."

She served Father and herself. Seeing Conner waited for her to begin before he did, she took a small bite, then waited while he tasted his.

He closed his eyes and sighed. "So good. I think I could about survive on your pies."

Pleased at his praise, she nevertheless laughed at the idea of him eating nothing but pie. "You'd miss meat and potatoes." She paused for emphasis. "And bread and eggs and bacon and carrots and beans and—"

He held up a hand. "Okay. I get the picture. I know I eat a lot."

Father chuckled. "Daughter, they don't grow that big without a lot of food."

They all laughed at his comment.

Conner finished and accepted a second piece of pie.

Father refused seconds. "Now if you'll excuse me, I'm going to have a Sunday afternoon sleep while I can." He glanced toward the office door. "Perhaps no one will need my services this afternoon."

Kate waited for him to go to his bedroom and close the door before she spoke. "His hours are so erratic. He sleeps when he can." Her comment served as a reminder why she couldn't…wouldn't…try to combine doctoring with mothering. What kind of life would such uncertainty provide? She knew, having experienced it firsthand. Often she would be wakened in the night by someone needing medical attention. Many times she'd been unable to go back to sleep, worried her parents would be called away and wondering who would greet her in the morning. Or she'd be whisked from bed and taken to the Bramfords.

Conner touched the back of her hand. "You've gone to a troubling place. Tell me about it."

She tried to shake away the darkness and uncertainty of those days, but the memories clung. "It wasn't easy being the doctor's daughter. Life was uncertain. And often shattered by things beyond anyone's control." His look, so full of sympathy, brought forth a burst of explanations. She told him of being wakened, of being frightened, taken next door, afraid her parents would not return. Her voice broke. "It's why I will not try to combine a medical career with family life."

"I'm sorry your life was so uncertain. But perhaps the feelings started before you were adopted by the Bakers."

"What are you saying?" She suspected he was going to suggest she was afraid of the risks of having a family but would pretend otherwise…as if it didn't matter enough for his earlier words to even form a memory.

"You lost your parents early and then lived with a grandmother you adored, but you knew she could die any day. That's a lot of uncertainty for a child."

She stared into his eyes. A shudder raced across her shoulders. As he suggested, her life had been full of fear. How had he been able to see and understand when she couldn't? "It wasn't as though I didn't have a happy life. I have lots of good memories and I love my father."

"Didn't he recently have an accident?"

"I was so scared he would die," she managed to whisper.

She didn't recall getting to her feet, but she stood in the circle of Conner's arms, her face pressed to his chest as he held her and murmured comforting sounds. Her racing heart quieted and his words broke through into her mind.

"You can't guarantee you won't face more pain by closing your heart."

She should argue the point. But she didn't want to put an end to the refuge she found in his embrace. Nor could she remain thus forever and slowly eased back.

He let her go. Said nothing. Together they cleaned the kitchen.

"Let's take Ellie for a walk when she wakens," he said.

"That would be good for her." And enjoyable for Kate.

Shortly thereafter, the baby stirred and they went to her. She rolled over and looked up at them, gurgling with pleasure. "She is such a happy baby," Kate said. "It's amazing after what she's been through."

"I'm hoping we can eventually learn a few details about what her short life has held." He scooped up the baby. Together they tended her and tied on her little bonnet.

"It would be nice to have a buggy for her," Kate said.

"I wonder if Uncle George has one. Let's go see." They headed for the door, but before they reached it, a wagon rumbled to a halt outside.

Kate sighed. "This will be for my father." Already, booted feet clattered up the wooden steps and the outer door to the doctor's office banged open. "Doc," a heavy voice called. "I need the doctor."

"Wait here," she told Conner, "while I see how serious this is." She hurried through the adjoining door to see a man holding a woman in his arms. The blanket wrapped about the woman had a growing bloodstain. Behind the man stood a little boy and a slightly bigger girl, both so frightened their eyes almost consumed their faces.

"Where's the doctor?"

"Put your wife there." She pointed toward the examining table. "I'll get my father."

She felt Conner waiting in the doorway. "I'm sorry. I can't go now. You go ahead. Have a good time." She didn't want him to go without her, to have a good time while she stayed behind to help her father, but perhaps it was for the best. He'd see firsthand how unsettled a doctor's life was. But the necessity of staying warred with a desire to accompany him.

How had she allowed herself to care so much for his company?

Chapter Ten

Conner looked at little Ellie in his arms. He'd been eager to take the baby for a walk as an excuse to escort Kate on an outing. It wouldn't be any fun without her. "I'll stay in case you need help."

"Thank you." Her eyes said far more than her words. If he wasn't reading them wrong, he would say she was as disappointed as he to cancel the walk and he was grateful he chose to not go without her.

The walk would have been his chance to make up for the way his observation had hurt her. He regretted causing her pain by pointing out that her guardedness might be as much to do with losing her parents and her grandmother as it was about the uncertainty of her adoptive parents' erratic hours. However, she hadn't denied it. He hoped it would make her see herself more clearly. As clearly as he thought he saw her?

What did he think he saw?

A beautiful young woman afraid to open her heart to love. Committed to following a path laid out for her by her grandmother and the Bakers. Why did he think it wasn't the path she would choose for herself if not for those outside influences?

He didn't know how he knew, just that he did. Perhaps it was the way her eyes darkened as she watched families or the longing that filled her face when she sat at the table in the Marshall home.

What did it matter what he thought? She must be the one to choose how she would live her life. *God, take her on a path that will lead her to peace and joy.*

Dr. Baker hurried from his bedroom into the examining room. "Kate, take care of the children."

She led two wide-eyed children from the room. A girl of about six or seven and a boy of maybe five clung to each other's hands. Fear palpated from them.

Kate bent over to face them at eye level. "My father is going to look after your mama. We're going to look after each other."

The children relaxed a great deal. Conner had to admire Kate's skill at dealing with the frightened youngsters.

"Let's begin by learning everyone's name. I'm Miss Baker. This is Mr. Marshall and the baby is Ellie." Her smile lingered on Conner and Ellie before she turned back to the children. "Now tell us your names."

The children drew closer together. Then the girl tipped her chin upward.

"I'se Mary Sue and my brudder is Jimmy Lee."

"Pleased to meet you. Welcome to our home." Kate straightened and looked around as if seeking a means of entertaining the children.

"Have you eaten?"

"We's fine," Mary Sue said.

"I hungry," her brother protested.

A rumble of voices came from beyond the door and the children's faces pinched with worry.

"I have an idea. We'll take cookies outside and have a picnic." Kate urged them forward as she spoke.

Conner followed.

She took the cookie jar and led them outside to a little bench near the garden. It barely held the four of them…five counting Ellie, who studied the newcomers with interest. After a moment, she clearly decided she liked them and leaned toward Mary Sue, babbling excitedly.

Mary Sue laughed and took Ellie's hand. "She's a nice baby." Sorrow replaced the amusement. "Mama said we was gonna have a new baby, but on our way here she told papa there'd be no baby now. She said she losted it. How can you losted someone, 'specially a baby?"

Conner hoped she wasn't expecting an answer from him. How did you explain such things to a child so young? He tightened his arm around Ellie. It appeared her mother had lost her baby. He repeated Mary Sue's question to himself. How does someone lose a baby? Or send it away? Unless it was in some kind of danger. He hoped Jesse would find Thelma very soon.

Before she answered, Kate handed each of the children another cookie. She and Conner took one as well.

"Did your mama say babies come from heaven?"

"Uh-huh." Both children nodded vigorously.

"Even me," Jimmy Lee said with a great deal of assurance.

Kate met Conner's gaze and they shared a smile over Jimmy Lee's need to point that out.

She turned back to the anxious Mary Sue. "Sometimes God decides the baby isn't ready to leave heaven yet, so they go back to Him."

Tears clouded Mary Sue's eyes. "So we's not gonna get a new baby?"

"Maybe later."

The girl considered the answer a moment. "That's okay, then."

"I have an idea," Kate said. "How would you like to pick some flowers for your mama?"

"Oh, could we?" Mary Sue bounced to her feet. "Come on, Jimmy Lee." She half dragged her little brother to the row of flowers, where she drew to a halt. "You's sure it's okay?"

Kate joined the children. "What is her favorite color?"

"Pink."

Kate broke off several pink flowers. "Here's a start. Now which ones do you want to take her?"

In a matter of minutes, Kate held a bouquet of pink and red and white flowers the children had plucked from her garden, leaving a hole of green where there was once a flood of color.

"Let's put them in water until your mama is ready to see you."

Conner followed her indoors, where she took a jar from the pantry for the flowers.

The pair rocked back and forth before the bouquet. Mary Sue looked toward the doctor's office, her face wrinkled with worry.

Conner had an idea. "Would you like to play with the baby?" He spread a quilt on the floor and the children lay down on either side of Ellie. She patted Mary

Sue, then turned and patted Jimmy Lee. The children giggled.

Pleased with their response, Ellie laughed aloud.

Conner laughed, too, surprised and pleased to hear her belly-tickling laughter.

He met Kate's gaze as she stood within reach. Something as warm and sweet as a piece of her best pie filled him. He could float in the enjoyment of their shared pleasure.

Mary Sue released a huge sigh. "I sure was lookin' forward to a new baby."

Kate sat on the floor beside the child. "I'm sorry. Is there anything I can do to make you feel better?"

Mary Sue sat up and faced her. "You can make sure my mama's okay. That's what's most 'portant."

"I'll go see how she is." She slipped away, closing the door quietly behind her. Mary Sue scrambled to her feet to wait.

A few minutes later, Kate returned. "Would you like to see your mama and papa now?"

"She's okay?"

"She's tired and will have to rest for a few days, but she's fine and anxious to see the both of you." She reminded them of the bouquet. Mary Sue carried it carefully as Kate took them in.

Conner picked up Ellie and went as far as the door so he could see how they fared.

Dr. Baker joined him. "Mrs. Harper is fortunate to be alive. Thankfully her husband ignored her protests that she didn't need a doctor and brought her here."

Conner thought of the children. "She'll be okay, though?"

"She's a strong young woman. A day or two of rest and she'll be back on her feet."

The woman lay on the cot against one wall. She took the flowers and thanked the children, then gathered them in her arms.

Mary Sue patted her mother's cheeks. Jimmy Lee looked awkward at first and then burrowed his head against her neck.

"I need to get back to the farm," Mr. Harper said, looking regretful.

"I'll be going, too," his wife said.

Mr. Harper shook his head. "You need to rest."

"I'll rest better at home. And these two will help me, won't you?"

The children looked from one parent to the other, and at their mother's question, they agreed eagerly.

"Make me a bed in the back of the wagon. I'll be fine."

Mr. Harper looked to the doctor. "What do you say?"

"So long as she rests for a few days, I see no reason for her not to go home. She'll be less anxious."

"She'll rest. I'll see to it."

Mrs. Harper blushed at the look her husband gave her.

Mr. Harper spread a fur in the back of the wagon and carried his wife to it. Mrs. Harper held the jar of flowers carefully.

Kate took the children by their hands and led them out. She lifted each into the wagon. "You mind your mama and don't give her any trouble," she said to them.

"I won't," Mary Sue promised.

Jimmy Lee didn't immediately respond.

"Jimmy Lee?" Kate prodded.

"I try to be good."

His parents chuckled at his answer.

Conner held Ellie. Kate and her father stood side by side as the Harper family drove away.

"I have to make some notes." Dr. Baker went to his desk.

Kate led the way back to the front room, where she folded the quilt and put it over the back of the burgundy armchair.

"You're good at this," Conner said.

"You mean helping my father?"

"That and reassuring the children." He pushed back his caution and spoke his mind. "You're a natural mother."

She stared at him, a protest forming.

He lifted a hand. "I know. I know. Motherhood, family and marriage are not part of your plans." She hadn't said all that, but he felt it was safe to assume she meant it. He had no right to feel sorry for himself, but he did. Would no woman ever see him as worth more to her than the expectations of parents or goals that excluded him? And not just any woman.

But he didn't want to ruin what was left of the day. "Forget I said anything. Shall we take that walk now?"

She hesitated but a second. "I'd like that."

They left the house, passed the school and proceeded to the town square, where two young women sat holding babies. They smiled as Conner and Kate continued on their way. He couldn't say who decided the direction they would take, but they headed toward the river.

"It's not easy," Kate said.

He wasn't sure what she meant, but before he could ask about it, she continued.

"I'm not supposed to get emotionally involved, but I can't seem to help it. I see two frightened little children and I want to push away every hurtful thing. I see pain in Mrs. Harper's face and it tears at me. Medicine can help, but so often it can't fix."

Her agonized admission made Conner want to stop right there to hold and comfort her, but they had not reached the privacy of the trees along the river. "How does your father deal with it?"

"He says we can alleviate some of the pain and suffering, but we have to accept our limitations." She seemed troubled by the notion.

"You don't agree."

"Of course I do, but it feels as if I die a little bit every time I see how little we can do or watch someone die or, like today, know there won't be a baby for that family."

It occurred to him to suggest she wasn't as suited to being a doctor as she thought. How much piece-by-piece dying could she do before there was nothing left of her? Would she become cold and unfeeling or would she become a shell of a person?

Would she come back broken and needing him?

It was the last thing he wanted. Not the needing part. That sounded good. The broken part did not.

But nothing he said would make her change her mind. She'd have to come to her own realizations.

Even if they differed from what he thought?

He didn't have time to ponder the question. Mrs. Grieves came toward them, a self-righteous look upon her face.

"Conner Marshall, what is the truth about that baby?"

He shifted Ellie so she looked over his shoulder. No need for her to see the harsh expression on the woman's face.

"I've told you all you need to know."

Mrs. Grieves sniffed. "Miss Baker, why are you with him?" Her eyes narrowed. "You can't be the mother, unless…"

Conner knew she was doing some mental arithmetic, then she turned her steely eyes back to Conner. "Where were you last spring? Didn't you disappear for a time?"

The only place he'd gone was to a ranch near the Canadian border to pick up some horses. Not that it mattered. "Ma'am, your question is offensive. I suggest you withdraw it."

A man might have been intimidated by Conner's size and the look on his face, but not Mrs. Grieves. With a sniff, she marched on by.

Conner let the frustration of such judgment seep away. "Kate, don't let comments like that offend you."

"I fear it is only the beginning. You've let people believe Ellie is yours."

"I simply didn't deny it. What they believe is up to them."

"That might be so, but when they learn that Thelma is the mother—and I suspect many people are already making that connection—they are going to expect, nay, demand that you marry her."

They had reached the shelter of the trees and he stopped to face her.

"I have to do what's right for Ellie."

"Of course you do." She didn't linger, didn't meet his eyes, didn't give him a chance to explain. Though what could he say? Not that it likely mattered to her. Her course was set. She was going to medical school. Nothing he decided to do would affect her.

He'd been anticipating some quiet time with her by the river, but any sense of sweetness between them had disappeared.

The walk that Kate had been looking forward to suddenly seemed pointless. He would do what was right for Ellie. Even if it meant marrying Thelma?

Kate knew he would not hesitate to do so. Why it drove such pain through her innards that she could barely keep back a groan, she was unwilling to admit. *You're a natural mother.* Those words and many others echoed through her. She could almost be convinced.

Child, don't waste the gift God has given you.

Grammie's words reminded her of the promise Kate had given.

When Conner suggested a walk, she had envisioned a quiet hour or two by the river, alone in the shade of the trees. They'd talk. He'd say—

She shook her head, denying the hope that he would say anything about his feelings for her.

He had Ellie and Thelma to consider and she had her promise to fulfill. A fresh thought startled her and she jerked to a halt to stare at the rippling water. If she said she was going to medical school because of a promise she'd made when she was ten, Conner would misunderstand. It wasn't the only reason for her plans. Becoming a doctor had been her dream since…

Well, since she was ten. Something about that confession unsettled her.

This confusion had to end and she pushed away every errant thought and focused on plans for the fair.

"Several people spoke to me after the church service about where they would like to help at the fair. We ought to go over the volunteer list and update it. The page is at home."

She finally allowed herself to look at him, saw the calmness in his eyes and something more…as if he understood her desire to rush back and avoid being with him. Little did he guess how much wanting to stay warred with needing to leave.

He turned and they made their way back to the house. She brought out the paper and wrote down several names. Two men had offered to help with any construction needs. One woman had volunteered to be in charge of a food booth. "Things are coming together." She tried to sound enthusiastic but guessed she failed. She just wanted to get the fair over with, get her letter from the medical school and move on with her life. The longer she stayed in Bella Creek, spending time with Conner and his family, the harder it was to think of leaving.

Ellie fussed and Conner fed her. When she'd finished the bottle, he got to his feet. "It's time for me to go home."

An unexplained, unexpected urge to hold him back came over her. She ignored it as she escorted them to the door, where she leaned over and kissed Ellie goodbye. She straightened, her face mere inches from Conner's. His eyes were watchful and perhaps a bit regretful.

"I'll be seeing you," he said.

She waved as he drove out of sight. He hadn't said

when he'd be seeing her. Were the words spoken without meaning? But of course they would have to spend more time together until the fair was over.

She found no comfort in the thought.

Three days later, she wondered when she would see him again. She began to turn away from the window where she spent an inordinate amount of time looking down the street, hoping to see a big bay horse or a buggy driven by a big blond man. What was wrong with her? She'd never thought she'd be pining after something beyond her reach.

A horse and rider passed the house and she stared after it. Sheriff Jesse had returned. A note at his office said he would be away on business for a day or two. Conner had said Jesse meant to follow up some clues about Thelma's whereabouts and she assumed that was the business that Jesse was away on.

Had he located Thelma? Where was she? Would she tell the truth about Ellie's parentage?

Jesse dismounted and strode into his office.

Kate waited several minutes, but he didn't come out again. Had he already been to the Marshall ranch? Would anyone bring her news of what he had to report?

But then why should they?

She went to the kitchen and began to prepare the noon meal. Not that it required much on her behalf. Soup had been simmering since breakfast and biscuits were ready to put in the oven. Father had been seeing patients in his office and would be at home for dinner.

The meal was a quiet affair. Father was often too absorbed in his work to converse. But the lack of conversation was a marked contrast to meals shared with the Marshalls.

Or even meals with her family before their passing. She held back a sigh as she acknowledged this was one thing she'd lost and still longed for.

Someone entered the waiting room and Father returned to his patients.

Kate wished he would allow her to help, but he insisted he could manage on his own. "Barring a disaster." And no one wanted to see that.

She cleaned the kitchen and faced a long, lonely afternoon. She could go visit Isabelle and knew she would always be welcome, but it wasn't Isabelle she longed to see. She must keep busy. It was the only way to keep her thoughts at bay. Thoughts of sitting by the river with Conner. Thoughts of the way her skin tingled when he touched her face.

She grabbed a pair of gloves and hurried to the door to work in the garden. She opened the door and jumped back. "Oh, I didn't hear you." It was a young woman she'd met a number of times. "Good day, Mrs. Abernathy. Are you needing the doctor?" If so, she should have gone to the door facing the street. She surely knew that.

"I've come to see you."

"Please come in. Can I offer you tea? Cookies?"

"No, thank you. I can only stay a moment. I have much to do. You see, my brother and his wife are coming to visit."

"That's nice." Though Kate wondered why the woman would feel the need to tell her.

"You said you needed some form of entertainment."

"Yes, I did."

"I think my brother and his wife would do it for you.

He plays the banjo and she the accordion. They both sing. They are very talented, if I do say so myself."

"Can you tell me what sort of music they offer?"

"Most anything."

Her answer wasn't very helpful.

"For a fair, they would likely sing rousing camp tunes."

"I'm sorry. I don't know what you mean by that."

Mrs. Abernathy cleared her throat. "I can best explain by singing a few bars of the kind of songs they'd sing. Do you mind?"

"Not at all. Go ahead."

She sang a few lines of *Oh, Susanna*, *Camptown Races* and *Rock of Ages* in a rich, full voice so clear and sure that Kate wondered why the woman wasn't volunteering for the job.

"That's beautiful. Would you sing for the fair?"

She colored up. "Not on my own."

"If your brother sings half as well as you, he'll be just what we need."

"I don't sing half as well as he and I know you won't regret having him do the entertainment." The woman rose. "I must get back."

"Thank you so much." She waited until Mrs. Abernathy was out of sight, then put the gloves back on the shelf, wrote a note to her father and headed for the livery station.

She had to share this news with Conner. Perhaps at the same time, she could discover what news Jesse had brought.

Not until she was on her way did she consider that Thelma might be at the ranch...reunited with her baby daughter and the man she claimed as Ellie's father. Curiosity overcame reluctance and she continued on her way.

As she approached the ranch, she decided to go see Isabelle first.

Ellie was with Isabelle. The fact eased Kate's mind greatly. Surely Ellie would be in Thelma's care if she was at the ranch.

She greeted her friend and kissed the baby, who seemed eager to see her, then followed Isabelle inside.

"You've come to see Conner?"

"I have come to discuss some developments regarding the fair. How is Ellie doing?"

"She's a sweet baby. Makes me long for one of my own." She saddened. "So far it hasn't happened."

Kate took Isabelle's hand. "We'll pray it happens soon." They clasped hands and prayed aloud—a practice the two of them had developed over the years of their friendship.

They went into the small living area. Isabelle sat Ellie on the floor. "She's sitting well on her own now." She proceeded to regale Kate with details of Ellie's accomplishments.

Although pleased to hear how the baby was doing and to know Isabelle enjoyed tending the baby, Kate had to admit she missed Ellie, missed taking care of her, missed seeing her do different things.

They were enjoying a cup of tea, admiring a cross-stitch picture Isabelle planned to enter in the fair, when the clop of approaching horses came to them. It was all Kate could do not to rush to the window—to sit calmly as Isabelle glanced out. "It's Dawson and Conner. They've seen your buggy and look curious. Now they're headed this way." She smiled at Kate. "It's been nice to have a visit with you. Now go and tell Conner all your news."

Isabelle didn't need to make it sound like Kate was that eager to speak to Conner. But Kate was on her feet and headed for the door before she'd completed the thought.

She stepped outside.

Conner reined his horse to a halt and stared at her. And then his eyes filled with sunshine and he smiled like he welcomed the surprise. He dismounted.

"I'll take care of your horse," Dawson said, a wide, knowing grin upon his face.

Conner tossed the reins to him, then strode to Kate's side. "What brings you here?"

Kate didn't bother saying she often came to visit. Plainly he understood she wasn't here solely to see Isabelle or Annie. "I have news about the fair."

"Tell me all about it." He tucked her hand into the crook of his arm and led her away, toward the grove of trees where she had fled not so long ago and where she'd found comfort in his arms. Did he recall that day?

She told him of all the volunteers but held the best news for last. "If Mrs. Abernathy's brother sings half as well as she does, they will be excellent entertainment."

They sat side by side on an old log and she pulled the volunteer list from her pocket. He moved closer, his shoulder pressing to her, his fingers brushing hers as they pored over the list.

"I have to confess I didn't think it would come together quite so quickly." He chuckled. "I half pictured us scrambling to get things done. So what more do we have to do?"

They discussed the fair for a few more minutes, then she changed the subject.

"I saw the sheriff return earlier today. Did he have news regarding Thelma?" It hurt to breathe as she waited for him to say Thelma was in the house even as they spoke.

Shouldn't it be a relief to have her here, to know she would take over her rightful role as Ellie's mother?

But what would Conner think was *his* rightful role?

Chapter Eleven

Kate stared straight ahead as she waited for his answer.

"He hasn't found her yet."

Why should the news ease the tightness in her chest? Wouldn't it be better to know the truth about Thelma? But would it hurt for Kate to enjoy a few more days of pretending?

Pretending what? How could she be so foolish?

Conner continued, "That lead proved to be a dead end, but he did find someone who used to be with the traveling show who recalled she had grown ill near Havre, Montana, and they left her there. Jesse has sent a message to the sheriff there to see if he can locate her."

They sat in contemplative silence for several seconds, then Conner sighed.

"I wish she'd turn up. It's hard to make plans until she does."

She made a noise that he could take as agreement.

"I'd go looking myself, but there's Ellie to consider and the fair to see to."

And nowhere in there did Kate fit. Which was, she firmly reminded herself, exactly as it should be.

The door to the main house opened and Annie banged the triangle to call the men to supper.

Kate sprang to her feet. "I didn't realize it was so late. I better be on my way."

Conner caught her hand. "Stay for supper."

She hesitated.

"Grandfather will want to hear the latest developments regarding the fair."

He invited her only for Grandfather's sake?

"Everyone will be disappointed if you leave."

"Everyone?" She studied his face, wishing for more. Despite knowing Thelma might have a claim on Conner and knowing he was prepared to do what was best for Ellie, she couldn't stop herself from hoping he might harbor a bit of sweet regard for her. Somehow or other, she managed to ignore the fact that she planned to leave.

He touched her cheek in a gesture so tender it made her eyes sting. "Everyone, but none more than me. Please stay."

She was powerless to refuse after that. "Thank you. I will." Feeling rather pleased with herself, she accompanied him to the house. "What about Ellie?"

"I've been leaving her with Isabelle until bedtime."

They joined the others around the table. Grandfather, Bud, Annie, Conner and Kate. It wasn't the usual crowd of a Sunday after church, but nevertheless a far livelier mealtime than the silent times at the Baker house.

Conner was right about Grandfather. He demanded a detailed update and Kate gladly provided it.

Grandfather nodded. "I was right in getting you two to organize this." His shaggy eyebrows knitted together as he looked from Kate to Conner. "Just make sure you don't mess it up."

Kate looked to Conner, who studied his grandfather. "Plans for the fair are under control."

"Harrumph. I wasn't referring to the fair." He turned his attention back to his meal.

Annie tried to muffle her amusement.

Bud concentrated on the food on his plate so Kate couldn't see his face.

Conner shook his head back and forth. "You're incorrigible, you know?"

Kate's mouth fell open. Just as Sadie suggested, the old man was playing matchmaker. "But—" Didn't he know it was impossible?

"No point in arguing," Conner said. "Like I said, he's incorrigible."

Annie brought out cake. "I'm hoping to win a blue ribbon with my chocolate cake. Tell me what you think." She served each of them a piece and waited for them to offer an opinion.

"You'll bring home a blue ribbon for sure," her father said. "Your ma would be so proud of you."

"Thank you, Pa." Annie's voice cracked.

"It's excellent," Kate said, and Conner and Grandfather echoed her approval.

Kate's fork fell to the table with a clatter. Everyone stared at her, no doubt wondering at how wide her eyes had grown and the way her lips parted.

"Kate?" Conner touched her arm. "Is something wrong?"

She swallowed hard. "Everyone will be expecting prize ribbons. Am I correct?"

Conner nodded.

"And where are we going to find these ribbons?"

Conner groaned and pressed the heel of his hand to his forehead. "I never once thought of it."

"It's too late to ask your uncle to order some for us. What are we going to do?" She didn't dare look at Grandfather.

"Uncle George has spools of ribbon," Annie said, completely calm in the face of the panic consuming Kate. "We'll make the prize ribbons. They're just rosettes with tails. That's easy."

It was nice to think Annie thought so.

"Why don't we get together after church Sunday and fashion them?" Annie said.

"Thank you so much." Kate's relief left her shaking.

Conner slipped into the pew beside Kate and settled Ellie on his knee next to her. The baby chortled her greeting. Kate smiled a welcome.

Since her visit on Wednesday and the arrangement for her to come out today and make prize ribbons, he had sought for a reason to hang around the house while she was there. He couldn't see himself making the award ribbons, especially when Annie illustrated how to make one. He could watch Ellie…which would give him an excuse to watch Kate, but he knew Beth liked to take care of the baby. He'd considered every option he could think of and failed to come up with something until Grandfather asked a question about the fair.

"Who do you have making the signs for the tables?"

He steadied his surprise. "What signs do you mean?"

Grandfather had given him a serious look. "Are you joshing me? You'll need signs to indicate the judging section."

"Yeah?" It still didn't make sense to Conner.

Grandfather sighed loud and long. "I suppose people would figure it out for themselves, but a little sign—like so—" he held his hands out to illustrate something about the size of a page from a letter "—would make it easier. *Baking. Preserves. Hay.* You get it?"

He got it and it provided the perfect excuse to join the ladies as they fashioned ribbons. He prepared boards the right size, each with a stand. Today, with Kate to help, he would letter the posters. Thanks to his mother for teaching him to print neatly.

Having Kate next to him in church, joining her voice to his as the congregation sang several hymns, made the day about perfect.

As the service ended, he grew aware of several ladies, Mrs. Grieves among them, with their heads bent together whispering. Their glances came his direction and he guessed he was the topic of conversation. His pleasure in the day was marred by thinking of the accusing words Mrs. Grieves had spoken to him and Kate. He had a mind to march over to the group and set them straight. But anything he said had the potential to bring judgment upon Ellie, so he held his peace.

Dr. Baker turned down the invitation to join them at the ranch for dinner. "I'm looking forward to a quiet afternoon at home."

Conner pretended shock. "Kate, you should not be so rowdy and disruptive. Your poor father needs some peace and quiet."

Kate faced him. Opened her mouth to protest, then noticed his teasing grin. "Oh, you." She gave him a playful push.

He caught her hand to protect himself, though her little push had not moved him even a fraction of an inch.

The excuse to pull her close to his side was too great to ignore. He leaned close to whisper for her ears only. "Come on out to my place and be as rowdy as you like." He laughed at the way she protested.

They made their way to the wagon. Grandfather waited for assistance and sat on the front seat by Annie. Conner and Kate sat on the second bench with Ellie upon his knee.

Grandfather turned to Conner. "This reminds me of when your ma was alive and we rode to church as a family. Ellie here is like Annie would have been. Sitting with your mama and papa."

Annie glanced back and winked at Conner. "I wonder what Grandfather is trying to say."

Conner groaned and pretended a great interest in the passing scenery and hoped Grandfather wouldn't feel the need to explain. He felt the old man studying him but ignored it.

"Harrumph. Do I have to spell out everything? Conner, what that child needs is a family. A proper loving family. Seems you might think about giving her that. You and Miss Kate here." With another harrumph, he jerked forward, leaving Conner stunned at his directness.

"I apologize for his behavior," he whispered to Kate.

She gave him a wooden smile and did not meet his look. "Not to worry. I'm not offended."

He watched her a moment, wishing he knew what Grandfather's suggestion meant to her. Did it cause her to wish things could be different? It certainly caused him to wish it.

He faced straight ahead, not letting himself form clear thoughts on what he wished could be different.

* * *

Kate tried not to think of Grandfather's comments. *You and Miss Kate.* Making a home for little Ellie. It sounded just fine until a person considered the objections and then it was nothing but an old man's foolish wish. She pushed aside the tangles of her mind and looked about at the passing scenery. As often happened, her gaze went to the mountains.

They soon reached the ranch and Conner handed Ellie to Kate before he jumped down to assist his grandfather. Then he took Ellie, held out a hand for Kate and smiled up at her. Her heart stalled at the welcome in his face. The world tipped and then righted as she sucked in air and reminded herself of the realities of both their lives.

Her heart and mind steadied, she took his big, warm, work-hardened hand and stepped to the ground. Immediately she slipped her hand free and adjusted her skirts.

The entire Marshall family had assembled.

"Looks to me like we're going to have lots of help," Conner said.

"I expect we need it. I've made a list of how many ribbons we need. It's going to take a long time to make them all."

Kate went to the kitchen to help Annie and the other ladies while Conner joined the other men in the sitting room. The children played together.

In a few minutes, the meal was served and the family sat around the dining room table. Grandfather looked around his assembled family.

"I am blessed beyond measure." His voice quavered. "I wish your grandmother had lived to see this day." He cleared his throat. "I'll ask the blessing."

Kate, seated beside Conner, bowed her head.

"Father in heaven," Grandfather began, his voice deepening, "we are grateful for Your many blessings. Our family, especially the children. And most especially little Ellie, who is growing stronger every day. We are also grateful for the blessings of this land, the abundance of the garden, and thank You for the bounty we are about to enjoy and the loving hands that have prepared it. Amen."

Kate raised her head. "My grammie would have enjoyed this," she managed through her tightened throat.

"And where is she today?" Grandfather asked.

"She passed away when I was ten, but not before she taught me to love God and thank Him for His blessings."

"She sounds like a good woman. I wish I could have met her."

As the food was passed, the Marshalls talked, telling of their daily lives, sharing and encouraging.

Kate listened. If her brothers had lived, they would likely be married by now with children. Would they gather together like this? Enjoying being with each other?

She rearranged the food on her plate. What might have been did not change what was. One of the things Grammie had taught Kate was to accept the facts of her life and make the best of them with God's help. And she would. She resumed eating and smiled and laughed at the comments the family shared.

As soon as the last crumb was gone, the last coffee cup emptied and the last dish washed, Annie put ribbons and glue bottles on the table. When the men headed for the door, she stopped them. "Many hands make light work."

Conner laughed. "I think my hands might make more work."

"Nope. Beth is going to watch the children and the rest of you are going to help."

Grandfather ignored her and retired to the sitting room. Kate sucked her lips in to stop from smiling.

Bud hurried outside, ignoring Annie's protests.

Logan and Dawson edged after their pa, but their wives gave them looks that stopped them in their tracks.

Kate tried and failed to contain her amusement. Conner, who had seated himself beside her, nudged her in the side. "Looks like we'll be getting lots of help."

The smile they shared was warm and seemed to be only for each other.

Dawson and Logan sat beside their wives. Annie placed rolls of ribbon before each pair.

"You men can cut it in these lengths." She gave them each the directions. "The women can pleat the rosette and glue on the tails. It's easy and straightforward."

Conner murmured, "She'll soon be eating those words."

Again Kate and Conner shared a private smile.

But Annie called for their attention and showed the women how to pleat the rosettes.

Kate felt Conner watching her as she did her best to create one. "It's harder than it looks," she complained as hers fell apart.

Annie glanced over at her. "Conner, hold the pleats in place until she can glue them."

"Sure." He reached across her to press the ribbon in place.

His arms were in the way.

"I can't see to glue it."

He got to his feet, stood over her, one of his arms at her side and the other across her shoulders so she was virtually within the shelter of his arms. It took a great deal of effort to concentrate on what she was supposed to do.

Carefully, hoping the tremors in her hands didn't show, she glued the rosette into place.

Conner kept his hands in place a moment longer, likely to be certain the ribbons weren't going to escape, but Kate couldn't help wondering if he felt the same awareness and was, like her, trying unsuccessfully to dismiss it.

He removed his arms and returned to his chair.

Kate pushed the rosette toward the center of the table. "It looks okay, doesn't it?" She glanced around. Why had everyone grown so quiet? Why were they all looking at her or Conner or back and forth? Heat stole up her neck and settled in her cheeks. Had they all seen her reaction? She grabbed another length of ribbon and began to fold it. She would make this one without help. She would not let anyone guess as to the confusion she felt.

The next rosette stayed together without Conner's help and each succeeding one grew easier. As she pleated the rosettes, Conner cut ribbons in the right length. The pile of completed award ribbons grew steadily. She began to relax.

After a couple of hours, she stopped to count the ribbons. "I think we have enough. Thanks, everyone." She carefully stowed the ribbons in a small crate Annie provided.

Sadie, Isabelle and Annie went to the window to check on the children. The men pushed back from the table. "Let's go outside." But Conner did not follow his brothers.

"We have another task," he said and went to the entryway to bring back a stack of boards all the same size. "Grandfather said we had to have signs." He explained it to Kate and showed her the list of those needed. He had prepared well and brought out a pile of thick paper, pens and ink.

"Do you need help?" Isabelle asked.

Conner shook his head. "We can manage."

"Then we'll leave you two to do it." Sadie hooked her arm through Isabelle's and they went to the door, Annie in their wake.

Kate watched them depart.

"Are you wanting to join them?" Conner asked.

"No, I'd like to get this done. There's only five days until the fair and I'd feel better if as much as possible is ready." Nor did she mind the sense of unity they shared at the moment.

It didn't take them long to finish lettering the signs, and as soon as the ink dried, Conner tacked the paper to the wood. He sat back with a pleased smile on his lips. "I think that's it until Friday when we'll be setting things up."

"Do we have enough help lined up?"

His grin widened. "All the Marshalls will show up. Grandfather has said they will. So yes."

She laughed. "So nice to have family to fall back on when needed."

"Can't argue with that. Now let's go find Ellie."

Ellie was happily entertained by the children but reached for Kate when she and Conner joined them.

Kate lifted the little girl, giving her a noisy kiss that brought forth a happy giggle.

"I can't believe this is the same baby I saw just three weeks ago. She'd done so well."

"Thanks in large part to you."

She acknowledged his praise with a nod. "Thanks in no small part to the love you and your family have given her."

Their gazes connected. She felt the power of his love for Ellie like an unspoken vow. Ellie would always be safe with him.

Kate's eyes stung at the intensity of Conner's gaze and she turned to Ellie. Love was such a powerful emotion. It would cause a man to marry a woman he didn't love to be father to a child he did.

It was love that compelled Kate to pursue a medical career.

That thought didn't seem right, but she couldn't think why not. She loved caring for people, helping them through an illness even though she found the limitations of medicine frustrating.

She shook her head. Why did being with Conner and his family always bring confusion? She knew what she wanted in life and would soon enter medical school to pursue that goal.

How long would it take to get her reply from St. Louis telling her the start date for classes?

Conner was up before the sun Friday morning. He fed Ellie and dressed her in a little cotton dress that Annie had found. Their ma had saved many of their baby clothes, which proved a real help in caring for

Ellie. She played contentedly while he prepared to go to town.

Too anxious to relax, he ate breakfast standing by the stove. Today would be busy with setting up for the fair. He couldn't wait to get started. He'd visited Kate just once during the week to go over last-minute details, but every day he'd tried, and failed, to find some excuse to ride into town.

Making rosettes and signs with her on Sunday, it had hit him that soon she would have no reason to keep visiting him…or Ellie or the Marshall family.

He'd always known their time of taking care of Ellie and then working together on the fair would end. She had a goal that took her away from Bella Creek, whereas he could not picture himself anywhere else than at the Marshall Five Ranch, making sure the family was safe and well cared for. Since Ellie's arrival, his reasons were even more important to him. She needed the sort of home he and his family could provide.

But, he promised himself, he would let nothing mar the enjoyment of this day of working together with Kate. Over the past few weeks, he had come to enjoy and appreciate her calmness under stress and her sense of humor. He grinned. Not to mention her pie baking.

Annie turned from packing a lunch to take with them. "What are you smiling about, big brother? Maybe the thought of seeing Kate again?"

"Didn't I hear you ask her to bring a couple of pies for dinner?" He smacked his lips. "I'm looking forward to that."

"Uh-huh." She chuckled as if enjoying a private joke.

"Well, shoot." He slapped his thigh.

"What's that all about?" Annie asked.

"Why did no one think of the best money raiser we could have for the fair?"

Annie turned and considered him with narrowed eyes. "And what would that be?"

"A kissing booth. You could run it. Maybe you'd be kissed by a handsome prince and fall madly in love."

She flicked a towel at him. "And then what? Would I leave you and Pa and Grandfather to fend for yourselves?" She hooted. "You'd all starve to death."

He shrugged. "Maybe Sadie and Logan would like to live here." At the troubled look on her face, he wished he hadn't mentioned the thought. "But not to worry, baby sister. You're too young to get married."

"I am not!"

He chucked her under the chin. "Any man who wants to court you has to meet approval from your brothers, your father and your grandfather. You think there's a man brave enough to try that?"

She narrowed her eyes and scowled at him. "Maybe I'll run away and get married."

"Don't even think of doing that. We'd all be hurt. You want that?"

She sighed. "Of course not. Can you take that to the wagon?" She indicated the box in which she'd stowed the food.

He carried it out. Grandfather waited on the veranda. "Help me up, boy."

"You're going? What are you going to do?"

"I'm going to make sure you do things right."

"Now, won't that be fun?"

Grandfather chuckled at Conner's dry tone. "I'm looking forward to it myself."

Isabelle and Mattie trotted over and climbed into the back of the wagon. He kissed Ellie.

"You be good for Auntie Isabelle," he said to the baby.

She gurgled a happy sound that he took for agreement, then he handed her over to Isabelle's care. Pa, Dawson and Conner swung to the back of their horses and the family made their way to town and the open pasture by the river.

Dr. Baker drove up in a wagon with Kate at his side.

Conner didn't even wait for his horse to halt before he jumped down and rushed over to help her.

"Are you excited?" he asked.

"My nerves are jumping madly, but I can't say if it's excitement or trepidation."

He squeezed her hand as Sadie, Logan and their children joined the crowd. "The Marshalls are here in full force, so you have no need to fear."

"That remains to be seen. I know I won't be able to relax until this is all over tomorrow evening. I would hate to leave town with the specter of a failed fair to trouble me."

He chuckled and pulled her closer to his side as the family gathered round.

She greeted each one and bent over Ellie. "How are you, little sweetie?"

The baby reached for her and Kate took her, her eyes bright with the joy of this little girl.

Everyone spoke at once, offering suggestions, asking questions. Conner leaned closer so she could hear him. "I assure you this fair is not going to be a failure." Had she purposely reminded him that she would soon leave? How long before that time arrived? It wouldn't be today or tomorrow and he wouldn't think beyond that.

"Conner." Dr. Baker called for his attention. "I brought the tent."

Conner and his brothers went to the back of the wagon to look at the mound of canvas and the stack of poles.

"The owner gave me instruction on how to set it up," the doctor said. "But they made little sense to me. I told him there would be plenty of men here who knew how to do it."

Conner eyed the makings of a tent. It couldn't be hard, could it? "Logan, help me unload this stuff." He grabbed the corner of the canvas and tugged. Nothing happened. It was far heavier than he anticipated.

Logan grabbed a corner and tugged. He grunted and pulled harder. Conner added his weight and, between them, they dragged the canvas to the back of the box. But if they dropped it there, they would have to wrangle it to the spot where it was supposed to be set up.

"I'll move the wagon before we lower the canvas to the ground." He drove the wagon to the arranged spot and returned to help Logan and Dawson, who seemed to realize they needed his assistance.

Grandfather had brought a chair and placed it a few feet away, where he sat leaning on his canes, looking like he expected entertainment.

Conner studied him a moment. "Do you know something you aren't telling us?"

"Nope." The word carried way too much amusement for Conner's liking. "But I'm going to enjoy watching this tent go up."

Somehow Conner didn't think that meant what Conner wanted it to mean. He glanced toward his brothers. Dawson eyed the old man, a wary look upon his face.

Logan shrugged. "Let him have his fun."

A crowd had gathered round. Kate stood with Isabelle, Sadie and Annie. Her gaze connected with Conner's. Did he see admiration? She smiled. He smiled back, unable to tear himself away from her look.

"Let's get at it," Dawson said.

Conner grabbed one side of the canvas, keenly aware of the audience of one, even though two or three dozen had assembled at this point. He only wanted admiration and approval from Kate.

The men lowered the canvas to the ground and began to unfold it.

"It's bigger than I thought it would be," Logan said, standing back to look at the material on the ground. "I've never set up anything this big."

Conner looked at the pile of poles. "It must be done the same way."

Grandfather chuckled and Conner again wondered if he wasn't telling them something they needed to know.

A handful of men edged closer, full of advice. "Start with the center pole."

"No, start with the edge poles."

"Go from front to back."

"No, no. The only way is to do it all at once."

Conner signaled his brothers to come closer. They bent their heads together. "Anyone have any idea of what to do?"

Neither of them did.

"How hard can it be? Grab a pole and let's get started."

There were six long poles and a couple dozen shorter ones. There were stakes. Well, at least he knew what those were for. A large pile of rope completed the materials.

He considered the various suggestions that had been offered. "We'll do it the same as we would a smaller tent." Logan and Dawson agreed. They waved forward some helpers to erect the four corner posts. It was harder than it looked and took several strong men pulling at the ropes to pull each corner upright.

Grandfather might have been watching a circus from the enjoyment on his face.

Conner slipped his gaze toward Kate. She smiled and nodded at him and he turned back to the task, feeling victorious.

"What next?" Logan asked.

"A center pole." Conner was far less certain than he sounded.

Logan dragged forward one of the longer poles. "We'll let you do the honors."

"Fine." How hard could it be? All he had to do was go into the tent and find the center. The door was before him, but after that he saw only canvas. He tossed aside his hat, fell to his hands and knees and began to fight his way through the material. It enfolded him. Trapped him. The musty smell of an old tent stifled him.

He stopped flailing at the heavy shroud. He had to think what he was doing. Had to be rational about this.

He felt suffocated. If only he could get in a satisfying breath. If the corner poles gave way, how long would it take for someone to get him out of there?

Chapter Twelve

Kate couldn't believe how much she enjoyed watching Conner take charge and work out how to set up the tent. He was so self-confident, so strong, and moved with such grace. She could watch him work all day and not get bored.

But then he crawled into the tent and disappeared from sight. She could see the canvas move as he made his way through it. She joined the others in laughing at the ludicrous picture it provided. Then worry began to grow in her. Wouldn't it be awfully hot in there? Was there enough air? As if to prove her worries valid, movement ceased. She caught her breath. Was he okay? Her heart pounded in her ears. Why wasn't anyone doing anything? They were all watching and waiting. How long did it take to suffocate?

She did not intend to stand by and learn firsthand. Kate handed Ellie to Isabelle. She was about to rush forward and fight the canvas off Conner, but the tent began to move and she stopped. The center slowly rose upward and steadied.

She sucked in life-giving air.

A cheer rose as Conner emerged. His hair stuck out every which way. Dirt and sweat streaked his face. He grinned and waved at the crowd, dusted himself off, then looked at Kate. It might have been her imagination that she saw welcome and relief in his gaze. Had he been in trouble for those few tense moments? She took a step forward, needing to touch him, reassure herself he was fine.

Behind her, Grandfather Marshall roared with laughter.

Conner shifted his gaze to him. "Why do I get the feeling you are enjoying this far more than you should?"

Grandfather gasped for air. He choked out his words. "It was like watching a badger dig a hole." He laughed some more.

Soon those assembled joined in the merriment.

Kate reached Conner's side, touched his arm. "Are you okay?" she murmured, wondering if the noise from the crowd would drown out her words.

He pressed his hand to hers. "I'm fine now."

She let herself read welcome and so much more in his gaze, smiled back her own welcome, and then people pressed in close. She stepped aside, satisfied things were right.

Everything, that was, except her own foolish thoughts, which had gone seriously astray.

The men grabbed poles, ropes and stakes and soon had the tent up amid much shouting and laughing and grunting.

While they worked, Annie and a handful of others helped volunteers choose spots for the various booths.

"Kate, come see." She turned at Conner's call. He stood at the doorway to the tent and she joined him.

They stepped inside. The interior had an unusual yellowish light. An odd smell filled her nostrils. She sniffed, trying to think of a way to describe it. Not quite musty. It had a definite masculine feel to it. In the future, she would always associate the scent with this day.

Conner pointed from one place to another, indicating where different displays would be. As he spoke, men trundled in with sawhorses and planks and set up tables.

"Let's put out the signs." Conner caught her hand and drew her out into the warm sunshine. He located the box of signs. "Do we have a plan as to where they should go?"

"I hadn't thought of it, but should the culinary entries be clustered together and the sewing entries in another group?" she asked.

"That sounds reasonable."

They could have each taken a handful of signs and placed them separately, but they worked as a team.

It was lunchtime before the interior of the tent was arranged to their liking and they stepped outside. The grounds had been transformed with many booths. Someone had thought to arrange flowers and greenery around the booths and in front of the tent.

Excitement filled Kate and she reached for Conner's hand. "It looks wonderful. Better than I dreamed."

He squeezed her hand and pressed his shoulder to hers. "Many hands make light work, as my ma used to say."

"It certainly does." For the first time she could remember, she felt part of a community. She would miss it when she left.

Nonsense, she told herself firmly. What tighter-knit

community could she expect to find than medical students at college?

Annie called them over. "We're stopping for dinner."

"I'll have to go get my pies."

"I'll go with you." Conner helped her to the seat of the Marshall wagon and they trundled across the field and down the street to the doctor's house.

Kate let out a gust of air when she saw no one waited to see her father. "Maybe he'll be able to enjoy the day."

In a few minutes, they were on their way back to the busy fairgrounds with three pies.

Conner eyed them. "Are you going to enter in the fair?"

"I kept one back for that very purpose."

"What kind?"

"I can't tell you. I might be accused of seeking special favor from you."

"I decided to judge the cookie entries so I wouldn't be prejudiced for either you or Annie."

"I'm sure that will be a real hardship." She kept her face expressionless.

He chuckled. "I might favor the ginger cookies if anyone enters them."

They looked at each other. Did he remember the afternoon he had ginger cookies with her and the Harper children? They had shared so many special moments. She was going to cherish each for the rest of her life. Again she scolded herself. Soon enough she would have other things to fill her mind. Studies, new friends, tests and city life. When did city life begin to feel so barren and lonely to her?

By the time they returned to the fairgrounds, a large

table had been set up and a bounty of food put out and she firmly dismissed her doubts and questions.

Conner went immediately to Isabelle to get Ellie.

Kate's smile stirred the depths of her heart as she watched the affection between the two. They deserved to have a future together. She swallowed hard. Even if it didn't include her? But of course it wouldn't include her. Why had the idea even voiced itself?

She struggled to control her breathing, but her air caught partway up her throat and she coughed a little. *Grammie. I have to remember Grammie and the future she saw for me. God's gift to me.*

Grandfather waved at the crowd to gather round, then struggled to his feet to offer a prayer of thanks.

She kept her head bowed a heartbeat after his amen. *Please, God, give me strength and wisdom to keep my word and honor You with my choices.* That meant going to medical school as had been planned.

Conner stayed at Kate's side as they joined the others filing past the table to get food, Ellie perched in his arms. He had his hands full, so Kate carried two plates and chose food for both.

"You sure you can eat all this?" She pretended to be doubtful about the amount of food he wanted her to take for him. "It's enough to feed a small family." She paused for emphasis. "And a couple of hired men."

He considered the pile of food on his plate. "I suppose it will have to do, but please don't complain if my stomach rumbles in a couple of hours."

She laughed. "I don't know whether or not to believe you."

"You'll soon enough know, won't you?"

The way he looked at her left her feeling as if several butterflies flitted about inside her.

They found a grassy spot a little distance away and Conner indicated they should sit. He laid Ellie on a blanket and edged close to Kate. She caught the scent of the canvas tent mingled with the aroma of fried chicken, potato salad and all the good things offered by this day. No wait, she only meant the things offered by the potluck meal.

They were about ready to go back for dessert when Mrs. Abernathy appeared before them with a couple at her side. "I'd like you to meet my brother and his wife. Barry Publisher and Joanne." The man held a banjo, the woman, an accordion.

"We'd like to play for you so you know what to expect tomorrow," Barry said, and without further ado, he and his wife began to play a lively tune. Soon the assembled crowd clapped in time to the music. When the pair finished, people cheered and applauded.

Barry and his wife continued to entertain as they strolled among the people.

Conner spoke close to Kate's ear. "They're good. Their music is going to add a wonderful touch to the day's festivities." His breath fanned across her cheek, disturbing a strand of hair. She was about to tuck it behind her ear when he caught it and drew his finger along her cheek.

His touch sent a flurry of tremors through her. Filled her heart with a suffocating longing. Her throat tightened as she leaned toward him. "Conner." His name was a whisper on her lips.

"Kate." His fingers lingered on her cheek, making it impossible to be rational.

Barry and his wife began to sing a slow, sweet ballad. A love song. The words and music carried Kate on their wings.

"What do you think of them?" Mrs. Abernathy had returned to their sides.

Kate jerked back.

Conner dropped his hand and turned away. It was he who answered as Kate could not find her voice.

"They're wonderful. I just told Kate that they would add a lot to the day."

"I'm glad." She moved away, seemingly unaware of the tender moment she had interrupted.

Kate could not believe how foolishly she had acted… in public, of all things. She hurried to her feet, ashamed of her weakness. "Are you coming for dessert?"

He joined her. "I wouldn't miss your pie for anything." He signaled Beth to watch Ellie, then he followed Kate back to the food-laden table.

Just her pie? Would he miss her when she left? *Kate, stop this silly way of thinking. You'll go to St. Louis and get immersed in your studies. He'll stay here. Give Ellie a good home and perhaps marry Thelma.*

She glanced back at Ellie. The baby played happily with Beth. Ellie would always be surrounded by the Marshall family.

Kate did not, she informed herself, feel like a spectator. A lonely spectator.

Conner chose three slices of pie, all of which he knew Kate made. What would he do when she left? No one baked pies as tasty as hers. And if he failed to convince himself that was the only reason he would miss her, he refused to acknowledge it.

What if Thelma didn't come back? Could he persuade Kate to stay? Her affection for Ellie was obvious and he let himself believe she held some sweet regard for him as well. The way her eyes darkened when he touched her cheek, the way she leaned toward him, the way she caught his hand when she was worried. And hadn't she been the only one who expressed any concern for his well-being when he was stuck under the tent?

All of which changed nothing. Hadn't she just this morning reminded him she would soon be leaving? How long would it take for her to get the response she waited for from the medical school?

They returned to their spot to enjoy the pie.

"Can I take Ellie?" Beth said. "The children are playing over there. She likes watching them."

"Go head, and thanks." He had the rest of the day to enjoy Kate's company. He would not let uncertainty about the future steal from today's pleasure.

She ate the narrow slice of peach pie she'd chosen and leaned back to watch him.

He paused in his eating. "You don't know what you're missing."

"I'm well aware of how those pies taste."

He enjoyed another mouthful. "You don't eat enough to keep a sparrow alive."

She eyed his plate. "I'd say you could feed a huge flock of sparrows, crows, blackbirds and pigeons combined with what you eat."

Her reply tickled him and he roared with laughter. "Are you saying I am personally responsible for starving several hundred birds?"

"I'm only making an observation."

They teased back and forth. Likely anyone overhearing them would wonder at their conversation, but then they wouldn't feel the underlying theme of their words. That they simply enjoyed being with each other, though he couldn't really speak for her. But he was willing to believe it was so.

He grinned at something she said. Had he ever felt this same enjoyment with any other woman? Certainly not with Thelma nor the occasional outings he'd had since.

Thelma. Always the thought of her quelled his enjoyment.

His plate was empty. One of the young girls sauntered past, collecting the used dishes, and took away his plate and Kate's.

"I suppose we should get back to work." Reluctantly he got to his feet and held out a hand to assist Kate. He retained his grasp on her hand as they returned to the tent. Once inside, he had to release her so they could attend to the tasks they had yet to do.

The afternoon sped past as they dealt with judging forms, let people know where to put things and gave various directions.

Finally, everything was ready for the morrow and they stood in the middle of the clearing. Grandfather had declared himself tired an hour ago and the Marshall family had departed, taking Ellie with them. The volunteers had completed their tasks and gone home.

Only Conner and Kate remained.

"We're ready," he said, pulling her arm through his and pressing it to his side. "How does it feel to know we did it?"

"Conner, to tell you the truth, I will feel a little more

jubilant tomorrow when it's all over and Grandfather expresses his approval."

Conner shrugged. "I'm confident we'll raise more than enough to buy the bell." Grandfather had said that wasn't his only reason for having them work together. But even an old man's scheming and hoping did not change the facts. Would anything? How would he know if he didn't ask? "Kate, aren't you going to miss all this when you leave?" He circled his hand to indicate the fairgrounds and the town beyond and brought his hand to rest on his chest.

Aren't you going to miss me?

But the aching cry did not leave his chest.

Miss this? If only he knew how often she'd thought that. How she'd miss the closeness of the small community, the cheerfulness of the large Marshall family and—

She swallowed hard, almost unable to admit the ache that sucked at her until she wondered if she was able to continue standing.

She'd miss Ellie, who would have her real mother back.

She'd miss Conner, who would feel bound to make a new family. Even if he didn't speak the words, she knew he would do anything to protect Ellie and keep her as his own.

Unable to answer him honestly, she turned full circle, taking in the tent, the booths, the decorations, the pens for the animals and an area for games. She could count on one delicious day to enjoy being simply Kate Baker. Not the doctor's daughter or his assistant or even the future Dr. K. Baker. She brought her gaze back to Conner, who watched her with a gentle expression.

"I think I am beginning to get a little excited. I've never been to a country fair." A troubling thought ended her happy anticipation. So many things could go wrong. Accidents, storms... *Please, God, don't let anything ruin tomorrow.*

"Your forehead just wrinkled." He stroked at the furrows, bringing a rush of longing that they could enjoy moments like it for many days...years? Even a lifetime.

"What are you worrying about?" He leaned closer, close enough she could see the sunshine captured in his eyes. "Maybe you're wanting to change your mind about St. Louis." His breath whispered across her cheeks. How had he guessed at her thoughts?

She fought to bring her mind back to reality. "I was praying nothing would go wrong." But she couldn't imagine anything disagreeable at the moment. Every thought overflowed with awareness of him so close.

He trailed his thumb over her bottom lip. "Nothing will go wrong. It's going to be a fine day. One that you and I are going to enjoy completely. Agreed?"

She was more than willing to believe him. More than willing to forget every troubling thought, every regret and every futile wish. "Agreed." Did that breathless, expectant whisper come from her mouth? Her arms seemed to have a mind of their own and she leaned forward and cupped her hands on his shoulders.

"Kate." Her name rang with promises and wishes that echoed in her heart. He lowered his head and caught her mouth with his. His lips lingered a moment, sweet and tender. He lifted his head a bare inch. Air filled with his scent drifted over her face. "Kate," he murmured again.

She stood with her eyes closed, her face uplifted, still feeling the touch of his kiss on her mouth and his warm breath on her face. A vast silence filled the air. Nothing moved or breathed or existed apart from the two of them. The seconds passed while she stood encircled in his arms, her thoughts going no further than this moment.

Toward the river, a twig snapped, the noise as sharp and intrusive as a gunshot.

Conner sighed and slowly—dare she think, reluctantly—eased back. "We have a long day tomorrow. I should get you home and get back to the ranch to take care of Ellie."

"Of course. I have left Father on his own far too long." Ellie would always come first in his thoughts—as she should. Just as her responsibilities could not be pushed aside for long.

Father had taken the wagon home. Conner caught up his horse and led him. Side by side, Kate and Conner walked back to town. He didn't seem to be in a hurry and she found her feet preferred a slow pace. They said little. There existed no need for words. Their kiss had spoken from their hearts. Or so Kate told herself.

They parted at the Baker house and she stepped inside, staying at the window to wave as he rode away. Only then did she admit that perhaps the heart was fickle and prone to believe what it wanted against facts and reality.

Father had left a note informing her he'd been called away to tend a baby with croup.

I should have been here. I should be helping him

more. Instead, she neglected her calling to enjoy a few minutes of deliriously delicious time with Conner.

Tomorrow was the fair. After that, there would be no reason for the two of them to see each other.

Unless…

Was it possible to contemplate an alternative?

She shook her head. That fickle heart of hers seemed determined to ignore the facts.

Saturday she bounded from her bed and rushed to the kitchen to prepare breakfast. All warning thoughts were forgotten. Today was the fair. The entries for the various competitions were to be delivered by nine o'clock to allow time for judging. Her rhubarb pie sat on the pantry counter. The golden-brown crust looked perfect. The filling never failed, thanks to Mrs. Bramford's instructions. Could she possibly win a ribbon for her entry?

Father joined her and they ate hurriedly.

"I'll take my bag to the fair. I expect there will be minor injuries to deal with. Let's hope there will be nothing major."

She felt again a tremor of worry. It wasn't like her to see trouble brewing and yet she did.

With a shake of her head, she dismissed the idea. Breakfast was a hurried meal. She cleaned the kitchen in record time, then climbed into the wagon with Father and together they headed for the fair.

She saw Isabelle and Mattie enter the tent and knew some of the Marshalls were there, but she didn't see Conner. Perhaps he hadn't yet arrived. He'd have no need unless he had something to enter for judging.

Dismissing her disappointment as unnecessary, she took her pie into the tent and filled out the entry form.

No one was allowed to stay inside until after the judging. She stepped out into the sunshine. It promised to be a fine day. In every way imaginable.

Isabelle joined her. "I'm excited and nervous," her friend said. "I entered a piece of needlework."

Kate gave her friend a sideways hug. "You do lovely work." She looked about. People hustled back and forth. Several ladies gathered at a booth set up to serve food. Two men waited where games of skill had been set up. "I thought you would have Ellie."

"Conner got her early this morning. He brought her and Grandfather to town." She looked around. "I don't know where they've gone to. You know Grandfather. He likely has something he wanted Conner to do." She patted Kate's hand. "Don't worry. You'll see him soon enough."

"I only asked about Ellie," she informed her friend, even though, in Kate's mind, Conner had been part of the equation.

Conner stepped from behind a booth, Ellie in his arms.

Kate's heart stalled at the sight of the baby in the big man's arms. Safe. Sheltered. Belonging. So long as Conner kept the baby, Ellie would always have a home.

Again a shiver of apprehension. What if Thelma wanted to take the baby away? But then why would she have sent Ellie to Conner and said he was the father?

Conner crossed toward Kate, his gaze holding hers. He smiled and Kate noticed the scent from the nearby flowers. She barely heard Isabelle murmur something about leaving them alone.

Ellie gurgled and waved her arms. Kate took her from Conner and nuzzled a kiss against the soft skin of her neck. Her heart turned to mush at her love for this sweet child.

"Have you entered your pie?" Conner asked.

She nodded toward the tent. "It's there along with about twenty others."

"No one has a hope of winning over yours." He took her elbow and guided her through the crowd.

"Thank you." His praise was enough. Blue ribbons a pale addition. "Where are we going?"

"The morning is for enjoyment. Let's watch some of the games."

They had discussed this part of the fair, but seeing the games set up and people paying a penny to take part made it more exciting than she had anticipated.

A young man with sandy-colored hair poking out at all angles from under his low-brimmed hat paid his penny. He got three balls to toss at a target with holes of three sizes—the smaller the hole, the higher the score. He toed the mark, shrugged his shoulders several times, then drove a ball hard enough to make a resounding whack when it hit the board...missing the hole.

He groaned.

Kate nudged Conner to indicate a blushing young woman watching. "He's trying to impress her."

Conner whispered close to her ear. "Will she like him less if he misses?"

"Impressing each other is part of the courtship routine." She tipped her head so she could meet his eyes, which sparkled with reflected sunshine.

"I'm impressed with your pie baking." His admiring smile did strange things to her heart. "Among other things."

She wanted him to tell her what those other things

were, but a cheer from the crowd drew their attention back to the game. It seemed the young man had gotten his ball through the target. Raising his hands in a victory gesture, he grinned widely as he went to the young woman's side, glowing with pleasure.

"I'm going to give it a try," Conner said. He paid his penny and took his place. He smiled at Kate. Did he mean to remind her of her comment about impressing each other being part of a courtship routine?

He threw his first ball. It went through the largest hole.

Another smile for Kate. And a shrug.

The second ball missed all the holes.

The sandy-haired young man called, "Keep your eye on the target. You can do it."

Conner squinted at the board.

"He's going to make it," she whispered to Ellie.

He wound up and threw the ball.

Kate held her breath. For some strange reason, it was important he succeeded. The ball caught the edge of the hole. A collective sigh and then the ball went through and everyone cheered, none any more pleased than Kate.

He joined her.

"No prize?"

"Just the pleasure of impressing you." He bent to look into her face. "Did I?"

She didn't need a mirror to know his attention had brought color to her face. She pressed her cheek to the top of Ellie's head and avoided looking at Conner...for about two seconds. Despite the warning bell clattering inside her head, she looked at him, smiled and whispered, "I'm impressed."

"Good." He draped his arm across her shoulders.

She wondered how appropriate it was to let him touch her like that but told herself he only meant to guide her through the crowd to the next game. And there were many.

Ring toss for the children. Rock toss for the men. They went from one to another. And each time he took a turn, she was suitably impressed.

They came to a food booth.

"I could use a snack. How about you?" he asked.

She nodded. Not so much that she was hungry as she wanted to enjoy every minute of this day, the time spent with Conner and Ellie. One day of pretend.

He bought a stack of cookies and took the offered water and they sat on the nearby crude bench. They lingered there long after the cups had been drained and Conner had consumed half a dozen cookies as they watched the townspeople and the country folk from a large radius enjoying the fair.

"It looks like they've opened the tent." He pointed. Indeed people were hurrying inside.

He helped her to her feet and they headed that direction.

"I wonder who won ribbons." Did he hear the doubt and hope in her voice?

"I know who has won the pie contest." He stopped and looked into her eyes. "You."

She lifted one shoulder. "We'll see." She couldn't help but increase her pace toward the tent. They had almost reached the entrance when Ellie started to fuss. "She's hungry. You go ahead. I'll take her to the wagon and feed her." The baby things were in the Marshall wagon.

"I'll wait for you." He glanced toward the tent.

"I know you're anxious to see the results." He had no reason to stay back. Many of the Marshall family had entries.

Sadie and Beth left the tent. Beth grinned widely.

"She won a blue ribbon for a picture she made from dried flowers." Sadie beamed at her adopted daughter. "I'm so proud of you."

"Congratulations," Kate and Conner said as one.

Ellie protested at the delay.

"You haven't been in yet?" Sadie asked.

"I'll have to delay and go feed this little girl." Kate jostled the baby, trying to soothe her.

"So you don't know?"

"Know what?"

"You need to see for yourself. Lots of our family won ribbons. Why not let Beth take Ellie?"

"I'd love that." Beth reached for the baby.

Kate hesitated. She wanted to spend as much time as possible with Ellie, but she also wanted to know how her entry had done. Knowing Ellie would be in good hands, she let her go. "I'll come and get her after I've checked things out."

"Take your time. I don't mind." Beth turned her attention to the baby. "I'll get you fed real soon and then you'll feel so much better. I know it's hard to wait when you're hungry." They made their way toward the wagon.

Sadie saw someone she wanted to talk to and left.

Conner grabbed Kate's hand and drew her into the tent. How different it looked now. The tables were laden with colorful goods—orange carrots, red beets, jars of bright green pickles, rows of luscious-looking cakes, bouquets of flowers, paintings and handiwork. But her eyes went to the pie table. She couldn't draw in a satisfying breath.

"Let's go see." Conner pulled her forward. Her eyes went to her pie. A blue ribbon hung from the edge of the plate.

"You won! I knew you would." He smiled, looking as pleased as if he had won the ribbon himself. "Congratulations." He announced to the crowd, "Ladies and gentlemen, this is the best pie baker in the whole area, Miss Kate Baker." He swept his arm in a welcoming gesture.

Those around them clapped and called their congratulations.

Kate's cheeks burned. "Thank you." She grabbed Conner's hand and dragged him away. "I'm embarrassed."

"No reason you should be. Being the best at something should make you proud." He pulled her to a halt and bent to look into her face. "It does, doesn't it?"

She grinned at him. Her eyes were warm. "Yes, it does."

He tucked her hand around his elbow. "Now, let's see how the others did."

They knew Beth had won a ribbon and admired her picture. Isabelle had won a red ribbon for her cross-stitch sampler.

"It should have gotten first," Kate said with some annoyance.

"I agree. We'll have to fire those judges."

She laughed. "How do you fire volunteers, especially when their job is done?"

"We'll certainly keep their mistake in mind for the next fair."

She barely managed not to stumble. Next fair? We? If there was another, she wouldn't be here. But the thought flitted through her mind and was gone, erased by the excitement of the day.

Annie had won the cake competition.

Grandfather had won the carving category with a rearing horse.

Conner looked surprised. "I didn't even know he was going to enter. Wily old man to keep it a secret."

"I heard that."

They spun about to face Conner's grandfather.

"What do you think I do all the time I'm sitting on the porch, watching you boys do my work?"

"Yeah, but I never saw you actually make anything. Well, except for the little doll you carved for Mattie."

"I been practicing." The old man fairly glowed.

Kate brushed her hand over his arm. "Congratulations. You deserve it."

"You're a sweet girl. And the best pie maker in the area, according to Conner."

"You heard?" She covered her face to hide her embarrassment.

Grandfather chuckled. "I expect half the people here heard. You deserve all the praise he can give you." He hobbled away to look at the exhibits.

Kate's heart felt ready to explode and she grinned at Conner.

As they stared into each other's eyes, his smile faded. "Let's get out of here." He pulled her toward the exit.

She blinked as they stepped into the bright sunlight. And blinked again as Beth passed between a food booth and a group of people. "There's Beth, but she doesn't have Ellie."

"I suppose Isabelle has her."

Kate pulled free of his grasp. "What if she doesn't? We need to make sure."

"We will." They hurried toward the Marshall wagon, but before they reached it, they saw Isabelle with a group of women. She disappeared in the crowd, but not before Kate saw Ellie was not with her.

She jerked Conner to a halt. "This doesn't feel right. Ever since yesterday, I've had a bad feeling that something would go wrong. What if Thelma sent the baby to you because she expected you to protect her from someone bad? We should have watched her better." This was her fault. She'd been selfishly pretending this was the life she wanted instead of keeping her attention on her Ellie. What if someone had stolen her?

Chapter Thirteen

"I'm sure she's safe," Conner said. Only, he wasn't. Kate was right. They should have been watching the child better. Hadn't he wondered from the beginning if Thelma had concerns about Ellie's safety? Why else would she send the baby to him? If anyone bore blame, it was him. "Let's find Beth and ask her where Ellie is." They edged their way through the crowd in the direction they'd last seen Beth.

Kate held his hand in a viselike grip. She vibrated with tension.

"We'll find her. I promise you." He caught a glimpse of his niece and trotted toward her, pulling Kate after her. "Beth," he called when they were close enough for her to hear.

She looked about at the sound of her name.

"Beth."

Seeing them, she stopped and waited. "Hi."

Breathless, he jogged to her. "Where's Ellie?"

"Isabelle took her."

He shook his head. "We just saw her and she didn't have Ellie."

Beth looked startled and then worried. "Isabelle was holding her when I left."

Conner turned to Kate. Her face was flushed from their run, her eyes dark with worry. "Come on, we need to find Isabelle."

Again they pushed their way through the crowd. He spoke. "It's nice to see such a good turnout, but I wish they would let us through more readily." He turned sideways and shouldered his way through a knot of men, shielding Kate as he brought her in his wake.

They reached a place where the crowd thinned and he stopped to look around. "There." The woman turned. "No. It's not her."

Kate raised to her tiptoes, clinging to him for balance. Given a different set of circumstances, he would have enjoyed the moment, but his worry for Ellie made any enjoyment impossible. A couple hundred yards away, he spotted a woman that looked like Isabelle and they were again edging past groups of people, giving hurried responses to their greetings. About all he could get out of his mouth at the moment was hello.

The woman disappeared from sight, but he didn't slow his pace. And then Isabelle was only a few steps away, staring at them like they'd sprung from the ground.

"What's wrong?" she asked, correctly reading the concern in both their faces.

"Where's Ellie?" he said.

"Beth said she left her with you," Kate added.

"Isn't she at the wagon? I left her there with Beth watching her." Isabelle broke into a run in the direction of the Marshall family.

"In the wagon? We never looked there." But no one

heard or cared what he said. The three of them had one thing in mind. Find Ellie.

He dropped Kate's hand and outran both women, skidding to a halt at the back of the wagon. Grandfather lay with his mouth open, snoring. Beside him, Ellie slept safely in her basket.

His relief made his knees weak.

Isabelle and Kate reached his side and sagged with relief.

"She's safe." Kate's words wobbled as much as Conner's legs.

Grandfather snorted and sat up. "What's all the commotion?"

Ellie opened her eyes and cooed. "It's nothing." Conner scooped the baby to his chest. He was never letting her out of his sight again.

"*Nothing* doesn't bring three adults galloping to my side." Grandfather squinted at them. "What's happened?" He patted Ellie. "Something about the baby?"

"False alarm." Conner explained the mistake.

"May I hold her?" Kate's forehead wrinkled.

He longed to smooth away those worry lines, but perhaps not in Grandfather's presence. Instead, he forced his arms to release Ellie to Kate.

Kate closed her eyes. Her worry lines disappeared. "Thank You, God." She murmured the prayer over and over, Ellie held tightly in her arms.

Isabelle reassured herself that all was well with Ellie. "I left Mattie with her father, but I feel the need to check on her whereabouts." She hurried away.

Grandfather eased to the ground, took his canes. "Fine lot you two are. Letting a baby out of your sight and then panicking about it." He hobbled away.

Conner waited until they were out of earshot to speak. "Easy to say we panicked now we know she's safe."

"I don't intend to let her leave my arms until you pry her out to take her home."

He saw the sorrow she'd feel when the time came. "You could come with me." He watched hope and longing flare in her eyes.

"Let's go." She pretended to understand he meant the few remaining hours of the fair. But he knew what he'd seen. And it gave him hope for a future shared with her.

What about Ellie? What would happen when they found Thelma?

He'd learn why Thelma said the baby was his and that would answer many questions.

They circled the grounds again, pausing to watch others play the games, but what he really wanted was to pull Kate and Ellie aside and hold them both in his arms. Talk to Kate about the options in her life. Make her see that staying was a good choice. But the fair was wrapping up. Dawson and Logan joined him and Kate to gather up the proceeds and tally the amount.

Grandfather found them. "How did we do?"

Conner told him the amount. "More than enough to buy a bell, I'd say."

"You've done good. Both of you. Now, don't go disappointing an old man."

Conner shook his head, refusing to acknowledge that he understood what his grandfather meant.

Kate's cheeks blossomed as prettily as any of the flowers on display and she buried her face against the baby.

Grandfather stood at the doorway to the tent. "Listen up, everyone," he bellowed, drawing the attention of the crowd. "I have an announcement to make." He turned to Conner and Kate. "You two come out here."

Conner practically had to drag Kate to Grandfather's side.

"I don't want to stand in front of all those people," she protested.

Grandfather took her arm on one side. Conner crowded closer to the other, stroking Ellie's hair to smooth it.

"We have enough money to buy the bell for the church," Grandfather said. "And it's because all you people supported the cause, but mostly it's due to the hard work of these two—a round of applause for Conner and Kate."

Not only did the people clap, but they cheered and whistled. The blossom in Kate's cheeks grew rosier.

The noise settled down and people began to move away. Some would linger to visit and share a picnic with friends and neighbors. Others would gather up their entries, their children, and leave.

Conner pulled Kate out of the way of people going in and out of the tent. They stood along the canvas wall. They could overhear the comments of people coming and going, the prolonged goodbyes and the invitations to come and visit anytime.

"They certainly make a nice-looking couple," a loud-voiced lady said. "And that little baby is so sweet. They make the perfect family, don't you think?"

Her companion laughed softly. "Conner is taking his time about asking her to marry him."

"I can't imagine Mr. Marshall Senior not doing his best to see them married."

"I remember he was gone for several weeks last

spring. You recall that? Plenty of time to father a child. Conner should do right by her and marry her."

Conner blanched as he realized they talked about him and Kate. He eased away from the tent, drawing the red-faced Kate with him. "I'm sorry you had to hear that." *The perfect family.* If only it could be so. But to have Kate's name linked with such gossip…

He clenched his fists. What else were people saying behind his back?

They made their way to the front of the tent, where they would be more visible and less likely to overhear unwanted comments.

He turned to Kate. Her gaze held his. He dared think he saw something different, as if the words they'd heard had made her see and believe the possibilities. They belonged together. He knew he saw welcome and hope and invitation in her look and reached out to touch her cheek.

"Conner." He recognized the voice. Jesse. Back from his latest trip in search of the missing Thelma. Conner hoped he had not met with success.

The sheriff stepped into view leading a woman. "I found Thelma."

Shock silenced Conner as he stared at the woman before him. Nothing about her seemed familiar. Yes, she still had light brown hair, swept up in a bunch of curls. Her eyes were still brown. He used to think them bottomless with enticing depth, but now they looked flat and lifeless.

"Hello, Conner," she said in her breathy voice.

Had he ever thought that was appealing? It seemed downright childish now.

Her gaze drifted to Ellie. She made no effort to take

the baby from Kate, and if he wasn't mistaken about the fiery look in Kate's eyes, Thelma would be forced to pry Ellie from her arms. "I apologize for not letting you know about our daughter sooner."

He gave her a narrow-eyed study. What was she hoping to achieve by continuing this deception?

Her gaze came back to Conner.

He knew he correctly read the challenge in them. She knew it was her word against his that he wasn't Ellie's father.

Jesse shuffled his feet. "It's been a long day. Miss Bird is tired. Perhaps we could go somewhere quiet where we can sit down to talk."

Jesse was right. A dozen people watched and listened openly.

Kate recovered first. "You're welcome to come to the doctor's house."

Isabelle joined them, a look of concern on her face.

Conner introduced her. "My sister-in-law. She married Dawson."

"Pleased to meet you." Thelma was all sweetness and smiles. "Jesse told me Dawson and Logan were both married now. How sweet."

Dr. Baker had noticed the commotion and hurried over.

Conner introduced Kate and her father. He wanted nothing more than to demand an explanation for Ellie's poor condition and Thelma's reason for lying. But not until they reached the doctor's house. They began the trek across the fairgrounds.

Their entourage grew to include Logan and Sadie and their children.

Pa joined them just as they reached Kate's place. She

ushered them inside, still holding Ellie. Conner stayed close to her side.

A wagon stopped in front of the house and then Dawson led Grandfather in.

Pa turned to Thelma. "You've finally come to check on your baby."

If she heard the hard note in his voice, she ignored it. She ducked her head and managed to look shy and coy. "And to marry Conner. I thought it was time."

Grandfather grunted and ignored her mention of marriage. "Maybe you can explain why this little one was doing so poorly."

Conner wanted to hug the old man for his bluntness. He was not the only one who looked at Thelma, waiting for her answer.

A beat of silence as if she expected Grandfather to withdraw his question. He didn't, and if she'd looked at him, she would have seen the way he stared at her, demanding an answer.

Thelma slanted a smile at Conner. "I was sick and couldn't manage her. I knew Conner would see she was taken care of." She hung her head as if to portray a regretful mother.

Conner didn't believe anything about her.

Conner didn't need to look around at the family to know none of them believed her story.

"Must have been sick a long time." Grandfather's tone was harsh, disbelieving.

Thelma shrugged in a delicate way, trying to portray her helplessness.

Conner studied her. She'd always been slender, but it did look like she'd lost weight and there were blue smudges below her eyes. They might have been makeup.

"I'm fine now," she said, lifting her head and looking from one to the other with a great show of bravery. Her gaze rested on Kate and her smile faltered.

Kate returned her look, revealing nothing. Oh, how Conner wished he could ask what she thought.

"Kate nursed Ellie through a few bad hours." What would Thelma say in response to that?

Her eyes narrowed almost imperceptibly and then she widened them. "I owe you thanks for taking care of my baby." She slanted a smile at Conner. "Our baby." She touched the baby for the first time, but her hand did not linger.

Kate's expression tightened. She looked at Conner and he saw the pain there. Perhaps at knowing she would have to release Ellie to this woman. Perhaps, too, at Thelma's insistence the baby was his.

Kate pressed her lips together and bent to plant a kiss on Ellie's cheek, earning a bright smile from the baby. Kate straightened and looked past him.

Annie, with Carly hard on her heels, burst into the house. She skidded to a halt as she saw Thelma and she scowled at the woman.

Thelma continued her sweet-person routine. "Annie, Carly, how nice to see you both again."

"Hello," Annie managed.

"Can't say I feel the same," Carly said. She had no father or grandfather present to scold her for being rude, so she spoke her mind...perhaps spoke for most of those present.

They pressed to either side of Kate as if to say they were prepared to protect the baby...and Kate, too? He had never seen her look so wounded. It was all he could do not to ignore Thelma, pull Kate and Ellie into his arms and shelter them from this situation.

Thelma smiled at Conner, the smile going only as far as the corners of her mouth. "I made a mistake when I left. But I'm back and I want to do the right thing for Elspeth and give her a father…" She paused dramatically. "*Her* father."

Conner's teeth protested at the pressure he put on them and he forced his jaw to relax. He didn't know what Thelma hoped to gain by her charade. Conner didn't doubt Thelma was Ellie's mother, but that was where the truth ended. If she continued this game, it was her word against his. If he refused to claim Ellie, what would become of her?

Thelma gave a reluctant smile. "It's been a long trip." She yawned. "Is there any chance I could rest for a bit?"

"By all means," Pa said. "You must stay with us while we sort things out. Let's be on our way." He paused at the door to speak to Kate and her father. "Thank you for allowing us to meet here…and for everything else." He nodded toward Ellie.

Thelma followed on Pa's heels. Logan, Sadie, Dawson and Isabelle hugged Kate on their way out.

"I'll take Ellie," Conner said to Kate.

She nodded, her eyes brimming with tears, and released the baby to his arms.

"I'll take good care of her."

"I know you will."

It about shattered his insides at the way her voice broke. "I'm sorry."

"This is something you have to work out." She carefully avoided his gaze.

If there remained anything inside to break, it broke at that point.

Grandfather waited at the door for Conner. "Why does Thelma pretend Ellie is yours?"

Conner rubbed his neck as the tension in him mounted. "I simply don't know."

"Then I suggest you find out."

"I certainly plan to try. But in the end, it could be my word against hers." He'd heard the gossip about Kate and now the gossip would include Thelma. He knew well enough that people often preferred the shocking falsehoods over the simple truth.

Kate closed her eyes and slowly eased out her breath so as not to make Father notice her distress. Thelma had returned expecting to marry Conner. What sort of game was she playing and why? Not that it made any difference. It was the only way Conner could truly become Ellie's father. She knew his love for the baby must come above everything else.

Kate had not anticipated how hollow she would feel at waving goodbye to Conner, though she didn't lift her hand or look out the window. Was it possible to avoid the Marshalls until she left for medical school? Avoiding them would be difficult, if not impossible. Her best friend lived at the ranch and she couldn't imagine avoiding Isabelle. Nor could she think there would be no more pleasant visits with Annie.

"I expect I will hear back from the medical school soon. I'm anxious to get at my studies."

Father nodded his approval. "That's good to hear. God has given you a natural ability as a healer."

What would he think if she admitted that at this moment her biggest reason for wanting to go was to get away from Bella Creek and the Marshalls? Especially Conner and his sweet little daughter…only, she wasn't his daughter and wouldn't be unless he married Thelma.

She made her cautious, calm way to her room. She sat on the edge of the bed and let her moans escape. She knew better than to grow fond of her patients. Father and Mother had both warned her of that. But she didn't see Conner and Ellie as patients. She saw them as…

She closed her mind to every other description and lifted her Bible to her lap. The pages fell open at the ninety-fourth Psalm and she drank in the words: *When I said, My foot slippeth; Thy mercy, O LORD, held me up. In the multitude of my thoughts within me, Thy comforts delight my soul.*

She read the verses over and over, letting them seep into her heart and mind until she felt ready to face her future. *Lord, You are my strength and comfort.*

She gazed about the room that not long ago she had shared with Isabelle. Would she meet someone back East who would be the kind of friend Isabelle was? She must believe she would or her insides would cave in with emptiness.

Over the next few hours, her resolve grew, her determination settled into the depths of her heart. She had always found daily comfort in God's Word. *For the Lord GOD will help me…therefore have I set my face like a flint.* Her face and heart and mind were set like flint to do what she'd planned to do her whole life.

If only tomorrow wasn't Sunday. How could she endure seeing Conner with Thelma, no longer able to sit at his side and enjoy both his presence and Ellie's? Her flint lost some of its steeliness.

She practiced putting a smile on her face. She would face this with grace and dignity and no one would see the tears that gushed forth from her heart, filling her with weakness and sorrow.

Sleep evaded her that night. When morning came, she felt put through the wringer. Perhaps she was coming down with something. She should stay at home just in case.

But she would not allow her weakness to rule her and she dressed with care. No one would look at her with pity.

"Are you ready?" Father asked, waiting at the door.

She'd been finding excuses to delay their departure, hoping they might slip in late and sit at the back. A wagon rattled by and slowed. She caught her breath. Was it someone needing the doctor? That would provide the perfect excuse to miss church. But no, the wagon had simply slowed because of a dog crossing the street and then it continued onward, stopping in front of the church.

"I'm coming." She donned her best hat, pulled on her gloves and left the house at her father's side.

"Are you doing okay?" he asked.

Her breath caught on its upward journey and she coughed a little. "I'm fine. Why do you ask?"

"I think I'm not mistaken in believing you have grown a little fond of Conner Marshall. And now Miss Bird has arrived to claim her child and a husband."

"But he isn't Ellie's father." He knew that and it surprised her to hear him speak as if he was.

"If he denies it, he accuses Thelma of lying. Besides, I have a feeling he loves that wee one enough to marry her mother. And perhaps that is for the best."

Somehow Kate made her wooden feet keep pace with him. How could it be for the best?

"You've delayed your medical training for me. I fear if you delay it for someone else, you will never get there. It would be a shame to lose sight of the dream you've had even before Mother and I adopted you." He gave her a beaming smile. "A choice we never regretted. We couldn't have asked for a better daughter. You shared our passion for medicine and have been so helpful from the start. I'm proud of you." He squeezed her elbow, a movement that went deep into her heart and pressed out great huge drops of sorrow. He was right. She had momentarily lost sight of her goal and her promise.

"I knew from the start that this would happen." That Thelma would show up and Conner would have to marry her in order to give Ellie the family she needed. Being forewarned should have caused her to be fore-armed, but instead she'd let herself fall under the spell of Conner's charm and personality.

They reached the church. A glance around revealed no familiar Marshall wagon or any of their horses. Odd. They were usually early.

She pointed out the fact to her father. "I hope there isn't anything wrong." Her heart kicked against her ribs. "Maybe Ellie—" What if Conner had been hurt?

"Now, now, daughter. There are many good and innocent reasons for being unable to attend church."

Her mind raced with some of those reasons as she and Father slipped into a pew. Accidents. Disasters. Her arms twitched. Had Grandfather fallen and done himself damage? Perhaps they had come on horseback. She looked about, but not a single person from the ranch sat in the pews.

Sadie, Logan and their three children were the only Marshalls in attendance. The pews in front of them remained empty and the adults glanced about several times. To Kate's anxious mind, it appeared they were worried about the absence as well.

She sang when the hymns were sung, she listened though she could not have repeated one word of Preacher Hugh's message. As soon as the benediction had been given, she was on her feet, standing in the aisle, waiting for Logan and Sadie.

Sadie told Beth to take the other children outside.

"Is something wrong?" Kate asked as soon as the children were out of hearing. The worried expressions in the faces of both Sadie and Logan said it all.

"We don't know."

Logan touched his wife's hand. "I'm going to ride out there now." He hurried down the aisle.

Kate grabbed Sadie's hand. "Please let me know when you find out."

Sadie nodded, distracted by her concern. "I will." She went outside, collected her children and rushed them home.

Father patted Kate's arm. "There's nothing you can do. Let's go home."

She knew he meant she had no need to involve herself in this. Her job as a medical provider was over. It had never been easy for her to help people and then move on. Would she ever be able to distance herself as she should?

Somehow she managed to put dinner on the table and eat a portion of what she'd put on her plate.

There was pie in the pantry and she served Father a

generous slice but didn't give herself any. She'd never be able to eat pie again without thinking of Conner.

"Doc. Doc." A man pounded on the door.

Kate hurried to allow him to enter.

"It's my wife," he said in a great rush. "She's been trying to have the baby for two days now. She's getting awfully weak. Can you come help?"

"I'll be right there." Father grabbed his bag from the office and joined the man. He paused only long enough to speak to Kate. "I'm sure everything is all right. Don't worry."

She knew he didn't mean the anxious man at the door. He meant Conner and Ellie and the rest of the Marshalls. But his words brought no comfort to her.

He closed the door behind him and she leaned against it. "Lord God, keep them all safe. And please, please heal my heart. Give me courage and strength to do what I must do. What I've always meant to do."

She pushed away from the door and returned to the kitchen to clean up the meal. It took longer than usual as several times she found herself with her hands idle in the dishwater and her eyes staring at nothing.

A little later, someone knocked at the back door, startling Kate from her thoughts.

She opened to admit Sadie.

Kate immediately became alert. "What did Logan find out?"

"Nothing too serious. Just a number of mishaps. The horses got the gate down and escaped just as they were about to leave, so they had to take care of that. Then there was a little fire behind the house. Logan says his pa thinks Thelma had been smoking out there. By the time they dealt with all that, it was too late to go to church and Pa didn't think it was safe to leave with the fire just out." She shuddered. "Fires always make people nervous, but even more so since Bella Creek suffered so much loss." She managed a weak grin.

Kate sat back, her lungs emptying in a whoosh. "I imagined all sorts of horrible things." She couldn't even admit them to herself.

"All is well."

"Join me for tea?"

"I'd love to. It's been a long time since I sat in this kitchen with you. Remember the night we played games so long and loud your father came from his room and suggested we put an end to the night?"

It was shortly after they'd arrived and normally Kate was very protective of her father. "I felt bad about forgetting to be quiet. It seems like such a long time ago."

For a while they talked about the early days when they'd first arrived in town. Kate carried her end of the conversation, but she really wanted to know about Conner and Ellie and Thelma. Not that she'd ever ask. It was not her business.

Sadie leaned forward, her face awash in sympathy. "I saw the way it was between you and Conner."

"There was nothing to see."

"If it's any consolation, he looks as miserable as you."

"No, it's no consolation." How could each word rip through her innards like a dull knife in a cruel hand? She did not want to think of Conner being miserable the rest of his life.

But what could she do about it? This was out of her hands.

Chapter Fourteen

The following Sunday morning, Conner joined the others for breakfast in the kitchen. In the week since Thelma had arrived, he'd kept Ellie with him at night. Thelma had taken over her daytime care for the most part, though he often came to the house to discover Thelma upstairs resting and the baby in Annie's care.

He'd thought of suggesting the baby spend her days with Isabelle as she had before, but shouldn't Thelma be taking care of her?

Ellie didn't seem as happy. He missed the baby's ready smile. At first he thought he was imagining that Ellie didn't smile for Thelma, but a couple of day's observation convinced him he wasn't wrong.

He'd tried to ask Thelma why this was so. She had no answer. Just as she refused to explain why the baby was so thin.

All she did was shrug. "Some babies simply aren't plump," she said.

Conner suspected there was more to it than that.

Thelma did not join them for breakfast this morning,

but then she had not done so since her arrival, straggling in as Annie finished dishes to demand a cup of coffee.

Conner had twice remained in the kitchen until she came down and watched her staring at her cup, unwilling to talk. The first day he had asked, "Are you okay? Will you be able to look after Ellie if I leave?"

She'd given him a burning look. "I'm perfectly capable."

He almost shrank back from the venom in her words but wouldn't give her the satisfaction of letting her know she had that much power over him.

Her gaze had gone to Annie, then as if remembering they weren't alone, she got sweet and apologetic. "I'm sorry. I simply can't function until I've had my coffee."

He'd learned to leave as soon as she descended into the kitchen without trying to make conversation with her.

When time came to leave for church, Thelma shook her head. "I'll stay home with Ellie."

Pa looked about ready to order her to accompany them. He never accepted excuses for missing church, but he nodded. "Perhaps it's for the best."

Conner would not ask what Pa meant, but he guessed his father might consider it to everyone's benefit to draw as little attention to the situation as possible until things were sorted out.

Conner rode into town and dismounted at the church. He had hoped that Kate would sit with him, but she shook her head when he tried to wave her over and sat two pews behind the Marshall family. He understood that she saw him as belonging to another woman and he sat with his family, trying to ignore the burning in the pit of his stomach at how complicated life had become. Thelma's lies and his concern over Ellie trapped him in a place he didn't want to be.

Preacher Hugh rose and began speaking. How could the man stand before them and proclaim God's faithfulness when his son was still missing?

Hugh directed them to the forty-sixth Psalm and read, "'God is our refuge and strength, a very present help in trouble. Therefore will not we fear, though the earth be removed, and though the mountains be carried into the midst of the sea; though the waters thereof roar and be troubled, though the mountains shake with the swelling thereof.'" Hugh continued to speak of God's trustworthiness in the midst of trouble.

Conner's spirit calmed. *God, You are all I need. You know the truth and have said the truth will make one free. Free me, Lord, from Thelma's claim and her demands.*

Kate hurried out before he could speak to her. Gone were the days they could spend the afternoon together.

Mrs. Grieves elbowed her way to Conner's side and faced him with royal indignation. "We all heard Miss Bird and know the baby is hers. I trust you are going to do what's right and marry her as she asked." She sniffed. "I rather like that baby girl. She deserves a name." She tapped Conner on the chest, a sharp annoying jab. "You created a bad situation. Now do what's right to fix it." She steamed away.

A dozen people watched and listened.

Conner sighed. At least his family had already left the church. He glanced over his shoulder. Hugh watched, his expression kindly. Perhaps the man was suspending judgment until he had *all* the facts.

Conner slowly made his way outside. His family

had departed. Conner remained alone a moment, then turned to the cemetery and went to Ma's grave and knelt on the warm ground. He tried to hear Ma's voice. What would she tell him to do?

The truth shall set you free.

Was God directing him? But he'd told the truth. Thelma hadn't. If there was the faintest possibility Ellie was his, he'd marry Thelma in an instant. Even knowing he wasn't the father, he'd marry her to give Ellie a home if there existed even a thread of affection between them. There didn't.

What could he do but hope and pray that Thelma would see how wrong it was to continue her pretense and her demands?

Feeling no closer to a solution than he had when he rose earlier in the morning, Conner went to his horse and swung into the saddle.

He studied the doctor's house as he passed, hoping for a glimpse of Kate, though to what avail? Thelma's accusations and demands must be dealt with.

But how?

It wasn't until he got to the ranch that he realized Kate had accompanied Sadie and Logan. He jumped from his horse and rushed over to help her, retaining her hand after he helped her to the ground.

"I'm glad you've come," he said, drinking in every detail of her features. Her hair was darker than Thelma's. Strands had escaped beneath her bonnet and he tucked one back from her cheek. Her coffee-colored eyes widened. He ignored the warning in them. "You look nice." She wore a dress the color of bluebells and, in fact, looked as fresh as one. No guile in her face. No worry about what hidden meaning existed behind her eyes.

"Thank you. I've come to see how Ellie is doing." She stepped away from him. "Your pa asked me to check on her. Said he had some concerns."

"Of course." He must clear up this whole misunderstanding. No, it was more than that. Both he and Thelma knew perfectly well what the truth was. He needed to convince Thelma to admit the truth. Kate also knew the truth, but Thelma's demands for marriage had to be dealt with before she created a public spectacle that would forever mar the Marshall name.

Kate had gone inside. Logan returned and the brothers took the horses to the barn and gave them feed and water.

Conner lingered, in no hurry to go to the house and face his unwelcome reality.

"What's up, big brother? You seem upset."

Conner shrugged.

"Why does Thelma say Ellie is your baby?"

"I don't know what Thelma's reason is, but I only want to protect Ellie. If people knew I wasn't the father, then what would happen?" It was the question that kept him from taking any action. Would Thelma be willing to let her daughter be known as illegitimate? Would she whisk the baby away? He shuddered at the thought. Not for his sake, but for Ellie's. Thelma didn't seem to have any natural affection for her child. He tried to explain his reasons to Logan.

Logan studied the house again. "You have yourself in a real pickle, don't you?"

"It's not my doing, but that doesn't make it feel any better."

They made their way back to the house. Sammy threw open the door. "Hurry up. Dinner's ready and I'm starving."

Logan planted a hand on the boy's shoulder. "You're always hungry."

"I know." Sammy gave Logan such a look of admiration that Conner had to turn away. Logan had already forgotten Conner's problems. His life had turned out to be very pleasant.

The meal was already on the table and Conner saw he was to sit by Thelma. She'd used the time the others were at church to curl her hair into ringlets that were tied up at the back of her head. She'd donned a pink satin dress with a lower neckline than he was used to seeing and he jerked his gaze from the view, heat stinging his cheeks. She'd applied some kind of makeup that made her look like a professional singer. Was that what this was about? She needed someone to care for the baby so she could return to singing?

He plucked Ellie from her basket, where he often found her in the daytime...as if Thelma had no interest in playing with her. He perched her on his knees and took the place beside Thelma.

Kate sat at the far end of the table between Sadie and Isabelle and they laughed together at something.

Thelma looked their way. "A private joke?" Her voice was gently chiding, though Conner knew she probably seethed inside that she wasn't part of the circle of friends.

Isabelle smiled sweetly. "Not at all. I was telling them how Mattie has been making a doll for Ellie." She turned to Mattie. "They said they are anxious to see it."

Mattie grinned. "I sure hope Ellie likes it." She looked at Thelma for approval.

Thelma said nothing.

"I'm sure she will." Conner turned to the baby. "Won't you, sweetie?"

Ellie met his eyes.

He could almost believe he saw pleading.

"Hi, Ellie," Mattie said, and the baby smiled at her.

The conversation turned to other things as the meal progressed.

Thelma, as usual, ate very little.

He'd mentioned it to her once and she had given him an icy look. He wouldn't mention it again.

He let the baby have a taste of his potatoes. The food dribbled down her chin and onto her gown.

"Now look what you've done." Thelma rose and found a cloth to wipe up the mess. Her actions were rough and Ellie whimpered a protest.

Thelma sat back down with a sigh of exasperation.

Conner cupped his hand over Ellie's head and pressed her to his side.

The meal finally ended.

Thelma rose. "I'm going to have a rest." She swung her skirts as she left the room.

Was it only him or did the whole room breathe out relief at her departure?

The silence that followed her exit erupted into everyone talking at once.

Sadie clapped her hands—always the teacher. "Children, why don't you go play while Aunt Isabelle and I help your aunt clean up this mess?"

The children scurried out.

"I'll help, too," Kate said.

Sadie pressed her hand to Kate's shoulder. "I think you have a more important task." She tilted her head toward Ellie.

Kate hesitated, but the longing in her eyes was more than evident. Conner handed her the baby and she cradled her closely. Ellie's gaze locked on hers and Conner knew he saw the baby relax. Ellie smiled and gurgled.

"She's missed you."

Kate nodded. For a moment, he felt like things returned to the way they'd been before Thelma showed up—he and Kate enjoying Ellie together. Allowing himself to think of a future shared with Kate. He closed his eyes against the pain that pressed to the inside of his head.

"Hey, Conner," Logan said. "Show us what you're doing with your horses."

Conner reluctantly went outside with the men. He'd made great progress with one of the mares, so he didn't mind letting the men see how well things were going. But he'd far sooner stay in the house and watch Kate feed Ellie. Hope for a chance to talk to her alone.

The visit to the horses took longer than he wished. He kept glancing over his shoulder toward the house. The women came out, Ellie in Kate's arms, and wandered toward the garden.

He excused himself and hurried toward them. "Kate, wait."

The other women eased away, leaving him alone with her. "Kate, I miss you. The baby misses you."

Kate looked past him. "I'm sure things will work out for you." She checked the position of the sun. "I need to get back." She handed Ellie to him, hurried to catch up to the others and spoke to Sadie.

"Of course," Sadie said and called to Logan.

Conner stood by helplessly, watching them prepare

to depart. Before the wagon dipped out of sight behind the hill, he turned and strode into the house.

Grandfather sat alone at the table.

"Where's Thelma?"

Grandfather looked toward the ceiling. "Still resting."

Conner hesitated. Should he barge into her room and demand to speak to her? He decided it wouldn't be proper. So he would have to wait for her to come down when she was ready. In the meantime...

As if in answer to his wish to see her, Thelma came into the room, yawning.

"Would you hold Ellie for me?" he asked Grandfather.

Grandfather took the baby and smiled at her. "We'll entertain each other. I can talk as much as I want without boring you, isn't that right?"

Conner watched the two of them, relieved to see the spark in Ellie's eyes, even more relieved when she gurgled and cooed.

He turned back to Thelma. "Can we talk?"

"Say whatever you want."

"Privately." Perhaps without an audience, she could be persuaded to tell the truth. "In the sitting room."

With a sound that clearly indicated his request required a great deal of patience on her part, she accompanied him.

He drew closed the seldom-used pocket doors.

She sat in the most comfortable-looking chair and studied her fingernails.

Grabbing another chair, he drew it close. "Thelma, why do you keep insisting Ellie is mine? We both know that's not even remotely possible."

"It's your word against mine."

"True. Who is the father?"

Her gaze slammed into his. A look of defiance darkened her eyes. "What do you mean? You are."

He leaned back with a sigh. "I mean who is *really* the father…not the person you are accusing of it."

She shrugged. "You'll never know." Her voice lowered. "He'll never know." She tilted her chin.

"Did you love him?"

The skin of her face tightened. Ice filled her gaze. "Love has nothing to do with it."

"I should think it has everything to do with it. And with marriage."

She puffed out her lips. "You're a dreamer. Always were. Always will be."

Suddenly he realized such words were welcome praise. "Thank you."

"I didn't mean it as a compliment."

"I know you didn't, but I'm proud to be seen as a man with dreams, a man with high ideals and a man with a tender heart. So you see, it was a compliment."

"Someday you'll see that life isn't for dreams."

"Or someday my dreams will come true."

She snorted. "Only if I'm part of them."

Reality slammed him in the ribs. "Why are you doing this? You know I don't love you. Even as I know you don't love me."

"You think you love that self-righteous Kate. Can't you see she isn't interested in you? Doesn't she plan to be a doctor?" Her voice carried a mocking note. "Seems to me that's worse than wanting to be a singer."

He ignored her comment, but the truth of her words sliced through him. Kate had been clear that she wanted to be a doctor. Had an obligation to be one.

Obligation?

Perhaps she hadn't used that word, but he was almost certain it fit.

"Did you register Ellie's birth?"

She gave him a sly, victorious look. "I did and on the registry she is Elspeth Marshall."

He could only stare at her, dumbfounded by her cunning.

Leaning forward, her eyes narrowed, she spoke firmly. "If you refuse to marry me, I will take Ellie away and you'll never see her again."

Conner could not speak. He was still trying to figure out what it meant that he was named the father on the birth certificate.

Thelma wasn't finished. "How long do you think she'd survive with me?"

"You're admitting you neglected her?" He dug his fingers into his knees as horror and anger mingled in his veins.

"It has nothing to do with me. That baby hates me."

"Then why would you take her from me? She is well loved here."

Thelma gave him a look that revealed nothing and yet he felt he had seen into her soul and it was a dark, awful place.

"Is this some kind of weird revenge because you are disappointed with your life?"

Thelma rose, crossed the room in her regal fashion, slid open the door and marched up the stairs.

Conner sat back in his chair. His head hurt, but it was nothing compared to the pain in his heart.

"Conner?" Grandfather called from the kitchen.

"Coming." He pulled himself together and went back to the older man and the baby.

He held out his hands to Ellie and laughed when she lifted her arms for him to pick her up. This baby wasn't his, but legally, with his name on the registry, she was. Perhaps Thelma had outsmarted herself. Did naming him as the father mean he had a claim to the baby even without marriage? He laughed again.

"What happened in there?" Grandfather asked.

Conner repeated the story. "I don't know what to do. I don't want to marry her, but I fear for the baby if Thelma takes her away. I don't want to put Ellie at risk."

"You have a big problem, but God is bigger than our problems. We'll pray and trust Him to provide the right solution."

Grandfather must have read Conner's struggle to have faith. "Remember how Sarah had a hard time believing God could do what He promised when He said she would have Isaac long after her childbearing years. She was told, 'Is anything too hard for the Lord?'"

Conner knew nothing was, but would God answer by giving him the courage to marry Thelma or would God provide a way to escape a marriage he did not want?

Chapter Fifteen

Kate firmly pushed aside memories of her many visits to the Marshall ranch. She would not recall all the happy times spent there. Conner must work out things with Thelma. She had some concern about Ellie. The baby got a blank look on her face when Thelma dealt with her. Kate had spoken to Isabelle and Annie about helping more with Ellie's care.

Conner had no right to speak of missing her. He had to deal with Thelma. Even if he did, there remained barriers. Most of all, her promise to become a doctor. No, not just her promise...her desire.

From now on, she would avoid Conner completely.

She heard someone talking to Father in the examining room and then he came to the adjoining door. "Kate, I'm going with this young man to check on his mother."

She bounded to her feet. "I'll come with you."

"There's no need. You'll be here in case someone comes."

It made sense and Father had been managing well on his own. Leaving her free to pursue studying medicine. Why couldn't she feel an ounce of enthusiasm over the idea?

Because she had allowed other things to fill her thoughts. One way to correct that. She went into the examining room and wiped off every bottle and dusted every book. Seeing the labels and reading the titles was meant to refresh her eagerness to learn more, but her efforts failed.

A buggy rattled by outside. She stopped to listen. It didn't pass. It could mean a patient. That would serve to make her remember her dream.

The outer door opened. "Come on in," she called.

From the sound of the footsteps, a woman had come to see the doctor.

She glanced up, a welcoming smile on her face. Her smile faltered. "Thelma, I didn't expect to see you. The doctor is away."

"That's fine. I came to see you." She plunked down on the chair with the air of someone who expected to have her plans fulfilled immediately. The look she gave Kate brought a shiver across Kate's shoulders.

"I know you fancy yourself in love with Conner, but you'll get over it." She shrugged so dismissively that it brought a flash of anger in Kate. As if love was no more than a passing fancy.

Not that she'd ever confessed to being in love with Conner. Ellie, yes. No question about that.

Thelma leaned forward, her eyes flashing. "I'm here to tell you to leave. Go to your medical school or whatever you want to do. If you interfere with my plan to marry him, I will take the baby and he'll never see her again. You wouldn't want to be responsible for breaking up a happy family, would you?"

Happy family? Was that how Thelma saw things? Blackmailing Conner into marrying her hardly seemed the basis for a happy anything.

Thelma leaned back. "I can't guarantee how well Elspeth will do under my care." There was no mistaking the warning gleam in Thelma's eyes.

Kate couldn't speak. Thelma was very clear that she would take the baby, but had she also threatened the baby's life?

"I see we understand each other. I speak to you as the doctor's assistant, so I know you will keep this in confidence." Thelma rose and swept from the room.

Kate stared after her. Why was she doing this?

Kate waited until the door closed, then bowed her head to the desk. "Oh, Conner, what will your life be like?"

If only the letter would come from the medical school. But would leaving make it easier for her to deal with the sorrow she saw coming for him?

Isabelle came to visit Saturday afternoon and found Kate in the bedroom, the trunk open and partly full. "You're packing?" She sounded shocked.

"I want to be ready to leave as soon as I get the letter confirming my start date at the college."

Isabelle sank to the edge of the bed where she'd slept a few months ago. "But I thought..."

Kate sat on the bed opposite. "You know my plan was always to go to medical school. I only delayed it because of Father's accident."

"I know. But so many things have changed."

"Some things have not."

"Kate, what about Conner?"

"When are he and Thelma getting married?"

"Thelma and Conner barely speak to each other. I think it would be a tragedy for them to marry."

Kate dismissed her friend's concern. "How is Ellie doing?"

Isabelle smiled. "We all take turns caring for her. Well, everyone but Thelma. She claims she's too tired. Honestly, I think that woman could sleep day and night."

Again, Kate wondered at the lack of mothering on Thelma's part.

Isabelle continued. "I'm not criticizing you, but I've always wondered if being a doctor is truly what you want in the depths of your heart."

Kate could only stare in wonder. "Of course it is. I can't believe you think it's not what I want." The idea stung. "Do you think I have an ulterior motive? Guilt? What else?"

Isabelle caught Kate's fluttering hands. "Maybe I'm just speaking from my own experience. My heart found its resting place with Logan. I had hoped…" She shrugged. "Kate, please don't go."

"I can't stay." Seeing Conner married would be hard enough. Seeing him unhappily married would be a thousand times more painful. And being responsible for Thelma taking Ellie away would be pure torture.

Isabelle sighed. "If that's the way it is…"

"That's the way it has to be. Believe me—" She could not say more. She had no right to wish things could be different.

Isabelle left after they'd shared tea and the news of the Marshall family and events in town. Isabelle had begged her to come to the ranch Sunday afternoon, but Kate refused.

* * *

Sunday morning dawned with a glare of bright sunshine promising a hot day. In fact, her room already held an uncomfortable amount of heat and Kate hurriedly dressed and went to the kitchen to make coffee. The heat from the stove added to her discomfort.

Father came from his room. "How nice to have an uninterrupted sleep." There'd been few enough of them for several days with three babies born and an older man suffering from stomach pains. "I'm looking forward to church today."

"Me, too." But with mixed feelings. The service always encouraged her and she hoped to get a glimpse of— No, she only wanted to see her friends and enjoy the service. She did not want to see Conner.

She would have lingered until the last moment before she set out, but Father stood at the door waiting for her to join him. The Marshalls had not yet arrived when they stepped into the church, but she knew where they usually sat and made sure she and Father sat several pews behind the spot.

She knew the moment the Marshalls arrived even before Isabelle and Dawson, with Mattie between them, slipped into the pew ahead of Kate. Then Bud escorted Grandfather down the aisle. Last came Conner, carrying Ellie. Annie joined Carly across the aisle. Kate waited, hardly daring to breathe, but Thelma did not follow.

Throughout the service, she fixed her gaze firmly on the front of the church, but there was no way she could avoid seeing Conner and his family. He shifted Ellie to his shoulder and the baby gazed at those around her. Her gaze found Kate and she smiled.

Kate forgot to breathe. She would soon say goodbye

to this sweet baby. How could she bear it? She wanted nothing so much as to see that smile every day, watch her grow and develop, laugh at her antics and kiss away her hurts.

Conner turned to whisper something to Ellie, allowing Kate to see his profile.

Isabelle was right. There was something Kate wanted more than to become a doctor.

But it was something she couldn't have.

As soon as Preacher Hugh gave the final benediction, Kate hurried from the church, not even waiting for her father. She ran all the way home and into her room, where she threw herself on her bed. She didn't cry. She hadn't known until this very moment that there existed a pain too deep for tears.

Father tapped on her door. "Kate, are you okay?"

"Yes, Father. I'll be out in a moment to make dinner."

"No rush."

She sat up and stared at her trunk. Packed and ready to go. Too bad she couldn't pack up her emotions and send them on a distant journey.

Forcing a smile to her face, she left her room and put out the meal she'd prepared the day before—sliced cold roast beef, pickled beets, potato salad and the last of the early lettuce with pie for dessert. "Peach, your favorite," she said as she served Father a slice.

She sat down to enjoy her own piece when the door to the waiting room opened. The sound of a man and a woman talking meant more than one visitor. A sigh escaped before she could stop it. What she wouldn't give to be able to enjoy an uninterrupted meal. An uninterrupted life. But that was a purely selfish thought. Doctors and nurses carried an obligation to serve others above their own desires. Even above family needs. Which was why, she reminded herself, she had made the deliberate decision not to try to do both.

Kate and her father went to the office to see what was needed.

Father recognized the man immediately. "Albert Stevens. Did I ever thank you for helping at the mine accident at Wolf Hollow?" Father had been called away a month ago to tend several men hurt at the mining town.

"No thanks necessary." He turned to the older woman resting on the bench. "This is my mother, Adele Stevens. We moved to Bella Creek a week ago so Mother would be nearer to a doctor."

Kate could see the woman struggled to breathe. "Come with me to a more comfortable chair." She helped the woman into Father's office. Father and Albert followed. Kate took in Mrs. Steven's swollen ankles, her puffy hands and her labored breathing and knew she suffered from heart failure.

Father listened to her heart.

"I know what's wrong with me," she wheezed. "I'm just hoping you can provide a little relief."

"I have something that will help with the swelling." He poured out the medication. "But you have to rest. Don't drink more than a moderate amount of liquids. Avoid the use of salt and keep your feet up."

"Thank you, Doctor," she said. "You know, Albert always wanted to be a doctor." She paused to catch her breath. "I'm afraid my health problems have dashed his dreams."

Father studied the young man. "That would explain why you were so eager to help at Wolf Hollow. You were invaluable. A man with natural talent."

"Thank you. I appreciate you saying that."

Father looked from Albert to Kate. "My daughter is planning to leave soon for medical school. I could use a young assistant if you're interested."

Albert grinned from ear to ear. "I am very interested."

"Very good." He turned to Kate. "That will make it easier for you to leave, won't it?"

She nodded. One more excuse erased. Perhaps God was trying to tell her something. That it was time to follow her goal and stop letting herself be sidetracked.

Albert and his mother departed.

Father said he meant to go visit the blacksmith, Augie East, who was also the undertaker. He and Father had become friends, often spending hours sitting with chairs tipped to the outside of the blacksmith shop as they talked.

Kate returned to her room after he'd left and stared at her trunk.

Conner had proudly carried Ellie to church. He'd decided his name on her birth certificate gave him the right to say she was his daughter even though she wasn't. He was proud to claim her as his own. Not so happy about having to take Thelma as part of the package.

He'd seen Kate seated with her father and fought an urge to turn around and look at her. He meant to speak to her after the service, but all he saw was her back as she hurried away.

If not for the fact he had to take Ellie home and look after her, he would have gone to the doctor's house. But he knew she wouldn't welcome him. He'd had plenty of time to think about the choices ahead of him as he worked with the horses, but seeing Kate run away after church made them suddenly clear.

He could not imagine his life without her. There was only one way he could hope to see her in his future.

Dinner was ready soon after he arrived at home. Thelma joined them, about half awake. She kept her eyes on her plate and said nothing. The family had learned not to ask her questions or try to involve her in the conversation.

She didn't notice when he fed Ellie from his plate. He wondered if she even cared.

He gave Ellie her feeding bottle, then put her down for a nap. Thelma had not returned to her bedroom. Now was the ideal time to do what he meant to do.

"Thelma, would you like to go for a walk?"

She gave him a startled look. "In this heat? No, thank you."

The others had disappeared except for Grandfather, who said he was tired and headed for his room.

That left them alone and Conner sat across the table from Thelma. "You're taking too much of that medicine you use." He'd seen her take from the bottle several times and wondered if she was addicted to laudanum. She refused to answer any questions on the matter.

She glowered, though it lost some of its power because she had a hard time focusing. "I don't see that it's any of your business."

"I expect you're right." He had no desire to get involved in an argument, not with something far more important to deal with. "Thelma, I can't marry you."

That brought her eyes into focus rather quickly. "Can't?"

"I'm not prepared to."

"I suggest you get prepared real soon."

He shook his head. "I am not going to marry you. We'd both be very unhappy."

"You're prepared to see the end of me and Ellie? I can tell you're very fond of her."

"I love that child as if she was my own, so, no, I'm not prepared to see the end of her."

"You needn't think I didn't mean it when I said I would take her and you'd never see her again."

"According to the registration, she's mine and I won't let you take her."

Thelma stared at him, her eyes turning almost black with fury. "You'll regret this. You'll see."

She pushed her chair back and marched upstairs, slamming the door hard enough to make the windows shudder.

He stared after her. He'd not let her take Ellie, and if she did, he would track her down and bring her back. The baby was his and he meant to keep her.

Thelma did not come down again that day. And she had not come down when Conner left the house the next morning. At church, a neighbor had asked if Conner had a horse he could buy. He had a mare ready to go and, knowing the man to be kind, Conner said he'd bring her over and, if he liked her, they'd make a deal. He saddled his horse and, leading the mare, rode away.

The man declared himself pleased with the animal. "She is spirited without being headstrong. A horse like that can be trusted." They struck a mutually agreeable bargain. Conner pocketed the money. It felt good to know his reputation was spreading.

Even better was knowing he was free from marriage

to Thelma. He could take the news to Kate and persuade her to give him a chance. He'd go see her this evening.

As he reached the barn, Dawson hurried toward him. "You might want to leave the saddle on."

"Why is that?"

"Thelma rode away shortly after you left. Said she was going to town to conduct some important business."

Good. Maybe she would leave town and resume her singing career in some distant town. He had no desire to ride after her and ask her to return.

"She had Ellie with her."

"What?" She meant to fulfill her threat to take the baby, did she? Well, she'd soon see he wouldn't stand by and let her take Ellie from him. He swung into the saddle and galloped from the yard.

At the knock on the door, Kate opened it and stared at Thelma, Ellie draped awkwardly over her arm. She took the baby. Thelma seemed relieved to let her.

Kate stared at the woman before her, uncertain what she expected.

Kate sat, Ellie perched on her knee. The baby seemed tense, as if aware of the strain in the room. Kate did her best to relax, but it wasn't easy with Thelma glowering at her. She tried to think why the woman would be angry at her but could not come up with any reason.

"Conner is refusing to marry me."

Kate could do nothing but stare as the announcement slowly made its way through her brain. "Why?"

"He says he doesn't love me." Bitterness dripped from every one of Thelma's words. "That's not what he said a year and a half ago." She lowered her gaze to

Ellie. "Not that I suppose he figured he'd be fathering a baby with his assurances of love."

"Why do you insist the baby is his? Everyone knows that's not true."

Thelma continued as if Kate hadn't spoken. "So he says. I say otherwise and now he must marry me." She changed her tone and grew pleading. "I only want little Ellie here to have a father who loves her and will take care of her."

Kate couldn't find anything to say. Not that it seemed to matter to Thelma.

"I thought we understood each other." Her smile did nothing to ease the ice in Kate's veins. Thelma rose. "I suggest you leave immediately. He'd soon forget you. I'll see to that." She batted her eyes…an action that made Kate shudder.

"We'll provide a nice home for Ellie." She made her way to the door.

Kate forced her limbs to follow.

Thelma stepped outside, then turned. "Give her to me." She took Ellie. The baby watched Kate until they drove away.

Kate closed the door and stared at the wooden panel before her. She would not be responsible for taking Ellie's father from her.

Her legs gave out and she crumpled to the floor. She had known better from the first. She did not belong in a family. She would never be a wife or a mother.

How long she sat there, she couldn't say, but her feet had gone to sleep when she finally pushed to her feet and she grabbed the back of a chair and hobbled to the table. She needed to get away from this place. The mail came in today. Perhaps her awaited letter had arrived.

She waited for her feet to come alive again before she hurried from the house and down the street to the post office.

"Any mail for the doctor?" she asked.

"Some letters for him and one for you."

She took the mail and ripped open the letter from the school. It informed her she had already passed all the entrance requirements and could start in two weeks' time. The weakness in her legs returned double-fold and she leaned against the wall for support.

"Bad news?" The man watched her with interest.

"Good news." Wasn't it? Then why did it feel like the bottom had fallen out of her world? She gave the man a weak smile and made her uncertain way back to the house to stand in the middle of the kitchen and stare at the stove.

She shuddered in a breath.

Father came from the examining room. She handed him the mail. "I heard from the medical school." Unable to relay the information, she gave him the letter to read.

"Well, Kate, you're finally on your way. Isn't that great? I'm sure you're excited."

"Yes, Father. I have many things to do in preparation for leaving." She made her way to her bedroom and sat on the edge of the bed. Shouldn't she be excited? There were others who wanted this and couldn't have it. Like Albert Stevens. It was what she'd wanted all her life. What her father and mother had wanted. What she'd been born for.

It was Thelma's visit that had her unable to think clearly. She would not do anything that would interfere with Ellie's future happiness.

Ellie needed a father. She needed Conner.

Knowing she would find strength and encouragement in the words of her Bible, Kate opened the pages and read until her resolve was returned. She knew the right thing to do and she would do it.

All she had left to do was put the last few things in her trunk. Soon she would be on her way and the events of the past few weeks would be but a memory. One she vowed would not be filled with the regret of making poor choices.

She'd leave Thelma and Conner to work things out and provide Ellie with the home she needed and deserved.

How long would it take for the pain of saying goodbye to abate?

Chapter Sixteen

Kate went to the kitchen, intending to— She couldn't remember what her plan had been.

She buried her head in her arms against the tabletop. Why was it so hard to think about leaving? Going to medical school? Because, she admitted sorrowfully, she had let herself think about having a family. To do so, she would give up being a doctor. She wanted a family where she wouldn't be constantly called away, where she'd be able to plan family events and celebrations and where she'd be home every day to greet a husband, to tend the children. A smile played around her lips as she let herself dream.

And then she slammed the door on such thoughts. *Don't waste the gift God has given you*, Grammie's words condemned.

She bent her head to the table again, praying for strength to face her future with courage.

"Kate, is something wrong?"

At Father's voice, she jerked upright. She hadn't heard him come into the room. "No, of course not." She rushed to the stove. "No patients? I'll make you coffee."

Father sat at the table.

She felt him studying her and kept her gaze averted for fear he would see more than she wanted him to. The coffee boiled and she poured a cupful and put it before him.

He caught her hand. "Something is troubling you. What is it?"

She shrugged. "I'm suddenly realizing how much I will miss you when I leave. I hadn't expected it to be so hard."

"I'll miss you, too, but once you're there and immersed in your studies, you won't have time to be lonely."

"I know you're right."

Father patted her hand. "I wish your mother had lived to see you achieve this. You know she wanted to be a doctor but ran into roadblocks because of being a woman."

"I know." And now Kate would fulfill her mother's dreams. And fulfill her promise to Grammie. A Bible verse flashed through her mind. *No man, having put his hand to the plow, and looking back, is fit for the kingdom of God.* "I'll be fine, especially as you're doing better and you have Albert to help you."

"God has provided as He always does. We can trust Him. He never fails."

Father's words sent strength to Kate's heart. "There's really no reason for me not to leave immediately. That will give me time to get settled before classes start." And it would get her away from Bella Creek and all the reminders of Conner and Ellie. It would remove any reason for Thelma to take Ellie away.

Father hesitated. "That sounds wise." His words were

laced with sadness. "It's not going to be easy to say goodbye."

"The stage heads east at noon." Now that she'd made up her mind, she couldn't wait to be on her way. "I could be on it."

Father stared at the door and swallowed hard. "It's sudden, but I know you've delayed for a long time." He nodded. "You do what you think is best."

She was packed.

No time like the present to get started. She told Father she would leave this very day, then rushed down the street to Sadie's house.

Sadie saw her coming and met her at the door. The children played in the backyard and called out hello to her. She greeted them, then joined Sadie indoors.

"I wanted to tell you I heard from the medical school and I will be starting studies in the very near future. I'm leaving today."

Sadie stared. "You're still planning that?"

"Why does everyone think I've changed my mind?"

"You want the truth?"

"Of course."

"Very well. For two reasons. First, because I see how things are between you and Conner."

"Don't you mean Conner and Thelma?"

"No, I don't."

Kate wouldn't look at her friend. If Kate was the reason Conner and Thelma weren't working out their differences, then all the more reason she should leave.

"But the second reason is even more important in my opinion."

Kate wished she hadn't asked for the truth because she had the feeling she wasn't going to like what Sadie said.

Sadie continued, "You don't talk about medical school like someone who can't see herself doing anything else in life. Being a doctor should be more than a duty." She paused and, when Kate said nothing, added, "Don't you think?"

"I am going to be a doctor." She could find no other answer.

Sadie sighed. "I'm going to miss you."

"You and Isabelle have families of your own now to enjoy. I wish you both lots of happiness."

"Thank you."

"I won't have time to say goodbye to Isabelle and the others. Will you let them know?" Not being able to say farewell to her friend left a bitter taste in her mouth, but Isabelle would understand and Kate would be back at Christmas.

Her chest refused to work as she thought of having to see Conner and Thelma together. But at least Ellie would be safe.

Kate placed one hand over the other at her waist. She'd done that all her life when she was upset or afraid. Hopefully no one else had noticed it.

Sadie studied her a long, silent moment. "Very well. I'll let her know. But don't you want to say goodbye to the others? What about Grandfather? Ellie? And Conner?"

At the mention of the others, Kate almost changed her mind. But she didn't know if she had the courage to see Ellie and Conner again. "I wish I had time, but the stage leaves at noon."

Sadie's disapproval hung between them like a barrier. Kate didn't stay long, using the excuse that she had many things to do.

* * *

Conner rode toward town. Where would Thelma go? It wasn't likely she'd remain in town, where Conner would easily find her and take the baby back. His heart kicked into a frenzied gallop as he realized today was Monday. The stagecoach came today. He glanced at the sky. Likely it had already left the mail and passengers and gone on to Wolf Hollow. It returned before noon to pick up anyone wanting to travel east. The sun was already directly overhead.

He urged his horse to a faster pace. He'd let Thelma leave if she wanted. But she wouldn't be taking Ellie with her. If she protested, he would demand she reveal Ellie's birth records.

A buggy traveled toward him. Hopefully it would not be someone wanting to visit…or worse, requiring he return to the ranch. Within minutes, he recognized the driver and pulled to a halt.

Thelma coming back? Ellie safely in her lap. His breath whooshed out, but his nerves did not relax. What was she up to?

She drew abreast of him and stopped. "Going somewhere?"

He didn't believe the innocence she tried to portray. She knew he was riding after her…or more specifically, after Ellie. "What game are you playing now?"

She pouted a little and batted her eyes. "How unfair you are to me. I merely went to town to visit Kate. Is there anything wrong with that?"

He studied her, congratulating himself at keeping himself in check when he wanted to order her to stop her nonsense, to think of someone besides herself. "I'm sure Kate welcomed your visit."

Thelma's chuckle revealed no hint of amusement. "I can't say that she did, but we had a nice chat." She paused, smiling thinly. "We are more alike than you realize."

They couldn't be more different if they'd been born on opposite sides of the moon, but he held his tongue, letting Thelma get her enjoyment out of this.

"You do realize that she wants nothing to do with becoming a permanent part of your life, so if you think tossing me aside will convince her to marry you, you are blind to the facts."

"What did you say to her?" Each word scratched from his throat.

"Nothing you would object to. Why don't you visit her yourself? You'll see that I'm not mistaken. I'll be back at the ranch waiting for you." Ellie squirmed as she tried to get Conner's attention. She wanted him to take her, but he couldn't. He had to talk to Kate.

"You go on home. I'm going to town."

"Yes. You do that." She flicked the reins and rode on with a mocking laugh.

He continued his journey toward town at a slightly less hectic pace. What had Thelma said to Kate? Why was she so certain Kate wouldn't be interested in what he had to say?

He reached town. The stagecoach rattled away, but he was no longer interested in its passengers.

He went down the alley to the back entrance of the doctor's house and slowly dismounted. His mind bounced back and forth between anticipation and dread. He knew she had grown fond of him. Now that he'd made it clear to Thelma that he didn't intend to marry her, he could ask Kate to consider marriage to him.

But Thelma's warning made him uncertain.

He wouldn't solve anything standing outside looking at the door, so he strode up to the house and knocked.

Silence greeted him. He knocked again. Not a sound came from the interior. His insides felt wooden.

What had Thelma done?

The bang of a door drew his attention back to the house. Someone had entered the front entrance. He banged his fist against the door.

Dr. Baker opened to his urgent knock. "Conner, come in. What can I do for you?"

He stepped inside and looked around. "I need to talk to Kate."

"I'm sorry, but it's too late. She left on the stage-coach."

"Left? Why?"

"Surely you knew she was going to medical school. It's always been her dream."

Conner's bones melted and he grabbed the nearby chair to keep himself upright.

"She left you a note." The doctor handed Conner an envelope.

Clutching the paper in his fist, he staggered from the house. He reached his horse and swung into the saddle. His first thought was to ride after the stage and yank Kate from it.

First, he must read what she'd written and he removed a sheet of paper and unfolded it.

To Conner:
I'm sorry I didn't have time to say goodbye. I am on my way to medical school just as I always

planned. Please tell your family goodbye for me.
Give Ellie a kiss from me. Take good care of her.
Sincerely,
Kate

He turned the page over, hoping for more. More than
a formal goodbye that included everyone. He stared
down the road. Then reined about and headed for the
ranch. She'd been clear there wasn't room in her life
for him.

"Conner, come to the house," Annie called.

His nerves twitched at the urgency in his sister's
voice. He vaulted the fence and trotted toward the house.

"Is something wrong with Ellie?" He looked at the
baby sitting on a blanket on the floor surrounded with
pot lids. Over the two weeks since Kate had left, the
baby had started doing so many things. He only wished
he could share each joy with Kate.

"No. It's Thelma. She hasn't been down all day so I
went up to check on her. She won't wake up."

"She's taken too much of that medicine." Conner
clattered up the stairs and into Thelma's room. Her
lips had a faint bluish tinge. "Is she breathing?" he
whispered.

He and Annie watched and both released sighs when
the blankets over her chest rose and fell. "She has to
wake up." He shook her. "Thelma, Thelma." Her head
lolled back. "Send someone for the doctor. Dawson is
out by the barn."

Annie rushed down the stairs. She called out to Dawson and in minutes a horse galloped away at a furious

rate. It would take time for Dr. Baker to get here…if he was even available. He might be out on a call.

The water jug was full and Conner dampened a cloth and wiped at Thelma's face. She moaned. He took it for a good sign and continued to sponge her face and wrists.

Annie joined him again. "I took Ellie over to Isabelle."

By now everyone within shouting distance had been alerted. Grandfather called up the stairs for a report and Annie went to tell him what she knew. Pa rushed into the room and stared at Thelma. He saw the brown bottle at her bedside. "Laudanum?"

"I would think so."

"How long has this been going on?"

"Since she arrived. I don't know how long she's been using it."

Pa crossed his arms. "We'll see that she gets help to get off it." Something crackled beneath the toe of his boot and he leaned over to pick up a paper from under the bed.

Conner paid him little mind as he continued to try to bring Thelma from her stupor.

"Do you know what this is?" Pa asked, shaking the paper he'd picked up.

Conner jerked up at the half-warning, half-cautious tone in his voice. "What?"

"It's a birth certificate for Ellie. She's registered as Elspeth Marshall."

"I was aware that Thelma had done that."

"You know what this means?"

"It means Ellie is legally mine."

"I don't understand why she did this."

"I don't either. Maybe she'll tell us once she regains

consciousness." Though none of his questioning had yielded a satisfying answer.

She stirred again as he put the cold, wet cloth on her forehead.

By the time the doctor arrived, she had opened her eyes, though she could keep them open only a second at a time.

"Wait outside while I check her over," Dr. Baker said, and Conner, Pa and Annie moved into the hallway.

They heard Dr. Baker's low voice and then Thelma's weak answer.

At least she was coming from the dark grips of that medicine.

They waited until Dr. Baker stepped out of the room.

"Is she going to be okay?" Annie asked.

"It's that medicine." Pa got right to the point. "She has to stop using it."

"I'm afraid it's not that simple," Dr. Baker said. "Can we go downstairs to discuss this?"

Conner did not like the somber sound of those words.

They clustered about the table and the fact Annie didn't offer Dr. Baker coffee signified the seriousness they all sensed.

Dr. Baker looked around the table. "There is no easy way to say this. I'm sorry to inform you, but she is dying."

Dying? The word exploded into stunned silence.

Dr. Baker hurried on. "She takes the laudanum to relieve her pain."

Annie recovered first. "What's wrong with her?"

"She has a tumor. It started here." He touched his chest. "But I can feel lumps here and here." He indicated his neck and under his arms. "It's spread throughout her body. It's just a matter of time."

"How long?" Again Annie asked the question.

"I'm afraid I can't say."

Conner heard the finality of the unfinished sentence.

"Is she able to talk now?" Pa asked.

"I believe she is. She'll have good spells and bad spells." Dr. Baker looked around the table. "You might need help caring for her." He sighed. "It's times like this I wish Kate was still here."

Every day I wish Kate was here. Conner's insides ached at the mention of her name. Not that he needed any reminders. Her name, her face, every remembrance of her constantly filled his thoughts.

"We'll do what needs to be done," Pa said. "But I'd like to talk to her right now."

The four of them returned to Thelma's room.

She looked at them. "To what do I owe this honor?"

Pa took the birth certificate from his pocket. "I found this on the floor. We'd like an explanation as to why you've claimed Conner as her father when he insists he isn't and we believe him."

"I had to," Thelma said, her voice still wobbly. "I knew I was sick and I didn't want her to end up in an orphanage if anything happened to me. I knew if she was a Marshall that you'd all make sure she was taken care of."

Conner found it in his heart to pity the woman. He sat beside her bed and took her hand. "According to this document, I am her father. She will always have a home with me."

Pa's gaze went from Thelma to Conner. "I agree." He turned to Dr. Baker. "Do you see a problem with this?"

"Not at all. Being part of the Marshall family is the best thing for Ellie." The doctor looked troubled.

Thelma's eyes drifted closed.

"Time to let her rest." Dr. Baker shooed them from the room.

They went back downstairs. Dawson and Isabelle, Logan and Grandfather waited in the kitchen for the news.

Pa told every detail.

"What are you going to do about Kate?" Annie asked.

"I don't think there's anything to be done. She's at medical school where she belongs. It's always been her dream."

"It's your fault if you let Kate go." Grandfather had no qualms about speaking his mind.

"She's gone. Left two weeks ago."

"The road goes both ways far as I can tell."

"Yeah," Annie said.

"Yeah," Isabelle echoed.

"They're right," his brothers added.

Ignoring them, he scooped up Ellie. "I have a daughter to take care of."

They were kept busy the next few days with Thelma's care until Pa rode to town and brought back Mrs. Gunderson. "She's going to help with Thelma."

Conner made a point of visiting Thelma several times a day and of taking Ellie to see her at least once a day.

On one of their visits, Thelma asked Mrs. Gunderson to leave the room. "I have something to tell you. You once asked why Ellie was so thin and why she didn't like me."

"I never said she didn't like you."

"Well, it was fairly evident. I didn't realize how much work a baby would be and I resented it. I had to give up my singing because she needed me so much. I was angry at her and she seemed to know it. It made me even angrier when she would stare right through me. I'm sorry. She belongs here."

"Who is her father?"

"You are. I made sure of that."

"I need to know if the real father will ever come looking for her."

"You can rest assured he won't."

"Does he even know about her?"

"No." She swallowed hard. "To my shame, I can't say for certain who the father is."

He kept his reaction to himself. Just as he'd keep that information to himself. When Ellie was old enough, he'd simply say her mother never told him who her father was.

She turned to him. With Mrs. Gunderson measuring out her medicine more carefully, Thelma was clearer in her mind much of the time. "Conner, when are you going after Kate?'

"Who said I am?"

"If you don't, you will regret it."

"You of all people should know that some people value a profession more than a family."

Thelma snorted. "You of all people should know that Kate isn't anything like me. For one thing, she loves you enough to walk away because she thought it was the best thing for you."

"You must have taken too much medicine. You aren't making sense."

"I'm perfectly clear in my mind. Listen to me." She told how she had made Kate believe that staying around would jeopardize Ellie's future.

"You said that already."

"You didn't listen. I told her we loved each other once when we made a baby together and we'd love each other again if she wasn't around to confuse you. Then I told her I would take Ellie away if you didn't marry me. Don't you see? She only wanted to do what she thought was right."

"Maybe." He wasn't ready to throw caution to the wind.

"If you don't go after her, I'll…I'll…" She threw an arm over her forehead in a dramatic gesture. "I will die right here and now."

He chuckled. "I think Mrs. Gunderson might have something to say about that."

"Promise me you'll think about it at least."

"Okay, I'll think about it." It wasn't as if he could avoid doing so.

His head said Kate had made her choice, been clear about it. His heart wondered if she might be regretting her choice.

Everyone urged him to go after her.

Was he going to let his pride stand in the way?

Chapter Seventeen

Kate sat at her desk and stared at the page of the text-book. The words swam mockingly. *Vanity of vanities. All is vanity and vexation of spirit.*

It wasn't that studies were difficult. But her heart simply wasn't in them. Her heart was back in Bella Creek with Conner and Ellie. How long would it take to get over them?

She pulled out a letter from Father. He wrote that he was pleased with Albert's help. That Mrs. Stevens was showing improvement. He told her that they'd had a rainstorm with lots of thunder and lightning, but the letter contained not a word about Conner and Thelma getting married. Shouldn't they be taking care of that? Ellie needed a forever family.

She tucked the letter back in her pocket and focused on the words before her. But again it proved a struggle.

Wouldn't Father be disappointed if she failed her courses? That could not happen and she forced herself to concentrate.

Day after day, she fought the same battle. It drove

her to her knees as she begged God to ease the way the memory of her days in Bella Creek tugged at her.

Slowly, as she expected, she learned to concentrate on the books and the lectures. She would become a doctor. She'd make her father proud. Her mind made up, her heart steadfast, she opened her notes on the latest lecture.

But the words swam before her eyes like frantic fish. Perhaps she could walk away her confusion. She'd discovered a park not far away, close to the nearest bus stop, and she grabbed a shawl against the autumn chill and headed outside.

She filled her lungs with the scent of fall. The air carried less appealing smells—smoke, animal, too many people—and served only to make her even more homesick.

God, help me to find contentment.

She turned a corner. A cowboy got off the bus.

Her heart slammed into her ribs, making her unable to breathe. Would she ever see a man in a cowboy hat and not have this visceral reaction?

Wanting to avoid seeing the man any closer, she angled across the street toward the park, seeking solace beneath the spreading branches of an oak tree. The leaves had started to change color and a red one fluttered to her feet.

Like an echo of her heart.

Closing her eyes, she tried to pray, but her pain could find no words. Only a long, agonizing ache for relief. Time would heal her wounds. But would she ever be completely whole again? No. Part of her heart would forever remain back in Bella Creek, at the Marshall ranch with Conner and Ellie.

"Kate." Her name came on the whisper of the breeze.

She sucked in air, trying in vain to still the raging turmoil of her heart.

"Kate." The voice grew stronger.

She struggled against her pain, wanting only forgetfulness.

"Kate." Why must the voice grow stronger, more insistent when she worked so hard to put those memories behind her?

"Kate, open your eyes."

Her eyes flew open. She stared. Was this a dream? "Conner?"

He smiled.

"Is it really you? What are you doing here?"

"I came to see you." He stood inches away. She drank in his features. The bronze of his sun-blessed skin, the sky in his eyes, the fringe of wheat-colored hair. If she wasn't mistaken, his gray felt hat was new.

She tore her gaze from him, settling it on another red leaf on the ground to the side. "When are you and Thelma getting married?"

He shifted to the right to intercept her gaze and waited for her to raise her eyes to meet his.

"Didn't your father tell you Thelma is dying?"

Her mouth worked, but not a single word made its way from her stunned brain.

"I'm sorry." She felt nothing but sorrow at the news.

"We won't be getting married. I never planned to. I don't love her."

She nodded. What did he expect from her?

"You were right when you said Ellie needed a mother and a father. Kate, marry me and we can give her that."

The pulse in her throat thudded sluggishly. "A marriage of convenience for the sake of the child?" It seemed noble and self-sacrificing. Could she do it?

He chuckled. "That is not what I have in mind." He edged closer. "Kate, surely you know it's you I love. Why else do you think I kissed you?" His gaze dropped to her mouth.

She rolled her head back and forth, unable to allow herself to believe his words.

"Kate, I've come to the city to find a job and a place to live. I'll bring Ellie and find a nanny for her."

"Why?"

He took her hands and pulled them to his chest. "Because I can't live without you. I'll follow you as you follow your dream."

"My dream?" What was her dream? She knew the answer. It stood right before her, within her grasp. All she had to do was believe it could be hers. She would not let her fears control her future.

"This—" she swept the area with her gaze "—is not my dream. I'm not even sure I want to be a doctor. I like helping people, but not in that role." Suddenly Grammie's words made sense. *You have the gift of caring.* Nothing would give her more joy than caring for those in her family—Conner, Ellie, Grandfather, each and every one.

She slipped her hands from his and pressed her palms to his cheeks. "Conner, I want to go home."

He wrapped his arms about her and pulled her close. "Kate, I love you. Will you marry me?"

"Conner, I have loved you a long time…in fact, maybe forever. You are the answer to the loneliness in my heart that is as old as I am. You are the fulfillment of all my dreams. I don't want to ever be where you aren't. But before I can say yes, I must talk to my father. He expects me to become a doctor."

"Then all you have to do is tell him the truth. When he sees how much you love me, he will give his blessing."

She chuckled as joy exploded in her heart, flooding her whole being. She loved him so much and could now let her feelings have life.

"You understand Ellie comes with me?"

Her merriment filled her eyes. "Your daughter is my daughter. I couldn't love her more."

She lifted her face to him, inviting a kiss.

His eyes were bright as a July sun as he accepted her invitation.

His lips were warm and possessive, laying claim to her heart, her dreams and her love.

She wrapped her arms about his waist, pressed one hand to his back and returned the same promises—her heart, her dreams, her love—for now and always.

Kate's return home was met with joy from the Marshall family and Father. "I've missed you," he said. "You're needed at the Marshall ranch. Mrs. Gunderson has been called away to help her daughter."

"Conner and I have already discussed it. I want to take care of Thelma."

Father hugged her. "It's good to have you back."

"I'm sorry about giving up on being a doctor."

"I'm sorry for causing you to think you should follow our plans. I'm happy to know you are going to have the family you've always wanted."

"Oh, Father, I have always had a family with you and Mother. I've always known I was loved."

Father smiled. "Yes, you are."

She moved to the Marshall ranch the next day to tend Thelma, shocked at how much she had deteriorated. Many days she simply slept, others she wakened for brief periods, often too weak to speak, but there were days she seemed driven to talk.

"I'm glad you and Conner are going to marry. You both deserve happiness. Tell me you will always love Ellie."

"I promise." She held Thelma's thin hands. "But you know I love her so much already that it brings tears to my eyes." Isabelle and Annie helped with the baby's care as Kate tended Thelma, but Kate spent as much time with the baby as possible, rejoicing over every new thing she did.

Ellie bounced with excitement when she saw Conner or Kate.

"I want to see you and Conner married before I go."

Conner and Kate had discussed it and decided it didn't seem appropriate to marry with Thelma on her deathbed. "We've decided to wait."

Thelma grabbed her arm. "You can't."

Kate blinked. "Why not?"

"I want to make sure everything is legal and above board for Ellie. You need to get married and then legally adopt her." Thelma grew agitated. "I want this done proper."

"Quiet down. I'll talk to Conner about it."

"Do it right away."

"I will." She waited until Thelma fell asleep, then went looking for Conner. She found him with his horses, as she knew she would. He found satisfaction in working with the animals. He saw her coming and vaulted the fence, trotting to her side. "Everything okay?"

She told him of Thelma's concerns.

"It makes sense. I know I would feel better to have every possibility covered. I'll talk to the lawyer." He took her hand. "Do you need to hurry back?"

Thelma was sleeping. Ellie was with Isabelle, so they walked hand in hand along the path that led to the creek and spent a pleasant hour talking about the future.

"I have no house for you yet. I had hoped to get a cabin built before we married."

"Does it matter where we live? All that matters is we are together."

"We'll have to stay here for you to take care of Thelma."

"That's fine with me."

He went to see the lawyer that afternoon. Preacher Hugh came to the ranch at Conner's request and he agreed he would marry them at the ranch as soon as they wanted.

Kate wakened with a burst of joy the following Saturday. This was her wedding day. The ceremony was to be simple and small. Only the family and a few close friends.

Thelma had insisted she must be awake and carried downstairs to the sitting room so she could witness the event.

Kate helped her dress and did her hair, applied makeup to hide how pale she'd grown, then hurried to her own room, where Isabelle helped her prepare. She had planned to wear her best dress—a pale gray satin—but Father had pulled out a box and lifted a white lace dress from one of his trunks.

"It's your mother's wedding dress."

"I didn't know you even had it. Why have I never seen it before?"

He grinned. "I kept it with my personal things. I guess I had a dream, too. One apart from you becoming a doctor. I hoped to one day see you married with a dozen children of your own." He handed her the dress. "That's why I kept this and why I didn't tell you."

Tears had clogged her throat to finally realize Father wasn't disappointed she had given up medical school.

Isabelle did up the row of satin-covered buttons that ran down the back of the dress.

"It's like having Mother here," Kate managed through her tight throat.

Isabelle turned Kate to face her.

"We're best friends and now we'll be sisters-in-law. I'm ecstatic."

Father waited for her outside her door. Isabelle preceded them down the stairs and into the sitting room.

Thelma sat in Grandfather's usual chair.

The family stood together, Carly and Jesse among them.

Conner waited by Preacher Hugh, his eyes so bright she blinked. But she did not turn away. She would never turn from the love blazing from his eyes.

"Dearly beloved," Hugh began.

They exchanged vows to be faithful for the rest of their lives. Preacher Hugh had them sign the papers making them man and wife and then the lawyer who had prepared the documents beforehand had them sign papers making Kate Ellie's legal mother. As soon as they finished, Annie handed Ellie to them.

With a huge grin, Hugh lifted a hand toward them.

"May I introduce for the first time Mr. and Mrs. Conner Marshall and their daughter, Elspeth."

The family surrounded them, hugging them and laughing.

Annie, Isabelle and Sadie had secretly prepared a special tea, but before they joined the others in partaking, Conner carried Thelma back to her bed and Kate followed, with Ellie in her arms.

"I can die happy," Thelma said with a weary sigh.

Conner and Kate tiptoed from the room. He pulled her close. "I'm glad we were able to ease her concerns." He kissed her briefly before they went to join the others.

A month later

Kate let Conner lift her from the buggy and they looked at the cabin before them.

"It's nothing fancy," Conner said.

She chuckled at the mixture of regret and anticipation in his voice. "It's perfect for our honeymoon."

"I'm sorry we had to delay it a month."

"I'm not. Now that things have settled down, we can relax without worrying about what's going on at the ranch."

"That's true."

She squeezed his arm. Two weeks ago, Thelma had passed away peacefully in her sleep. They had both sat by her bedside that last night, reassuring her that Ellie would always be loved and cared for.

As she drew her final breath, they both wiped away tears. In the weeks of caring for her, Kate had grown fond of Thelma. Despite her behavior when she first arrived, Kate knew Conner was as grateful as she that the woman had given them Ellie.

"I'll miss her," she said, wiping away tears.

"Me, too. But no more suffering for her."

Thelma's last request was for them to celebrate their marriage as they had not had a chance to do yet.

"You're always so busy taking care of me and Ellie."

Conner and Kate had promised they would do as she requested. It was a promise neither of them minded making and keeping.

Conner suggested a line cabin that wasn't being used. "We'll be completely on our own."

Kate shivered in anticipation of this time alone.

He swept her off her feet and carried her across the threshold. "It's not home, but welcome anyway, my dear sweet wife." He kissed her before setting her on her feet.

She looked around. One room, a bed, a stove, a table and chairs. Plenty of supplies in the buggy. "It has everything we need." She turned into Conner's arms and kissed him thoroughly.

Everything she needed was right here in the circle of his arms.

* * * * *

Dear Reader,

As many of you know, my husband and I have adopted ten children. My goal and dream and wish for them has always been that they find healing and wholeness in the love and support of a large family. Psalm 68:6 says God sets the lonely in families. I believe strongly in the power of family. May this story help each one to see how important family is. If you don't have a family unit like I am talking about, I pray you will find it either through the acceptance of a welcoming family such as the Marshalls or in the warmth of an accepting church.

You can learn more about my upcoming books and how to contact me at www.lindaford.org. I love to hear from my readers.

Blessings,
Linda Ford

Get 2 Free Books,
Plus 2 Free Gifts—
just for trying the Reader Service!

Love Inspired HISTORICAL

SPECIAL EXCERPT FROM

Love Inspired HISTORICAL

When the wrong mail-order bride arrives with another woman's baby, Trace Warren's marriage of convenience brings back the memory of the wife and baby he lost. Can Katherine help him love again?

Read on for a sneak preview of
WEDDED FOR THE BABY by **Dorothy Clark**,
part of her STAND-IN BRIDES miniseries.

"I'm sorry I've gotten you into this uncomfortable position, Katherine. I never meant for you to be embarrassed or—"

The baby let out a squall. Katherine rose, then lifted Howard into her arms. "You owe me no apology, Trace. I chose to stay to help you keep your home and shop for Howard's sake. I'm not sorry." She looked over at him and met his gaze. Tears glistened in her beautiful eyes. "I may be hurt by my choice, but I'll never be sorry." Her whisper was fierce. She bent her head and kissed Howard's cheek. The baby nuzzled at her neck, searching for something to eat. It was the perfect picture of what he had longed for, prayed for and lost.

His chest tightened; his stomach knotted. He looked down at his plate, picked up his fork and forced himself to take a bite of salmon loaf.

"Trace…"

He braced himself and looked up.

"Please hold Howard while I warm his bottle." She handed the baby to him.

He looked at Katherine standing by the stove, holding a towel while she waited for the bottle to warm. Her lips curved in the suggestion of a smile. His heart lurched. She was so beautiful, so kind and softhearted, so brave to take on the care of an infant of a woman she didn't even know. Katherine Fleming was an amazing young woman.

He jerked his gaze away and stared down at his plate. He had to think of an acceptable excuse to leave as soon as the baby's bottle was ready. It was far too dangerous for him to be here alone with Katherine every day.

She set the baby's bottle on the table. "I'm sorry. I just realized I forgot to pour our coffee. I'll get it now. Would you please start feeding Howard before he begins to cry?" Her skirts flared out as she turned back toward the stove.

He swallowed his protest, clenched his jaw and shifted the infant to the crook of his arm. The baby's lips closed on the offered bottle; his tiny fingers brushed his hand and clung, their touch as light as a feather. Pain ripped through him. The pain of a broken heart vibrating to life again. It was his greatest fear coming true.

Don't miss
WEDDED FOR THE BABY by Dorothy Clark,
available August 2017 wherever
Love Inspired® Historical books and ebooks are sold.

www.LoveInspired.com

LIHEXP0717